THE CAPTIVE'S
Song

The Captive's Song

© Amanda Deed, 2024

Cover Design by Carmen Dougherty.
Layout by Rhiza Press.

978-1-76111-146-4

Published by Rhiza Press, 2024
PO Box 302,
Chinchilla QLD 4413
Australia
www.wombatrhiza.com.au

A catalogue record for this
book is available from the
National Library of Australia

AMANDA DEED

THE CAPTIVE'S Song

rhiza press

To my beautiful dad.
Sorry you didn't get to read this one.
Thank you for all your support over the years.
May you rest in the arms of Jesus.
Till we meet again.
Amanda.

CHAPTER
One

Olivia Cruikshank
April, 1841—Hobart Town, Van Diemen's Land

Olivia pastes on a smile as they lead her into the docks once again. She is good at smiling.

'Who is the defendant?' the magistrate asks. You'd think he'd remember her by now. She's been here often enough. Maybe it's not the same man presiding, she hasn't exactly paid attention.

'Olivia Cruikshank, convict,' the clerk drones.

Olivia schools her face into a look of boredom. She knows what to expect.

'Charges?'

'Absconding from her place of assignment. Theft of a length of ribbon.'

The small courtroom is dark, what with all the wooden panelling, wooden fixtures, and the small windows high on one wall. Olivia is not sure how the clerk can even read the charges. And it smells close—musty with the bodies of the unwashed—but she still catches the scent of leather and paper. Better than some places she's been, that's for sure.

'Who is the prosecutor?'

'Mr William Lambert, farmer.'

'Mr Lambert, please state your case.'

Olivia's former master stands to his feet, his chair scraping the

1

wooden floor, and clears his throat. 'Sir, I would urge you not to let this girl's looks deceive you. While she seems to be pretty and friendly at first, she is anything but.'

'I am not here to be swayed by a fair face, Mr Lambert. Please state your grievances.'

She tries not to grin. Take that, Mr Lambert.

Olivia stops paying attention while Mr Lambert tells the magistrate what an insubordinate harpy she is. They won't be interested in her side of the story. They never are. How his wife whipped Olivia for dropping an egg. How he made her rise and prepare the stove fires before dawn, even when she had the fever. How for punishment he made her sleep in the chicken coop. Horrid man. But she deserves such treatment, doesn't she? She is a convict, after all. The heavy shackles digging into her wrists and ankles attest to that.

Olivia consoles herself thinking about the loot she has tucked inside her stays. A few coins, some preserved meat, and a small square of lace. Items she has hidden away, little by little over the past few months, the Lamberts none the wiser. The scratch of the small leather purse against her skin reminds her of its presence. The women back at the Factory will be pleased. Pity they caught her with the ribbon. It would have been a welcome gift for one of the girls.

'Miss Cruikshank, do you have any defence?' The magistrate draws her back to the proceedings.

Olivia offers him her sweetest smile. 'No, sir. Exceptin' I were just borrowin' the ribbon to tie up me hair.'

It's a pity her long hair is braided and pinned beneath her mobcap, so she can't prove how hard it is to manage. Not that Mrs Lambert cared an iota about that. So, yes, Olivia ran away, even though she knew they'd find her. It was the only way to get away from the Lamberts and back to the known and reliable torment of the Factory.

The magistrate stares at her for a long time, and she glues her smile in place with defiance. Then he shakes his head and sighs. Looking down at his papers, he scrawls something in his notes, then looks back up at Olivia.

'You know, Miss Cruikshank, it is a shame. I see here a long list of similar offenses. Do you deliberately create a bad name for yourself? You came to Van Diemen's Land for petty theft, and you have served six of your seven years imprisonment. In another twelve months you may be released, providing you don't continue adding to your crimes. Is this the pattern you want for your life? Do you want to keep returning to gaol? Perhaps you should take a hard look at yourself and think about your future.'

He glances around at the others in the room, then down at his papers again.

'Five days of solitary confinement followed by a month's hard labour.' He raps his gavel down and it is over.

A constable grabs Olivia by the upper arm, his fingers pressing uncomfortably into her skin, and leads her out. All she can do is shuffle with the dratted cuffs on her legs, careful not to stumble. If she falters, she will likely hit the ground. The officer is not about to catch a falling convict, even if she is a girl. At least he's not trying to hurry her like others have done. Olivia chooses to walk in compliance. She is not in the mood for further trouble today. Besides, something the magistrate said made her think.

But Olivia doesn't want to think. Thinking is dangerous.

She breathes in the fresh air outside the courtroom. 'Lovely day for a walk, eh, sir?' She wonders if this man is the conversational type.

'You may keep your tongue, miss.'

Nope. He's not. Although that doesn't stop Olivia.

'I'm just sayin', it's a pleasant day, don't ya think? Not too hot. The sun is shinin'.'

'Well, enjoy it while it lasts. You'll be in a dark cell soon.'

He smirks at her, but she feigns ignorance.

'I intend to, sir.' Olivia turns her face to the sun and drinks in the warm rays. For sure, she won't see it again for a week.

Soon, he removes the shackles from her ankles and herds Olivia, with a few other prisoners, along the two mile walk down the rutted streets to the Valley of the Shadow of Death, otherwise known as the Cascades Female Factory. There are only two constables escorting them, so they are free to get acquainted. Sometimes Olivia finds herself with another familiar face, but today they are all new. Scared looking women. Must be a first offense for all of them. She tries to reassure them in her happiest voice that they will be fine. They'll probably go to Class Two for picking and carding wool for a while and soon be on their way to assigned work. That is, *if* they behave themselves. This mob look like they will. Olivia, she's down to Class Three now. She runs out of cheer and falls silent. She keeps her eyes on the uneven ground as if she's focused on not falling.

What if she'd *behaved* herself all these years? Where would she be now? Ha. Probably married to some overbearing landowner without a choice of her own.

Or dead.

It's hard to believe she's been here six years already. The magistrate's words come back to Olivia again. In another year, she could be free. It's a hard notion to accept. *Is this the pattern you want for your life? Do you want to keep returning to gaol?* Did she even have an answer for that? Olivia has not contemplated a free future since before her transportation. It seems like an impossibility. When did she become so used to this circle of life? Punishment and imprisonment at the Female Factory, assigned labour until she becomes insubordinate or runs away, back to the magistrate on charges and returned to the Factory to learn her lesson again through hard labour.

Olivia laughs to herself. It sounds harsh even in her own ears. The only lesson she's learnt is she cannot trust anyone, and her life is destined to be a series of failures and tragedies.

Regret.

The taste of it is foreign in Olivia's mouth. Why should she regret the choices she's made? Most of them were forced upon her, anyway. And yet, it is there. The strange thing is, she cannot imagine her life any other way. If she faced the same moments again, the same choices, she is sure she would decide the same way. Except perhaps for the very first one. Would Olivia have said 'no' to her mother? Would she have had the mettle? Perhaps now she would, but back then, when she was only seven? Not a chance.

And so, there is no point in regret. Just like there is no point in hope. This is her life. The magistrate spoke without knowledge, without understanding what it is like to be a prisoner. She does not really have a choice.

The constables halt the mob, and Olivia raises her eyes to the familiar stone walls of the Factory. She turns to face all the women. 'Well, ladies, welcome to the Cascades. If you've never been 'ere before, enjoy your stay.' She lifts her shoulders and paints on a bright smile. As though they are arriving at a house in Grosvenor Square. She giggles at her own joke. But none of these ladies will find it funny when they are inside.

As they line up at the gate, Olivia takes one last glance at the blue sky, squinting against the brightness. She will miss it, that southern sun, even if it burns her pale skin. She will miss the greenery of trees, the hazy blue of Mount Wellington above them, so often shrouded in cloud. She will miss the peaceful sound of the rivulet trickling as it passes by. And she will most definitely miss the fresh air.

***

Michael Reeve - Turnkey

Mick watches with Matron and the overseer as the trail of women from the courthouse arrives in front of the Factory. A fresh group of prisoners to incarcerate. Not that he knows much about it. He's only worked here a few weeks.

''Nother bunch o' nemmos, I'll wager.' Fred spits on the ground in contempt. He is the crime class overseer. 'They prob'ly thinks they's all nobby an' such, but they's just gutter filth, if ya ask me.'

Mick grunts in reply. 'Where's your humanity, man? They're not disease-ridden rodents.' The way he figures it, they just made a mistake somewhere along the line, but there's always a chance to change.

The constables escorting them line them up at the gate. One by one, the Matron ushers them inside for searching and allocation. But Mick notices all the staff keep glancing at one particular convict, a petite girl with a pink mobcap.

'You can watch her, Reeve, I ain't touchin' her.' Fred screws up his face.

'Least, not until she's in the yard when I don't 'ave a choice.'

Mick shrugs his shoulders. It doesn't make any difference to him. Fred chuckles like he's missing half his brain.

One of the constables hands over some papers to the Matron—Mrs Hutchinson—and gives her the run-down. Eventually he nods toward the girl with the pink mobcap. 'That one's bound for the dark cells. Five days.'

The pint-sized convict is nearing the gate and Mick wonders what she could have done to find herself in the dark cells. Her head only comes to his chest, and he reckons he could close his fingers about her arm, she is that small.

She squints up at him, the sun in her large brown eyes, and grins. But those eyes, they are like flint. Like stone. Cold and hard. 'Hello guv'na. I ain't seen you 'round 'ere before.'

So, she's a returning convict to the Cascades. She looks so young, but her face bears the signs of experience. Too much of it, by Mick's guess.

'No. I'm new here. The name's Reeve. Michael Reeve. But most folks call me Mick.'

She nods. 'Nice to meet ya, Micky.' She makes up her own nickname, offers him a mocking curtsy, and he's convinced she thinks meeting him is anything but nice.

'What? Are you the new cook, then? Better be good tucker, else the girls will use it fer ammunition.'

A chuckle escapes him, even though he's supposed to appear stern. 'No. I don't know that I could even cook an egg.'

She grimaces and is at that moment taken inside for the search.

Ten minutes later, the women are all accounted for, and Mick is requested to take the small prisoner down to the dark cells. He wonders again why Fred doesn't want to have anything to do with her. She seems harmless enough. They walk through to the yard, where the other prisoners are busy at the washtubs. The smell of lye soap and wet linen tinges the air, the rhythmic slosh of the stick in the tub the only sound. However, the women's silent work becomes a murmur and from the murmur grows a rhythm that becomes louder. At first, Mick ignores it, but as he listens, he realises the women are chanting.

'Shank. Shank. Shank. Shank. The Shank's back. The Shank's back.'

They're banging on the copper pots and stomping their feet and getting louder by the minute. Mick realises he's stopped walking to watch, stunned. What are they chanting at?

'Hello girls!' His prisoner gives them a big hearty wave, well, as much as she can with cuffs on her wrists and makes a show of a deep curtsy.

This is about her? They are cheering for her?

'Are you The Shank?' Mick stares at her, incredulous.

'Olivia Cruikshank, at your service.' She bobs another curtsy and winks at him. Then she launches into song, her voice following the rhythm the other prisoners have set. She sings a satire lyric about the Cascades Female Factory while bouncing around on her toes, her chains jingling. Mick suspects that if she wasn't in leg-irons, she would dance a jig. When she gets to the last line, all the women join in with her. *Life is always grand inside the Female Factory, hey!*

Who *is* this girl? Footsteps approaching on the stone pavement draw Mick out of his stupor. It's the matron, her slack mouth flapping as she runs, or rather waddles. She is heavy with child.

'What are you doing, Reeve? Stop standing there like a bludgeoned rabbit and get her out of here!'

Yes, yes. They must maintain the peace. More like control.

Matron continues. 'Cruikshank. You know better. Do you want to make it seven days in the dark cells?'

'No, Mrs Hutchinson.' Her answer is meek, but her face reads anything but.

Mick finds it amusing and somewhat pleasing to see the reception Miss Cruikshank has received. There is camaraderie within the prison. But he turns her around and leads her away, while she is still humming her tune, the matron behind him hollering for the prisoners to desist.

As they move away, Mick notices one woman standing apart, no smile on her lips, no hand clapping, stomping, or singing. In fact, her face looks frozen in an expression of contempt, and her hands are balled into fists at her side. Her dark hair peaks out from underneath her mobcap, and gold rings hang from her ears. He's met her before. Ellen Smith. She seems to be the only one who doesn't appreciate Miss Cruikshank's arrival. Well, her and the group of women standing with her. He'd even go as far as saying her eyes cast icy daggers at Miss Cruikshank. Do they know each other? Has Miss Cruikshank offended Miss Smith in the past? There is obviously something between them, something unfriendly in nature.

Mick cannot dwell on this curiosity, as Miss Cruikshank's humming draws his attention again. Does she not realise the terrible time she will have in the dark cells? She walks as though she has not a care in the world, almost as though she doesn't wear shackles at all, as though no-one stared daggers at her. There is a spring in her step and a melody on her tongue. It is the oddest thing.

'So, Micky, what are you in for, eh?' She chortles up at him, an impish grin on her face.

He hides his amusement as he replies. 'You know, I don't think they ever told me.'

She cocks her head so she can study him from beneath her mobcap. 'Hm. I reckon you must be a danger to society. Bein' as yer such a bang-up cove an' everythin'.'

She is brazen. He'll give her that. He tries not to look shocked at her bold flirtation. Maybe she is deliberately trying to get him off-side. An attempt to anger him so he'll punish her, perhaps. Testing him to find his measure. Little does she know his determination to raise no more than an eyebrow. It saddens him that these women, some of them girls, are so familiar with harsh treatment. And yet, he still doesn't know what crime she committed to be sent to Van Diemen's Land.

'Thank you for the compliment, Miss Cruikshank.' He nods to her. 'We must be guilty of the same crime.' Let's see what she thinks of that.

Strangely, she goes silent. Stiffens even.

Perhaps he should not have done that. Pretty as she is, she may have received unwelcome advances more than once during her stay.

'I apologise, ma'am, I spoke out of turn.' Prisoner or no, she is a person and, therefore, worthy of respect.

She almost chokes on a laugh then, the stiffness gone. 'Ma'am? That's gotta be a first. Ya think I'm a lady of the ton, do ya?'

'Whether you are nobility or no, you are first and foremost a lady.' They pause in front of the cell she will inhabit for the next five days. No light, no fresh air, and about seven feet by four feet to inhabit.

She angles her head again, staring hard up at him. She doesn't know what to make of him, he can tell. Mick unclips the keys from his belt and opens the heavy wooden door, waving her inside. She shuffles past him, still staring at him, then sits on a small cot along the wall. He crouches down to undo her leg irons and cuffs.

'Will you be all right in here?' He considers it a courtesy to ask.

'Nothin' I 'aven't done before.' She looks bored.

It seems incredible that such a petite and intriguing creature can have done anything deserving of solitary confinement. Yes, she intrigues him, this Olivia Cruikshank.

'They'll bring your supper soon.'

She scoffs at that. 'I wouldn't call stale bread an' water supper.'

'Fair enough. Well, I'll leave you to it, then.'

'See ya, guvna,' she nods cheerfully.

Mick nods, backs out and locks the door, sure of two things: one, he needs to know more about Olivia Cruikshank and two, what does Ellen Smith have against her?

CHAPTER
Two

Olivia

Thank goodness he's gone. Olivia sighs, grateful she's alone at last.

She stretches herself out on the foul-smelling cot, breathes out and does her best to relax. It might be dark and cold, but here she can be herself.

That guard was too friendly. Olivia doesn't trust him. He might be good-looking, but he'll be as heartless as every other officer she's ever met when it comes down to it. They're all the same.

He doesn't bear thinking about. Nothing bears thinking about.

Olivia wriggles her fingers under her stays and tugs the hidden purse of contraband free. She grins to herself, knowing it escaped detection when they searched her. Matron wasn't watching carefully, and the girl searching gave Olivia a wink. She is a Class One prisoner, assigned to responsible tasks, but they're still mates when it is important. Not that they would have searched in Olivia's stays anyhow. They never do. For now, she secrets her purse away beneath her threadbare blanket. In five days, she'll share her meagre bounty with the other girls.

She turns her attention to the stone walls, her friends, every one of those bricks. It may not be the same cell as before, but it all feels the same in the dark. Olivia has named each stone in the wall, although most of them are John and Mary. She doesn't know that many different names to do it properly. They are like Olivia's audience, and she sings to them as though she is Guiditta Pasta. Guiditta sings opera and is famous. Olivia heard her singing once in London from outside the theatre, and she still remembers every note. She thought she'd be famous like the opera singer by now. But she doesn't want to think about what might have been.

What she has now is her brick wall audience, so she stands and faces all those Johns and Marys and she sings. Softly, mind you, because she doesn't want the guards, or any of the others to hear. The guards would likely beat her, or take her thin blanket, or refuse her food. And the other prisoners, they are happy with the merry, facetious songs she entertains them with, content for Olivia to be their court jester. But the opera, this Aria from Rossini's *Semiramide*, this is what she loves to sing. She never understood the Italian words, but she remembers the tune. And if there are parts she has remembered wrong, she just makes them up, anyway. The stone wall doesn't care whether Olivia is wrong or right. Bricks are silent listeners, happy to accept her every note, and she can imagine them as enthralled concert-goers if she wants to. The only thing they don't do is applaud.

Olivia steps closer to the wall, running her hand across the rough surface and twirls in a pirouette as she hits one of the higher notes. A noise outside the cell stops her, and she holds her breath. Did someone hear her? Is someone there? Olivia quickly sits on the narrow cot again, schooling her features into a bored expression, just in case.

Minutes pass, but she remains undisturbed. She launches into her aria picking up where she left off. The singing helps keep her mind away from troubling memories and haunting thoughts.

The grind of a key in the lock halts her song again, and she waits for the door to groan on its hinges as it opens. It's Micky, back with her staple bread and water. She smiles at him in the dim light that comes with the opening door.

'Yer back. I thought a different turnkey would bring me food.'

'I offered to bring it. I'm on my way home.'

Olivia nods. Fair enough. 'Well, what delicacies are ya providin' tonight, then?'

The twitch of his whiskered lips shows her he appreciates her absurd humour.

'I thought you might like some devilled kidney and an excellent red wine.'

A man who plays along. She likes that. But it doesn't mean she likes him. He is still Olivia's gaoler. He has to duck a little to get inside the doorway. An amusing idea hits her. 'Hey, was you arrested on account of bein' too tall?'

'Now that's a new one,' he says in a droll voice. 'Were you arrested for being too short?'

Olivia pouts, pretending offence. But is he fishing for her criminal history or what? This is the second time. She doesn't want to talk about it, not with the likes of him. Then she would have to talk about her mother, and that is not an option. Olivia doesn't even want to think about *her*.

'Sorry. I overstepped again, didn't I?' He looks sheepish.

'Just give me the food an' go.'

Drat the man. He's put the thought in her head now, but she doesn't want to think about the past.

Micky places the plate next to Olivia and withdraws in silence, apart from the resistant noise the door makes. And she doesn't blame it. That door was probably sent here for no reason, either.

No. She must think of something else. What did that magistrate say today? Is this what she wants? This cycle of punishment? But here she is accepted. Here, she is one of the girls. Here, she can get her hands on anything she wants. If Olivia tries to do better, she will lose all that. They would despise her, well, those who don't despise her already. She doesn't want that. They are her family. Better family than she's ever had, ever since Papa, anyway.

She can't think about this. She needs to do something. Olivia gets up and leans against the wall at an angle, pressing herself back and forward. She needs to keep the strength in her arms. You never know when she'll need it. And the same with her legs. When she's spent a long time on the wall presses, she starts on squats. No-one will find Olivia weak and vulnerable. She can take care of herself if she needs to.

Images crowd into Olivia's head. Images she doesn't want to give any time to. She paces up and down the few feet she has, trying not to kick either her bucket of water, or the bucket provided for her—waste. Heaven forbid she mistakes the difference in the dark. She hates solitary confinement. She hates it. Hates it. Hates it. Just let her back out there with the girls, where she can work and sing and make them laugh. Anything but this silence.

Olivia sits down once again, pulls off her mobcap and unpins her braid from the knot at the back of her head. Fully unwound, it reaches below her breasts, and when she unravels it and runs her fingers through the strands, it reaches her waist. They used to cut Olivia's hair short as a punishment, but they have now realised it is more of a punishment to leave it long. It grows back too fast, anyhow. And now she must deal with terrible tangles without a brush, constant problems with head lice, and the difficulty of keeping it clean. It wasn't so hard when she was out on assignment, but in here? In here, it will be bad. Olivia spends a long time combing through her hair with her fingers, and then carefully braids it again, although she leaves the braid hanging loose down her back. A long time ago, Mother used to take the time to braid her hair every day. Mother. Why is Olivia thinking about her again?

She jumps to her feet and paces again. It would be good if she could just go to sleep and forget, but she's not tired enough. Olivia considers eating the stale bread, but it holds little appeal. She feels weary just imagining chewing the bland crust. She tries singing to the wall again, but it's not working. Thoughts are crowding in. Memories. Memories she wants to avoid. Memories she wishes were not there at all.

Olivia is only seventeen, and her life is going nowhere. There is no future for her. And it is all because of her. Because of her selfish, manipulative, inconsiderate mother. She lies down, clutching the coarse blanket to her chest, and lets the memories come. There is no way she can hold them at bay for five days.

***

Olivia
London 1835

Her stomach gurgles with hunger. Her family has travelled all day, only stopping to rest once or twice. But Papa wants to be at Covent Garden before sunset so he can set up their market stall ready for the morrow. Olivia's legs

13

ache from walking, even though Papa sometimes allows her to ride in the cart. Mama says she needs to learn to walk long distances so she can be strong. To Olivia, that just seems cruel and unfair. She's not a grownup like them.

'Are we nearly there?' she asks Papa. It seems like they will never arrive.

'Stop yer whinin', girl.' It is her mother who replies.

Papa puts a hand on Olivia's shoulder and points to the sky. 'See how the sun lowers to the horizon? When it sits just above the buildings, we'll be in London.'

Olivia smiles at him, thankful for the encouragement.

'You'll notice the buildings gettin' bigger an' better the closer we get, too.'

'Why, Papa?'

'Well, because many people live in London, an' where we're headed is where the richer people live in their fine houses.'

'They're the ones who'll buy our fruit for the best prices,' Mother adds.

'I'm hungry.' Olivia's stomach growls again.

'You can wait.'

The thing is, Olivia knows there are baskets and baskets of freshly picked fruit in the back of the cart.

'Why can't I just 'ave an apple?'

Papa reaches under the cover, but Mama slaps his hand away.

'One piece o' fruit won't hurt.'

'That's one less piece o' fruit we can sell. She can eat when we get to the market.'

They go on arguing while Olivia imagines living in one of the fine houses Papa mentioned. It would be a simple matter to sneak a nectarine or apricot while they're not looking, but that is wrong. And Mama would give her a severe lashing if she found out. Olivia doesn't understand why Mama is so strict about it. *She* steals all the time. Especially olives. Mama loves olives. She loves them so much she named her daughter after them. But Papa says olives are too expensive, so Mama steals them whenever she gets the chance. The second she hears someone hawking French goods, she is there like a moth to a bright and dangerous flame. Anything French is her weakness, but particularly olives.

14

Papa once told Olivia that her Grandmama worked in one of those big houses and would sneak Mama some French delicacies from time to time. That's where it started, where she got the taste for olives. As she grew, she swiped them for herself. So now, she has no hesitation. When she wants olives, she steals them.

But if Olivia ever stole anything from her… well, Mama would find some horrible way to punish her. She is so unfair.

The last time after Mama stole some olives, she disappeared for several weeks. Some men took her away. When Olivia asked Papa, he said she went to visit a relative. Olivia is not sure she believes him. Mother didn't seem pleased to go, and isn't it supposed to be fun to visit relatives? It was always fun to visit Grandma and Grandpa. Papa's explanation didn't ring true.

At first light the next morning, after they have slept, huddled in blankets, on the back of the cart next to the sweet-smelling fruit, they get busy setting up the stall. It was not a frosty night, being that it was summer. But it is a little uncomfortable when squashed between her parents and forced to listen to Papa snore and Mama murmur in her sleep. Already tired, Olivia is now made to help Papa make the display of their fruit look pretty for the customers. Mama says if they make it pretty, it will draw customers to their stall. And so, they decorate the stall with fresh flowers and try to stack the fruit so that it doesn't look like a mess.

Soon the market square fills with noise: more carts trundling by, horses clip-clopping on the cobbled street, dogs barking, chickens squawking. Next comes the street cries of hawkers advertising their produce, and customers haggling over prices.

There are people everywhere Olivia looks and besides the sweet smell of their fruit, she recognises the odour of manure, slabs of cut meat, the earthy smell of animals and the people themselves. There is so much to absorb. Sometimes she just stands there, staring, drinking it all in. It is so different to their life on the outskirts of a small village, where they live on a farm. There, it is much quieter and peaceful.

They spend two days selling all their fruit. Papa is always pleased if they sell it all. During the summer, they bring fruit to the market every week—apples, pears, strawberries, and cherries. The money will see them through the winter months until the next crop comes in. When they have nothing left to sell, they take their turn to be customers, buying other fruit and vegetables they can take home for Mama to preserve. Usually, the prices at Covent Garden are too high and they go to one of the cheaper markets to buy their goods. But Mama spotted jars of olives at a nearby stall yesterday and she insists they need to get some.

Olivia knows what this means. Papa frowns but says nothing. Olivia supposes he has given up arguing with her. Mama always gets her way. She says Papa doesn't really love her if he doesn't help her get the olives, that if he really loved her, he would do anything for her.

They go over to the stall where the olives are, and Papa starts up a conversation with the stallholder. This is the way they work it. Papa distracts the owner, while Mama slips a jar of olives into her bag. Only this time it's different. As soon as she turns away from the stall, she hands me the bag.

''Ere, you look after it.'

Instinctively, Olivia knows this is not a good idea. Stealing is wrong. She knows it. And Mama knows it, Olivia can tell by the way she scans the crowd.

'Why, Mama?'

'Because if I get caught with that bag, I'll be forced to visit them relatives again, for longer this time. And then who'll make you an' Papa dinner? Who'll wash yer clothes? Who'll look after ya when yer sick, or mend yer cuts an' scrapes?' She gives Olivia one of those sad smiles. 'You love me, don't ya cherub?'

'Yes, Mama.'

'Then do this one thing fer me.' She holds out the bag again. Olivia swallows the lump in her throat and takes it. The lump in her throat grows and her hands are slick with fear. She twists the handle of the bag around her fingers, so it won't slip. Her heart pounds.

'But what if I get caught?'

'You won't.'

'But what if I am? Will I 'ave to visit yer relatives?'

Mama rolls her eyes but leans down to Olivia.

'O' course not. What're they gonna do? You're a little seven-year-old girl, with big brown eyes.' She pouts her lips. 'They won't do a thing. Yer just an innocent child.' She straightens. 'Besides, I will be with ya, right by yer side. Ya got nothin' to fear.'

But Mama is wrong, so very wrong. It was a god-forsaken lie. Within moments, big hairy hands encircle Olivia's arm, and a gruff voice hisses in her ear. 'Come 'ere thief.'

Olivia whips her head around. 'Mama? Papa?'

But all she can see is the stallholder Mama just stole from and he isn't about to let her go. She screams at the top of her lungs, pulling against his grip, desperately searching the crowd for a glimpse of her parents. But they are gone. Flown.

Terror takes hold of Olivia, and she can barely walk. The stallholder doesn't care. He half lifts, half drags her away. She doesn't know where they are going, but she is sure of one thing: it is *not* to visit relatives.

Soon, the paralysing terror dissolves into hopeless tears. Where are her parents? Why did they run? Why did they leave her to be taken away by a stranger? Olivia cannot make sense of it. She is too little. They are not supposed to leave her alone. Are they?

The stallholder takes Olivia to another man, whom he addresses as constable. 'This waif just stole me olives, sir.'

'But I didn't. It wasn't me.' Olivia shakes her head hard, her heart beating as fast as Mama's arm when she whips the cream. But, drat it, she still holds the bag, which the stallholder wrenches from her frozen hands. He opens it and shows the constable the jar and Olivia starts to sob again. 'I didn't do it. I didn't do it. Where's Papa?' Why didn't he stay and protect her? Olivia is bereft. She doesn't know what to do.

Next thing, the constable and the stallholder take her somewhere else. Olivia finds herself in an important-looking room with a bench at the front and various rows of seats. A man with a wig sits at the front bench and bangs a wooden hammer on the desk.

'Next,' he calls.

The constable leads Olivia to the front.

'Who is the defendant?'

'Olivia Cruikshank.'

'Charges?'

'Theft of a jar of olives.'

'Witness?'

The stall holder stands up and tells his story again, while Olivia stands there, trembling and crying. She can't even think she's so scared. What are they going to do to her?

'Do you have any defence, girl?' The man at the bench asks Olivia. He looks bored.

She can't think. She can't think. All she can manage is to sob and shake her head.

The man looks down at his desk for a minute, then back at Olivia. 'Since this is your first offense, miss, I will extend mercy. You may go home, but be warned, stealing has serious consequences. Think twice before doing it again.' He raps his hammer down again, and it is over.

But Olivia is still alone. She steps out of the building, not knowing where she is or how she is to find her way home.

CHAPTER
Three

Mick

He starts his day as he always does, on his knees with his Bible before him. Mick needs His strength to see him through these days at the Female Factory. God loves these women, no matter who they are or what they've done, and Mick endeavours to see them through His eyes. Not a simple task, given that they can be vulgar or aggressive. He prefers to assume that is not who they really are, but a show they put on to protect themselves. He wants to see *them*, the people behind the masks, and only his heavenly father can show him that.

There are a few inmates who make him want to search out their true nature. He is curious about them. Miss Cruikshank, for instance. Every time he brings her food or water in solitary, she seems cheerful to a fault. They have quickly formed a pattern of banter between them, not unpleasant, but he cannot but wonder if it is all pretence on her part. And if she pretends, then why? Truth be told, each time he sees her, she is a little less exuberant, so he suspects the hours alone have affected her, despite her attempts to convince him otherwise. And sometimes, when he passes her cell, he hears singing. Beautiful notes of a soprano quality. He has stood there, mesmerised by her song, wondering if he imagined it. It seems such a contrast to everything she shows.

And then there is Ellen Smith. She is quiet of late—since Miss Cruikshank returned. She does what is required of her but is a little subdued since the petite blonde arrived. Today, Mick intends to seek her out, see if he can unearth what goes on inside her pretty head. There is one more day until Miss Cruikshank is released from solitary, and Mick would like to know what to expect, if anything. He got the distinct impression that Miss Smith does not like Miss Cruikshank. Is there trouble in the wind?

He voices all his concerns and curiosities to God, leaving his day in His hands, and prepares to head to the Cascades.

The Female Factory is nestled in a valley near the base of Mt. Wellington, alongside a stream. A picturesque spot if one doesn't know the horrors that go on inside the prison. Indeed, that is why the prisoners have nicknamed the place the Valley of the Shadow of Death.

Mick enters the gaol, collects his keys, and begins his rounds. His job is to assist the Matron to keep order in the yards. She seems frustrated most of the time. Mick suspects her husband, the Superintendent, does not fulfil his duties well, leaving her to carry much of the load. And she is already carrying a child. It seems an enormous burden she must manage.

Mick has not been here long, but he has noticed that there is a sort of club among the women. People call them the flash mob. He supposes they signify their membership by a 'flashy' accessory they wear, perhaps a red ribbon, or a shiny ring. He does not know too much about this group, save that they stick together. Like sisters.

Miss Cruikshank, he reckons, is one of them, with her pink mobcap. And Miss Smith, with her gold earrings and colourful buttons. Today Miss Smith works at the washtubs, as all the crime class prisoners do. Hard labour. They lift and carry gallons and gallons of water every day, rub and scrub and wring and beat. Wet linen is heavy, and he is certain that by the end of the day their arms must ache severely. Especially during the warmer months when the sun sets later, and they therefore work longer.

He may have sympathy for these women, but by the rules of the institution, they must not slacken off. The problem is there are more workers than there is linen to wash, leaving them idle for several hours. That idleness breeds corruption, and with so many of them filling the yard, no wonder people are horrified at the moral decline of these women.

Mick goes over to Miss Smith on the pretence of checking her work. He scans the yard quickly to make sure he is not being watched too closely.

'Be sure you scrub those stains out, Miss Smith.'

'Yes, sir.' She narrows her eyes at him. She knows she's not to be impudent for fear of punishment, but Mick needs to get her talking.

'How much longer do you have in the wash yard?'

'Two months.' She doesn't look up but keeps rubbing linens on the washboard.

'Do you think you'll be assigned again after that?'

'Maybe.' She shrugs.

I suspect she will not talk, even though Fred, the overseer, does not look in this direction, but then a strange thing happens. Suddenly she looks up at him and lets a little honesty out.

'But maybe I'd rather just stay here.'

Her dark eyes are fierce with determination. He can tell she will make sure she never gets out of crime class, not that he knows why. This seems to be a pattern with many of the women here. But Mick knows there are more opportunities for these ladies than they think right now.

'My parents were convicts.' Mick tells her after checking around the yard again.

He waits for her to acknowledge that statement. After a moment, she glances up at him again and nods. Is there a modicum of respect in her eyes?

'There is life after prison, you know. My family is content and flourishing now. They married, received a land grant, built a farm, and had several children. They would never have had that if they were back in the motherland.'

She watches him for a moment. Does she wonder if he's genuine? She opens her mouth a few times and then closes it again. In the end, she shrugs again.

'I'm happy for 'em.' She goes back to scrubbing.

He's not about to convince her to aspire to that life in one conversation, but the seed is planted. That is enough for now.

Mick glances at Fred again. He is busy laughing at one of the other convicts who has just slipped over with a pail of water and is now soaked through. Mick doubts she will get dry today; it is not warm enough. How these women are supposed to stay healthy is beyond him. Not surprising, the infirmary is always full.

Mick turns his attention back to Miss Smith. There is still something else he wants to know.

'Are you acquainted with Miss Cruikshank? The Super will release her from the dark cells tomorrow.'

Her reaction to that name is both immediate and extreme. She freezes at first, her hands turning white around the washboard. She looks up at him with her teeth clenched and the fire of rage in her eyes.

'Never speak that name to me!'

Mick checks over his shoulder. That cannot have gone unheard. He needs to settle her down immediately.

'Hush now. I meant no harm,' he urges her in a whisper. Aloud and with a stern voice he commands her. 'That's enough, Miss Smith. Do you wish to be locked in solitary?'

He pulls his baton from his belt for good measure, not that he would ever strike her. But her reason has fled, and she rushes at him with clenched fists, knocking into his chest and taking him by surprise.

'I hate her! I hate her!'

She beats on his chest, and he has no choice but to grasp her wrists and force them back behind her waist.

'Calm yourself, woman, before the Super and Matron are called in.'

In truth, he can hear the other women gasping, and Fred is always eager to call for help. Mick's words fall on deaf ears, however. Miss Smith continues to spit and use profanity against him and against Miss Cruikshank, even while Fred tries to grip her shoulders and pull her away.

Next thing Mick knows, he is being called to the Super's office.

'What did you do to set her off, Reeve?'

He is truly at a loss. He merely mentioned Miss Cruikshank's name. How does that turn a person into a spitting, raging firebrand? He cannot admit to instigating a conversation, as he's not supposed to. But he cannot lie either. He opens his mouth to give an answer, but the Super interrupts.

'They said she was screaming about The Shank.' He stares at Mick, expectant, his mouth grim.

'Yes, that's correct.'

'There is history between those two. I'm guessing you know nothing about that.'

Mick shakes his head, no.

'No, otherwise you wouldn't have mentioned her name.'

How does he know?

'I've seen your type before. Too curious. It doesn't pay to be curious about these prisoners, Reeve. They're here for a reason, and that is all you need to know.' He dabs his face with a handkerchief, and Mick notices the pallor on his face. He is unwell.

'Yes, sir.'

'In this instance however, so you don't make the same mistake again, I'll give you the basics of the situation.'

'I appreciate that, sir.'

'When Cruikshank first arrived, she was placed as a bedfellow with Smith. Smith took her under her wing, so to speak and I suspect grew overly attached to Cruikshank. An attachment Cruikshank didn't reciprocate if you catch my meaning.' The Super stares hard at him.

Mick mouths an 'oh.'

'Right, so, then Smith goes out on assignment, falls in with a fellow who gets her pregnant, and she's been back here ever since, paying for her indiscretions. But she blames it all on Cruikshank. In fact, she blames everything on Cruikshank. Her mind has become twisted, especially after having the baby. Her son is in the nursery, kept away from her.'

Mick grimaces. It's certainly a volatile situation. And it explains Miss Smith's reluctance to leave.

'Now, since it was your folly that set her off, it will be your responsibility to discipline her. I've already sent her to the dark cells for a couple of days. You can administer the iron collar for tonight and give her horsehair to pick tomorrow.'

Mick gulps. Disciplining prisoners is not something he ever wanted to do. And yet, if he doesn't, he will lose his job and any chance of giving these women hope.

***

Olivia

Olivia is sick of the dark cell. She is tired of her silent audience, the stale bread, the virtual darkness, and the smell of herself. But most of all, she is sick to the death of the voices in her head, the memories of her mother and what she did, the memories of her father and what he didn't do. She hates Mama, and Olivia is glad she will never have to see her again. She wishes she could forget, but these four walls constantly remind her of the past. Olivia once had such dreams, such plans.

Even after that close call the first time, it didn't stop Mama from insisting Olivia hold her stolen goods. When she was nine years old, Olivia stood before the magistrate again. Once again, Mama didn't show her face, although she promised to stand by Olivia. And once again, she insisted they would not hold Olivia for long. She tried to cry as she had the previous time, hoping this judge would also be merciful. But when he heard it was her second offense, he locked her up in gaol for seven days. Seven long and lonely days.

When Olivia was ten, her sentence was thirty days with hard labour. She did the time, knowing she would eventually be free again. But she learnt during those times never to trust the word of her mother again. And if she couldn't trust her own mother, whom could she trust?

She couldn't even trust Papa in the end. He died and left Olivia at the mercy of all Mama's selfishness.

Olivia planned to run. She aimed to make a name for herself. But then she ended up in Van Diemen's Land. All because of Mama. The woman who called Olivia 'daughter'. And now she is trapped. No matter what anyone else tries to tell her, there is no going back. It can't be undone. She just wants to get out of this cell and find some distraction with the other girls.

Finally, after what seems like an eternity, the latch grates open, and Micky's friendly face appears. Olivia doesn't know why he's always so amiable. Probably some kind of trick he's playing at.

'Time to go,' he says with a wiggle of his eyebrows.

Olivia can't get to the door quick enough. She already has her bag of goodies stashed in her stays, and she tucked her braided hair beneath her cap.

'As much as I enjoy this luxurious hotel room, I reckon it's about time I saw another human face.' Olivia winks at him as she passes.

'Righto. I would never presume to be human, of course.' He rolls his eyes.

'Sorry, Micky. Officers is never human.' Olivia shakes her head. Isn't that the truth? More like monsters, she'd say. Perhaps a very handsome monster, but a monster all the same.

'I would hope you'd see me differently,' he mumbles, the pleasant expression gone from his face. Is that a sigh Olivia hears as he locks the cell behind her?

'What's got you all sullen today, eh?'

'Nothing.' He straightens and takes Olivia by the upper arm to lead her out into the yard. His grip isn't tight as many of the others.

'Sure, an' I didn't just spend five days in solitary.'

He stops walking and turns to Olivia.

'You really want to know?'

Does she? Truthfully, she hadn't thought about it. It was all about banter as usual. But something in his eyes makes Olivia nod. Listening to him yabber on has to be better than the yammering in her head of the last few days.

'Yeah, I guess so. You got secrets or what?' She tries to lighten the mood.

He gives a half laugh, half sigh. 'It's about Ellen Smith.'

Oh. Now Olivia is serious, too. This can't be good.

'I, er,' he clears his throat, 'mentioned your name to her yesterday, and she became agitated—riotous, in fact.'

It's Olivia's turn to sigh. 'I ain't surprised.'

'Well, it surprised me. I've not seen such a reaction before. The Super made me see to her discipline. It's not a duty I would choose to discharge.'

'Wait. Are you sayin' ya dislike punishing girls?' Olivia finds this hard to believe. They're all ruthless.

'Yes, I am. And I don't understand why anyone should enjoy such brutality.' He frowns, then glances behind him before continuing. 'Anyway, I went to her cell and begged her to desist. But she still shouted profanity and behaved violently—not towards me, you understand—but about you, it seems. In the end, I had no choice but to gag her and put the iron collar on. She is in the dark cells for insubordination and misconduct for the next few days.'

Olivia watches his face. He seems shaken, regretful. Ashamed?

'Well, I don't see why you're mopin' about it. She deserved it.' Olivia shrugs and turns to walk toward the mob of women waiting by the washtubs. She's not really into serious conversations, especially not with prison guards.

'But don't you see? It's *my* fault.' He jogs up beside her. 'If I hadn't mentioned you, it wouldn't have happened. She suffers for something *I* did.'

Olivia almost chokes and turns away as her eyes suddenly well up. What is going on? Mama never had that kind of compassion for her own daughter, and here is Micky, wanting to take the blame for a *stranger*.

'She don't deserve yer sympathy,' Olivia grinds out, keeping her face averted. 'She didn't have to react like that. Besides, she's as bad as they come.'

'I don't care what she's done, or what you've done. Everyone needs grace.'

Olivia quickens her steps. What is he on about? She's not heard anyone speak like this since Newgate. She presses a hand over her heart where she has a folded piece of paper tucked beneath her stays. A gift from one caring woman amongst a thousand indifferent faces. A gift that Olivia can't even read.

She lets out a scornful laugh.

'What happened between you two, anyway?'

'Why do you even care?' Olivia stops to let him catch up, but she still doesn't look at him.

'So I don't make the same mistake again.'

She sucks in a deep breath and pushes down the weird feelings his words have stirred. Then she looks up at him, this tall, confusing man.

'Ellen is here fourteen years for robbery and assault. She were here before me an' she were the queen of the flash mob when I arrived. Ellen has, um, strange inclinations towards others. She turned her attentions on me, but I refused her. Now, that shoulda made me an outsider, but,' and Olivia shrugs, 'for some reason, the other girls like me.' She preens herself for good measure and winks. 'Must be me charismatic nature.'

He stands there for a minute, taking this in. 'So, you mean to say she's jealous? You've knocked her off her throne, haven't you?'

Olivia shrugs again. 'Make of it what ya like. I just wanna mind me own business. But I'll give ya this warnin'. If she sees ya talkin' to me all friendly like, you'll make an enemy of her. She's brain sick I reckon. She'll tell ya I done stuff to 'er that ain't even possible.'

Olivia makes a gesture indicating Ellen is cuckoo, then turns to go straight to the washtubs. Partly to end the conversation with Micky, and partly to be around the other girls again. She has some wares to share with them anyhow. They whisper greetings and mouth secret words to each other, passing the wink, as Ann hands Olivia a wet sheet to put through the wringer.

Olivia looks back over her shoulder one more time at Micky, who is now trying to make clandestine conversation with one of the other inmates. He's an odd one for an officer. She doesn't know if she believes his caring talk, but so far, he's not shown any other side. She shakes her head. If he's soft, he's going to get himself in a lot of trouble. Not that Olivia cares, of course. There's no use in paying attention to him, and she forces her eyes back to the others.

'What do ya got for us?' Ann hisses.

Olivia checks around the yard to see if any of the officers are watching them, then reaches into her stays and pulls out the small purse. Olivia gives Jo the nod—she will distract any turnkey that comes close or shows interest. Several of the girls crowd around to have a look. Olivia spills the contents on the stones and shares around the coins and salt pork. The square of lace is for Ann—she has been the most like a friend of recent times. Although you never know when that can change.

The girls shove bits of dried meat in their mouths in delight, tucking coins in their stockings or stays. They will use the coins to buy other food, or tobacco, or tea or even whiskey. There is a good trade available over the walls, or via the cookhouse, or via the coves that bring firewood in. They pass the money to the right person and smuggle the goods in or toss them over the wall. As long as they are careful and don't get caught, it works well.

With her goodies distributed, Olivia starts up a song. A tune with frivolous lyrics, which the other ladies join in. It won't be long before the turnkeys shut them down and threaten them with gagging, but it is worth it for the few seconds of laughter they gain. Olivia glances over at Micky and finds him staring at her, and he wears a frown. But not an angry frown or even a warning, but a frown of puzzlement. She sends him a wink and a swish of her skirts before she bends to the wringer again.

CHAPTER
Four

Olivia

'I need to get me a knife,' Olivia whispers to Ann and presses a few coins into her hand. 'You know someone, don't ya?'

Ann checks their surroundings and looks back at Olivia, her eyes wide. Good old Ann with her broad hips and full chest. She's here for theft too, as is most everybody. She reckons her boss back in the motherland didn't pay her enough, so she lifted some silk stockings and lace handkerchiefs, then tried to sell them on. As a maid, she says, it was easy enough to do, since she had to clean and dust in the mistresses' rooms every day. Trouble came when she tried to sell them. One handkerchief had initials embroidered on the corner, making it recognisable. One fool mistake had her sent to Australia.

'You sure?' she asks.

'Yeah.' Olivia's been thinking about this for a while now. Ann has a beau on the outside, and he'll do anything for her. She reckons he's gonna marry her as soon as he can get approval from the governor. She just has to throw a note and the coins over the wall, and a couple days later, he tosses back the goods. Olivia is aware this will be more dangerous for Ann than usual, but Ann reminds her anyway.

''Cause ya know what happens if ya get caught with it, or if I get caught smugglin' it in? I mean, it's one thing to be discovered with tobacco or whiskey, but you're really riskin' your neck if you wanna get caught with a blade.'

'Well, I'll 'ave to take that risk then. I need it. Ellen's dangerous.'

Ellen will be out of solitary soon and Olivia's dead sure she's got it in for her. More than usual. She needs a knife to defend herself. Ann knows it, so Olivia's pretty sure she won't argue too hard. Ann's friend enough to stick up for her, and she's seen Ellen cause a ruckus before.

It's been fine since Olivia left the dark cell. Business as usual at the tubs. Worn out and aching all over, but no real trouble to be had. But when Ellen gets out, Olivia would wager her left arm she'll stir up all kinds of noise. Olivia voices her concerns to Ann, hoping she'll get it.

'Fine. I'll get you a knife,' she says with a shake of her head, 'but ya better think hard before usin' it.'

Twenty-four hours later, Olivia turns her new blade over in her hands. It's evening, and they're locked in for the night, so no-one's gonna see. Except Ann, of course, who shares a cot with her. It's too dark for any of the other girls crowded in the cell to see what she's holding.

Ann slipped it to Olivia as soon as the turnkeys locked the dormitory door. The edge cuts Olivia's finger as she tests its sharpness. She gasps and sticks the nicked finger into her mouth, tasting blood. It's not a long blade, but long enough to do damage.

Ann whispers another lecture about what will happen if she uses this dagger against Ellen. It's true. It will set some serious dominos falling if Olivia brings it out. But what else is she supposed to do? Let Ellen beat her to a pulp? Let her send Olivia to the infirmary? Ellen wants her dead, she is certain about that. And Olivia is prepared to defend herself.

But if she uses this knife and cuts Ellen, there is no way to avoid discovery. It will mean being locked up for the rest of her life.

Olivia can't go to bed like this, so she paces the cell. Their cell. The girls in the other cots whisper quietly together and Ann lets Olivia think through her words. That magistrate's voice is in her head again. Is this what she wants? Olivia crouches on the floor and leans against the side of the cot. It's the only life she knows. The magistrate said she could be free, but what is freedom, really? She'll never be free.

30

No, the only choice she has if she uses this blade, is to use it properly. Commit herself all the way. Finish Ellen. That will bring the death penalty and then Olivia *will* be free.

Then why does she suddenly feel sick? Sweat makes her hand slick, and she drops the dagger. Her gut clenches. She doesn't really want to do this. Olivia never even wanted to be a thief. And now she premeditates murder? What has she become?

The question remains unanswered as she presses her head between her knees. The walls suddenly feel like they're closing in on her and she can't breathe. She is trapped. Trapped!

Olivia gasps for air. Why can't it all just go away? Why can't she wake up to find it was all just a horrible nightmare? All along, she might have been happy with a mother who loved her and a father who protected her.

Without warning, the key grates in the lock and the door opens. Olivia quickly shoves the knife under the folds of her skirt and raises her arm against the glare from a lantern the visitor holds. She didn't even hear footsteps outside. Was she so lost in her thoughts?

'Are you all right?' Micky sounds concerned. She knows his voice but can't see his face behind the light. The question is, should Olivia believe his kindness is real? She must pull herself together, quick. No-one sees her like this. Blast him, he might make the other girls suspicious, too.

'I'm fine. What are ya doin' here?' Olivia glares at him.

'I am on my last round before I leave. I thought I heard you cr…' he coughs, maybe realising the position he's about to put Olivia in, 'I thought I heard something.'

'It's a windy evenin', I don't reckon you heard right. The floor just makes a change from the crowded bed. Nothin' spectacular in that.' Olivia shrugs. Hopefully, he will leave her alone. She's grateful for the shadows in the cell, hoping they will hide her face.

He places the lantern on the floor and crouches next to her. 'Are you worried about Ellen?' He whispers. Drat him! There are like, fifty other women in the dorm.

'Just drop it, Micky. You're lookin' for somethin' that ain't there.'

31

He squats there in silence for a long time. Olivia is not about to say another word. That would only encourage him to stay. And his presence and attention undermines all her work with the girls.

'You can trust me, you know.'

Olivia lets out a laugh that probably sounds more like a snort, but she's still not talking. Not to him anyway. 'Hey girls, can we trust the guvna?'

A round of boos and hisses rises from multiple cots.

A random thought occurs to Olivia that Micky could probably read that piece of paper she has folded in her stays. That thought is highly unwelcome, and she dismisses it. Olivia would have to trust him for that and she doesn't, despite him telling her she can. Despite him acting like she can.

'So, I'm getting the message you don't want to talk.'

Smart man.

'But I want you to know something. I'll be keeping my eye out for you tomorrow. Especially once Ellen joins the crime class yard.'

What does that mean? Is it a threat? A warning for Olivia to behave herself? That's what she would expect from the other turnkeys. So, he's the same as them after all. Olivia doesn't even bother to acknowledge his words. What seems like minutes pass before he collects the lantern, and his feet shuffle back to the door. Olivia lets out a long breath, picks up her dagger and tucks it into her empty shoes, then climbs onto the cot.

'Don't say a word, Ann. Not a word.' She'd better not lecture her again. Olivia's not in the mood.

***

Mick

Mick has a sense of impending doom today. As he walks the rounds, the tension in the wash yard is palpable, quieter than normal despite the number of prisoners in here. He wonders if the other women feel it too. They released Miss Smith late this morning and since then she and Miss Cruikshank have watched each other. It reminds him of two dogs when they're ready to fight—stiff bodies, hackles up, teeth bared and growling in the back of their throats. He expects one or the other of them to pounce soon. After expressing his concerns to Matron, she tells him in no uncertain terms to make sure he gives Fred full support in the event there is trouble.

Miss Cruikshank concerns Mick most. Not a song has departed her lips today. She seems agitated and fidgety. And several times today he has seen her touch her waistband, particularly when she looks at Miss Smith. She has something hidden there. He'd wager a dozen sheep on it.

Mick prays under his breath that this confrontation does not happen. Somehow, he must stop it before it starts. He has no way of knowing who else might join in defending one or the other. And then he shall be forced to intervene. He is obliged to take actions for which he has no desire. He is conscious of the baton sheathed at his waist. There's not one fibre in his body that wants to use it. And yet if he doesn't, he will soon have Fred, Matron and the Superintendent down on his head.

He stays as close to Miss Cruikshank as he can without making it obvious. He fears she might make things worse for herself, and if he can stop her, he will. It is late afternoon when Mick sees Miss Smith and two of the other prisoners head toward Miss Cruikshank. Miss Cruikshank has seen them too, and her hand immediately goes for her waist. Mick does not hesitate but goes up behind her and lays his hand over hers within the folds of her skirt.

'Don't do it, Miss Cruikshank,' he whispers in her ear. He only has a few seconds to disarm her. Miss Smith has paused, rethinking her actions with Mick in the picture, but it won't be long before she continues her advance.

'Don't do what?' Miss Cruikshank says through clenched teeth.

'Give me whatever it is you have hidden before you do something you regret.'

She grunts.

'I can make sure no-one ever knows you had a weapon in your possession. Just slip it to me now. But I promise this will not go well for you if you use it.'

He can sense her body tense.

'How do I know I can trust ya?'

'You don't.' What else is he going to say? This must be her decision. If

33

she surrenders the weapon, Mick will do his best to protect her, but she has no way of knowing that.

It feels as though the next few seconds tick by so slowly, but next thing, he feels hard metal slide into his hand. She did it. She let it go. He breathes out in relief.

'Well done, Miss Cruikshank.'

While he is still this close to her, he slips the knife into his waistband, sure that no-one saw the exchange. In fact, Fred leers at him, reading his actions in another way altogether. Well, let Fred make vulgar conclusions if he wishes. It will keep the truth hidden.

Mick backs away from Miss Cruikshank, relieved he has downgraded the oncoming battle. He reckons it won't end well yet, but Miss Cruikshank may have just saved her own life. Even so, Mick stays nearby, sure he will need to break up an imminent fight.

'Did ya cop a good handful?'

He turns to see Fred grinning at him with a lascivious smirk. Mick makes a grimace at him.

'Looks like she were enjoyin' it.' He chuckles.

Mick imagines twisting his filthy ears so hard he screams in agony. Instead, he fakes a laugh.

'She's a pretty thing, ain't she?' He licks his lips, and Mick is disgusted. 'Just a word o' warnin' to ya, though. Others 'ave tried an' got their nose broke for the effort.'

Mick raises his eyebrows at him.

'Yep. Kinda surprised she didn't crack 'er elbow into yer face just then, actually.'

Was this the trouble they all hinted at when she first arrived back from assigned labour? Was she violent? Yet, she had handed over the knife with little resistance. That must have been a big step for her. Mick realises he is still gaping at Fred, when high-pitched screams fill the yard.

Miss Smith has chosen their moment of distraction to make her attack. Mick swivels back to see her charge at Miss Cruikshank, knocking her to the ground. He bets Miss Cruikshank wishes she had that knife right now.

Yes, there. She glances at him briefly with a scowl as she scrambles to her feet. Fred and Mick are already on their way over.

Heedless of them or their roared warnings to desist, Miss Cruikshank simply walks up to Miss Smith and while the latter swings her arm back for a blow, rams the ball of her hand into Miss Smith's nose with force. Miss Smith hits the ground without the chance to land a single punch. It's kind of impressive, but Mick cannot afford to show his appreciation of such fighting skills. He wonders why Miss Cruikshank thought she needed a knife.

Miss Cruikshank stands there, calm as a summer's day. Even though Miss Smith's friends are now ready to rush her, she doesn't move. He supposes it's because she hears Fred yelling for backup as he tries to hold them back, standing between them and Miss Cruikshank. Meanwhile, Mick approaches her and grasps her upper arms from behind. She flinches, but she doesn't fight him off.

'You know I must cuff you and take you to a holding cell, don't you?'

She flicks her head up and around and winks at him. 'That's what they pay ya for, eh, Micky.'

And just like that, her agitation is gone. As Mick leads her away, she hums a tune. As though nothing happened at all. This young woman both intrigues and confounds him. More than ever, he wants to know what brought her to Van Diemen's Land, to the penal colony. Is she a cold-blooded killer? It would appear so from some of her actions, and from others' reactions to her. But he is certain he has seen vulnerability in her face, although she does her best to hide it. And he is sure he has heard her weep at night.

As he unlocks a cell and guides her inside, he stares into her eyes. *Who are you, Miss Cruikshank?* She holds his gaze for the briefest of moments and then looks away with a smirk. But as fleeting as it was, he thinks he reads gratitude in those wide brown eyes, and perhaps a little relief. She sinks to the floor and lets out a long breath.

'Were ya serious about the knife?' She scratches at a scab on her arm—a nervous habit, perhaps?

'What knife?'

With that familiar sideways tilt to her head, she looks up at him and her mouth opens, then shuts again as understanding dawns. She nods and swallows. She knows he holds the power to destroy her future right now, but he's not sure she entirely trusts him with it.

'You know you'll have to go before the Principal Superintendent, don't you?'

She nods again. 'Nothin' I haven't done before.'

Does she mean she is familiar with the process or familiar with attacking women?

'I'll most likely be required to testify to what happened.'

She curses.

'You can trust me, you know.'

'Hmph.'

'The thing is, Miss Cruikshank, I want to help you. But if I speak in your defence, I need you to do something for me.'

''Ere it comes. I knew it.' She gets up and walks to the opposite wall, facing away from me. 'Whatever it is, you can be damned,' she hisses.

For a moment, Mick is not sure what she means. Until he remembers, he is working in the prison system. Prisoners and staff exchange favours all the time. Corrupt favours. Unsavoury favours. He closes his eyes, troubled by her assumption.

'It's not what you think. Please look at me, Miss Cruikshank. Please.'

Time ticks by slowly, but eventually, she turns. He takes a deep breath, hoping she will really take this in.

'I want you to promise me you will try to do better. You *are* better than this. You can be free soon and have a life outside these walls. There is a wonderful future out there for you, but only if you believe it.'

She lets out a scornful laugh and opens her mouth as if to say something snide, but then she shudders and sighs. 'I'll try.'

CHAPTER
Five

Olivia

She's never been nervous about standing before Mr Spode before, or about being condemned. Not since she was a little girl. Olivia always knows exactly what to expect. But not today. Today, she doesn't know what will happen. What possessed her to give Micky the knife? He says she can trust him, but hey, her mother said she could trust her too. Why should he be any better? He says he will defend her, but he could just as easily produce the knife and condemn her to death. And Olivia doesn't see why he wouldn't. What is she to him? Just another filthy prisoner, that's what.

The prison carriage trundles along the streets to the courthouse. The sun shines outside, but she is not in the mood to enjoy it. It will take all her energy to show a strong face today. Olivia bleeds from several places where she has picked her skin raw. It's a terrible thing she does, but she can't help herself. Sometimes the pain of a few small wounds feels better than the agony of uncertainty, of never being free.

If only Ellen had let go of the past. How was Olivia to know the other girls would choose her over Ellen? None of this is her fault. Ellen should be the one standing in court today, and yet Olivia is the one who suffers the consequences. No good can come of this, and she is a fool if she expects anything else.

The carriage pulls up and next thing Olivia knows, Micky's muscular arms help her down. Anxiety makes her knees weak, and she stumbles slightly. Did he notice? His grip on her arm seems to tighten, but his face tells her nothing. Why is he so good to her? Or is he? It's probably just a front, and he's waiting for the perfect opportunity to do her in. That would be any moment now. Olivia takes a deep breath and stiffens herself. She cannot afford to show weakness. But she doesn't have the strength to make her usual light-hearted banter either, so she remains silent and lets him lead her inside, doing her best to keep her head held high.

The courtroom is just as she remembers it—dark and wood and paper and leather. They sit in the back and wait for her name to be called. Her fingers find the scabs on her arms again. Waiting is the worst part. Olivia just wants it to be over, so she can go on with whatever it is Mr Spode, the Principal Superintendent, decides for her life. Strange to think that one man has control over her destiny. Why do people insist Olivia needs to make the best of her life? Whatever she does, someone else messes it up for her. She is not in control of her future at all.

Olivia feels a nudge on her arm. Of course, Micky sits right next to her. It's hard to forget that. Another person who holds her life in his hands. He oozes strength, and not just because he's tall and muscular. Why can't Olivia lean on such support? Because she doesn't believe his strength is for her. She knows it as surely as she knows she is a prisoner. He will use his power to squash her like an annoying insect. Olivia turns to him reluctantly, expecting to see the glint of victory in his eyes. Instead, he nods, his eyes… encouraging? As if he says *it will be all right*.

It's not fair. How dare he try to make her feel hope? Olivia frowns at him and turns away. *Please hurry and call my name.*

When they finally call her up, she is so nervous her knees have lost their ability to work. She must grip the stand to keep herself from falling.

Mr Spode looks her over and seems to shake his head, although that might be her imagination.

'What are the charges?'

'Disorderly conduct and assault.'

'Witnesses?'

Fred Peterson, the overseer from the wash yard, gets up.

'Olivia Cruikshank has a long history of violent attacks, as ya will see in 'er file. The same in this case. She assaulted another prisoner, Ellen Smith, in an unprovoked attack.'

Unprovoked, he says. Lying piece of filth. Just as Olivia suspected, the guards have it in for her. She digs her nails into her skin even harder to stop them from trembling.

'What kind of attack?'

'One punch to the face, sir.'

'Thank you. Next witness.'

It's Micky's turn now. Olivia feels like she might vomit. She can already hear the creak of the rope as she swings in the wind. One mention of the word knife and it's all over. He takes the stand.

'Name?'

'Michael Reeve.'

The big Super looks up at him for a moment, as though studying him and then continues.

'Position?'

'Turnkey in the wash yard.'

'And what did you see?'

'Sir, I have observed animosity between Miss Smith and Miss Cruikshank over the past several weeks. Yesterday, I suspected there would be a confrontation and so there was. Miss Smith moved to attack Miss Cruikshank, pushing her to the ground. Miss Cruikshank punched her once, as Mr Peterson testified. It is my belief, however, that this was self-defence.'

Olivia can't believe her ears. He kept his word. Why would he do that? Now she feels sicker than ever. Not because she thinks it's going to go badly for her, but because she doesn't want to hope it might go well. Looking at Micky, she's not sure what to think. His face has paled, and he keeps glancing over at Mr Spode's assistant. Did that not go as well as it sounded? The swirling in her stomach kicks up a notch.

Mr Spode dismisses Micky and turns to her.

'Do you have anything to say in your defence, Miss Cruikshank?'

Normally Olivia says nothing, or happily admits to her supposed crime.

Today she is tongue tied. Her mouth has gone dry, and she finds it difficult to breathe properly.

'I … it … is as M … M … Mr Reeve says.' She's got to stop stammering. 'Ellen's had it in for me for a long time. I hit 'er to stop 'er attackin' me, is all. I feared she'd kill me if I didn't knock 'er out.'

That wasn't easy to say. Olivia's never admitted to fear in her life. But if it helps her, she supposes she needs to use it. Now Micky and the others will know how weak she really is. She'll have to play it tough even more when she gets back to the Cascades.

Next, he calls the Superintendent up.

'The history between Smith and Cruikshank goes back for years. The antagonism between them is a disruption to the Cascades Female Factory. I am concerned that if we do not separate them, a riot will eventually ensue. I would ask you to consider that in making your judgment.'

More reason to hope? Will they move Ellen away? This gets better by the minute. And here she thought the gallows would be her destiny earlier today.

The big Super goes quiet for a time, while he re-reads over everything and weighs up all the options. When he's done, he folds his hands together and looks up at Olivia with gravity, although she notices he keeps glancing over at Micky.

'Although I believe you acted in self-defence, Miss Cruikshank, assault is still a very serious matter. Normally, I would sentence you to a long stint in solitary confinement on rations of bread and water, followed by several months of hard labour. However, I must also take into consideration the well-being of other prisoners at the Female Factory.' He takes a deep breath and leans back in his chair. 'I have recently received a request for a convict to work at the Iron Pot Lighthouse. While it is unconventional to send a woman to this position, I believe it would be best for all concerned.'

Amidst shocked whispers, he ends the proceedings. Olivia's own thoughts have fled, except for his words repeating in her head—the Iron Pot Lighthouse. It's not Ellen who is to be sent away, it's her. And this might be worse than hanging.

***

Mick

They're to send Miss Cruikshank away. Just when he thinks he is finally getting through to her. It makes him wonder if it is worth all the effort. The one prisoner who he thinks he's made headway with is gone, while he remains with all the hard-nosed women, including Ellen Smith, and prison staff who are sure to see him as soft now.

For a moment he thought Mr Spode would be lenient, but then, the Lighthouse. There is something very familiar about Mr Spode's assistant, though. He looked at Mick longer than courtesy allows. As though he knew him. And for a second, Mick thought he recognised him, too. *Raff?*

But it couldn't be. Raff, an employee in the legal system? Mick hadn't seen him in almost ten years, since that fateful day in school. The first time he ever took a stand against injustice, and suffered for it. And today, while defending Miss Cruikshank on the stand, it all came back to him. Has he just made things worse for her by standing against injustice?

He shakes his head. No, he is certain her punishment would have been worse if he hadn't intervened. Oh, but the Lighthouse? She will be out of reach now. His heart sinks as he leads her outside. Somehow, he must find words of encouragement for her.

'I'm sorry, Miss Cruikshank,' he whispers, checking to make sure no-one is in earshot.

Her chains rattle as she turns to him, looking up at him with a quizzical expression.

'Sorry? For what?'

'That they're sending you to the Lighthouse.'

She looks at the ground and twists her cuffed hands together, then clears her throat, before glancing up again.

'Don't be sorry. Ya told the truth. That's more than anyone's ever done for me.' Her voice is little more than a murmur and she turns her head away, as if to watch the passing traffic. 'I don't know why ya've been nice to me, but thanks.'

41

Mick can feel a lump developing in his throat. He could help this young lady, he knows he could, if only she remained at the Factory.

'You are more valuable than you know.' He swallows past the lump. 'Even when you think no-one else cares, God cares. Deeply. That's what I've been trying to show you. There is freedom for you, but you must believe it first.'

She stares at him with those brown eyes, and they even seem a little glassy. *Am I getting through?* He knows she doesn't want anyone to see her vulnerable, so he lightens the mood.

'Try to stay out of trouble, you fearsome beast.' He gently cuffs her on the chin.

She rises to the occasion and grins.

'An' you too. Such an evil prison worker you are. 'Ave fun keepin' Ellen Smith under control, won't ya?'

A carriage rolls around and pulls up in front of them.

Mick feigns a sigh and mutters under his breath. 'If only she were as amiable as you.'

She chuckles and winks at him. 'Trouble is, Micky, yer just not friendly enough.'

And with those words they pack her into the carriage, doors shut behind her. She doesn't even look back at him as they drive away.

As he stands there watching the empty street, he senses someone approaching and he turns. It's Mr Spode's offsider.

'Michael Reeve? Is it really you?'

He has his hand stretched out in greeting. Mick takes it and shakes. 'Yes.'

'Raphaelo Cardamone. Do you remember me? From school?'

It *is* him.

'Yes, of course I do. But I thought … you never returned to school after, after that day.'

'Correct. So I never got the chance to thank you.'

'For what?'

'You stood up for me to Mr Foresythe.'

'And made it worse.' The teacher had given Raff a whipping because

42

his pencil rolled off his desk. It was not fair. The punishment did not fit the crime. When Mick stood and begged Mr Foresythe to leave Raff alone, the teacher then turned on Mick.

Raff pressed his lips together. 'Only for you, and I'm sorry you suffered. You took the beating I was about to receive.'

Yes, and those bruises had lasted a long time. 'But you never came back, even though Mr Foresythe was replaced.'

He laughs. 'No. My papa was the one who had Mr Foresythe sacked, and after a terrible meeting with the board, sent me to another school.'

'And now you're a … ?'

'And now I'm a lawyer,' he nods, still grinning. 'Because of what happened that day.'

Mick is astounded. He'd never realised his actions were of any help. 'You've no idea how good it is to hear you say that.'

'Are you finished for the day? Would you join me at the coffeehouse? Tell me about your life and how you ended up working in the penal system.'

'Great. I'd love to.' He never expected this to come out of a day of tension, but it is a welcome surprise. Raff crosses the street and Mick follows, keen to learn more about his story.

CHAPTER
Six

Olivia

May, 1841—Iron Pot Lighthouse—11 months remaining

Why is she here? Olivia did the right thing and gave up that damned knife and look where it got her. She's now stuck on this tiny rock island with a few other convicts, Henry Douglas, the head keeper, and his wife. They tell her the lighthouse is forty-odd feet high, a whitewashed tower with an enormous lantern at the top. Forty-odd feet of stomach-churning steps to climb. Other than the lighthouse, there is a small, two-room hut for the accommodations. Mrs Douglas and Olivia sleep in there during the night, along with one of the three men, depending who is on shift. During the day, the men take turns to sleep as well. There is no escape and there is no solitude. Except perhaps when she works in the lighthouse. If Mrs Douglas finishes with Olivia for the day, she is sent into the lighthouse to wash the walls. Those walls are the only thing that separate her from a long fall to the rocks below, and anything higher than the first half-dozen steps makes her swoon.

Olivia can see the mainland in the distance, so close it torments her, but the surging ocean separates them, making the distance insurmountable. And she is sure, as sure as that stretch of water would drown her, that trouble will find her here, just as it has everywhere else. As she stands out here, the cold south wind stinging with brine in her face, she prepares the fowl as Mrs Douglas bid her. Olivia pulls at the feathers with force, imagining she is tearing the hair from her mother's head, from Ellen's head, from the head of everyone who has made her life hell. Even from Micky's head.

No. She recants that. Micky is one person who has tried to help her, even if he is misguided. He's the second person she can remember who stood on her side. Pity she's not at Cascades anymore. She might have learned to like him. Or not. Maybe she got out of there in time, before she found out he's not as good as he makes out.

Then again. He had that same look in his eyes as that lady back when Olivia was in Newgate. Compassion. Such a rare commodity, she doesn't even know if she can believe in it. Olivia puts the bird down and reaches her fingers beneath her stays for the piece of paper she keeps there. She takes it out and unfolds it. It is worn and stained, but it is a treasure she has never departed with. Olivia wonders if the words the lady put there are even readable anymore. Not that she could ever read them. She closes her eyes and tries to remember.

Newgate—London, 1835

While kicking her heels in Newgate, waiting for her ship to sail, Olivia has plenty of time to think and to fret. Part of her feels guilty for leaving Mama on her own, but she pushes that feeling down quick smart. Mama deserves it. She deserves to suffer as much as Olivia. But, knowing Mama, she'll find someone else to manipulate soon enough. Will it be another bloke, or another kid like Olivia?

Newgate stinks like the worst kind of filth. Sewage, unwashed bodies, and foul clothes. The cells are crowded, with barely enough room to find a spot to sit, let alone lie down and rest—not that she wants to sleep on that rank floor. And there is no food. They must beg from passersby on the street. And of course, the loudest, strongest women get the food, not a scrawny twelve-year-old like Olivia. She goes hungry most days, her stomach cramping. They don't keep the kids in separate cells; they are with the grown women, and every one of them looks after themselves. All caught up in their own fears of the future. It is a holding place—Olivia suspects just like Hades, the holding place of the dead—or maybe worse. These women have no life, they might as well be dead.

The only light in these terrible weeks is a woman on the outside who comes daily with a basket of bread and hands small loaves to the starving prisoners, and on one of those days, she sees Olivia huddled in the corner. Olivia's given up trying to get food. She doesn't have the strength to fight the older, larger women, and apart from a few crumbs one or the other leaves for her, she hasn't eaten in days.

The light is dim in the cells, so she doesn't know how the lady sees her, but she tells the other prisoners to get out of the way and let Olivia through. Then she puts a loaf directly in Olivia's hand. She is almost afraid to take a bite. It is so soft and fresh. When another woman tries to snatch it from her, the lady jabs her with a stick she carries. 'Get away from her. She needs to eat.'

Tears well in Olivia's eyes as she nibbles slowly, savouring every mouthful. The lady stands there and watches her eat, her eyes gentle. Does this woman actually care? It is the first time anyone has ever looked at her that way since Papa died.

Every day after that, the lady makes sure she has bread to eat. It is never enough, but it is food, and it helps keep her spirits up a little. Olivia finds herself looking forward to her visits. And the lady talks to her, asks her questions about her life. Olivia has little to say, however. Her story sticks like a lump in her throat. If she tries to speak of her misfortune, she will no doubt end up in tears, and she cannot have anyone see her cry. That will make her look weak and vulnerable, which they already think due to her size. No, she must keep it inside.

But the lady keeps trying. One day, she hands Olivia a piece of paper.

'Do you read, lovey?'

Olivia nods. Not because she can read, but because she thinks if she says no, the lady will take the paper away again. It is the only gift Olivia's received in a very long time, and no matter that she can't read it, she wants to keep it close. To remember the lady's kindness.

Olivia unfolds the paper and pretends to read. She can make out a few words, of course. Papa taught her a little reading and writing, but not much. She recognises several numbers and a few of the words, but after scanning it, she folds it carefully and presses it to her chest, so the lady knows it means much to her.

The lady reaches a hand through the bars and grasps her hand, her grip warm and gentle. 'Have faith in God, lovey. He is your hope. He has good plans for you.'

God? Isn't he the one who never answered Olivia's prayers when she begged for the stealing and manipulation to stop? He ignored her, just as Olivia's pleas on Mama's ears were ignored. Just as her pleas to Papa fell on deaf ears. And now she is on her way to Van Diemen's Land, on the other side of the world. How can the lady say God had good plans for her? Olivia knows the truth. The trouble has just begun.

1841

Olivia folds the paper and tucks it back into her stays. That woman meant well, she's sure. And Olivia is still as convinced now that the lady is wrong as she was then. But now Micky has said the same thing. *God cares. Deeply.* Olivia honestly doesn't know how they can believe that. Are they blind? If God cared, she wouldn't be out here on a rock, wasting her life with hard labour.

Anger wells inside her again. Olivia picks up the bird and starts pulling feathers, harder than ever. If the world—and God—want to punish her for nothing she's done wrong, then she's going to make it as hard as possible for them. Freedom be damned. Freedom is just a pipe dream.

***

Mick
New Norfolk

Mick pushes the plane along the golden wood, then runs his fingers along the surface to appreciate its smoothness. This is the first board of a tabletop. Part of a dining setting he is building for a wealthy client. As much as carpentry generates income, it is also calming. Cathartic. The smell of freshly cut pine, the energy expended in sanding or wielding a saw, the sound of hammer and chisel biting into the wood—it all centres him. While he works, he digests the week's events. Especially when he is troubled by those events. As he is now.

The yard at the Factory seems so empty without Miss Cruikshank there. He doesn't understand why he is so drawn to her, but it is not the same without her. He must focus his attention on Miss Smith and the others now. Miss Smith, however, is far more difficult to work with. He is certain she tries to use his desire to help against him. She approached him yesterday, while some of the other guards were changing shifts.

'Why did ya take sides against me?' she hissed.

'I am not about taking sides, Miss Smith. I merely called it as I saw it. You made the first move.'

Her dark eyes narrowed at him, while she circled about him, reminding him of carrion circling its prey.

'So, if I'd waited for her to attack me, then ya would 'ave defended me?'

'I would have acknowledged that she instigated the fight, yes.' Mick wasn't sure where the direction of her thoughts lay.

'But ya weren't here when it started. When it *really* began. Shank started it all, ya know.'

She poked a finger in his chest, baring her teeth. Mick found Miss Smith's insinuations hard to believe, but since he had just declared himself to be fair, he felt obligated to hear her out.

'Tell me about it, then. I shall listen.'

'When The Shank arrived in Van Diemen's Land, I helped 'er, looked after 'er. She paid me back by attackin' me. Then, when I finally got assigned, I found a lover. The father of my wee boy in yonder nusery. We was gonna marry, ya know. But Olivia,' she spat the name out, 'took a fancy to 'im an' seduced 'im away from me. She took *everything* from me. I had respect 'ere before she came. I had friends. Now I got nothin'.'

Her story does not quite line up with the Super's version, nor Miss Cruikshank's for that matter. Who is speaking truth? Either way, Miss Smith is still a woman in need of grace and support.

'Depends on how you look at it,' he told her.

'What do ya mean?' She narrowed her eyes again.

'You have a child whom I can see you love. If you apply yourself to good behaviour, you can finish your sentence and find a good life outside these walls, with your son.'

Miss Smith rolled her eyes and cursed.

'It's true,' Mick continued. 'This is not the end. There is a future for you, and I am here to help you find it.'

She stared at him for several moments and then offered him a sly grin. She ran a finger along his forearm.

'Why, that's very gentlemanly of you,' she purred. 'I'll remember that.'

Mick walked away from that conversation wondering if he had made any impact at all, or if he'd just dug himself a deep hole that he'd likely fall into? She confirmed his doubts soon after, when she pulled another prisoner's hair, hard, right in front of him. Mick talked her out of her behaviour, rather than strike her or take her to the cells as the others do. She gave him another sly grin and minced away.

Mick grips the edge of his workbench with both hands and hangs his head. *What am I to do?*

'Hard week?'

It is his father. Come to check on him, he suspects.

'You could say that.'

'You've been out here for hours. What's troublin' ya?'

Mick turns and leans against the workbench, crossing his ankles and folding his arms across his chest.

'When you were at Norfolk Island, did you listen to the chaplain or anyone who gave you advice?'

Dad chuckles and moves to a stool that stands by the work area.

'No. But then, I can't remember the chaplain or anyone else being kind like you. Maybe I wouldha' listened if they were. They were more about making us realise what worthless mongrels we were. Sinners to the end, deserving of every lash of the Cat we got. I didn't see as I had any value until after.'

Mick rubs his chin and sighs. 'I feel like they're just taking advantage of me. And the other officers think I'm soft. The Super called me in again yesterday.

Said I need to be tougher with the prisoners.' He looks at the roof beams and groans. 'I don't see how violence and suppression will help them reform.'

'Son, just remember, you are there because you chose to be. You don't need to pursue this course if you don't want to.' He gestures to Mick's woodwork. 'You can make a decent living from your carpentry. Your pieces are not just useful, they are handsome, and from what I hear, in higher demand all the time.'

Mick drops his head.

'I know. I know. But these women, they are so lost. If I am not there to show them hope and compassion, who will be? I can't let it go, Dad.'

He eyes Mick for a while and then nods. He gets up from the stool and heads to the door.

'You know, there are other ways to fight the system.'

'Yeah, the anti-transportation movement, for one.'

Dad raises his eyebrows in surprise.

'You know about that?'

'Yeah. Didn't I tell you? I ran into Raff—Raphaelo—remember, from school?'

'The one you took the beating for?' Dad shoves his hands in his pockets, uncomfortable with the memory, no doubt.

'That's him. He's a lawyer now, and he's involved in the anti-transportation movement. He invited me to one of their meetings.'

'A lawyer, eh? Good for him. And he's against the system too?'

It's Mick's turn to chuckle.

'Seems we have a lot in common. He lives in Hobart Town now, but his family is around here somewhere. They are simple farmers like us, but he had an uncle who sponsored him to higher education. I can't believe we haven't met before now. I thought I'd ruined his chances for learning. All this time, I've been blaming myself for his loss. But it actually turned out for good. He went to a better school and was very successful.'

Dad is thoughtful for a time.

'So, you going to go to the meeting?'

'I think I might.'

'We can go together then.'

'You going too?' Mick is surprised to hear this.

'Well, even though our lives have probably turned out better than they would have had we stayed in England, the penal system is far too harsh given the level of crime of most prisoners.'

Of course, Mick already knew he felt this way. It's Dad who taught him to believe along the same lines. So, it really shouldn't be a shock. Mick offers him a welcome smile.

'Sure, we can go together then.'

Dad nods and heads back outside. Mick returns to his plane and starts working again, but this time he feels a lot lighter. He is doing the right thing. These women need hope.

CHAPTER
Seven

Olivia

This island is too small for the five of them. Olivia cannot escape the menfolk, except when they're asleep, and that seems to be a pitifully short time. It's only been two weeks and already she's climbing the walls. *Is this what cabin fever feels like?*

Sing a song for us, Shank.

She doesn't know why she ever opened her mouth. But one of them heard Olivia humming one day and now she's their entertainment. It's not like she can say no. That would go against her happy-go-lucky pretence. And singing those bawdy songs seems to keep them happy—most of the time.

One of them—they call him Brick, probably because of the way he's built—looks at Olivia in that way that spells trouble in big letters, if she could spell, of course. She is careful not to encourage him, but everywhere she turns, he's there.

The one solace on this rock is Mrs Douglas. She's not friendly exactly, but neither is she antagonistic. Olivia supposes the fact Olivia's another female here appeases her, so she is not alone in her womanhood. But Mrs Douglas doesn't trust her, she can tell. And Olivia doesn't blame her. Olivia doesn't trust any of them, especially not the convicts. Who knows what depravity they are capable of?

In the two weeks Olivia has been here, she has counted two boats that have arrived with rations, half a dozen ships passing on their way to Sullivans Cove along the Derwent or back out again, several fishing boats every day, and countless gulls that spend time on this rock island. Sometimes she sees a few dolphins playing in the waves around the rocks, leaping out of the water. Those moments give her some peace. The dolphins are untroubled by crime and the hardships of life.

Mr Douglas wasted no time explaining to Olivia the importance of the lighthouse. Before they built the Iron Pot, he told her, several ships were wrecked near the mouth of the Derwent River, causing much loss of life. In the last dozen years, he says, there have only been three that he knows of.

'The Iron Pot saves lives, miss.'

'I'm sure it does, Mr Douglas. It's good to know I'm a part of that.' Maybe that's true, maybe it isn't. Most of the time, Olivia just says what she thinks people want to hear. And she reckons guiding ships to safety is up there with growing crops or farming stock.

'Don't get too close to the edge,' he tells her another time. 'Especially when it's rough. The waves can wash a man out to sea without warning.'

It's true. Olivia has seen the waves crash so hard the spray reaches as high as the lighthouse. When the sea is calm though, you'd think you could dive right in and swim across to South Arm. It seems so close. But it's not close enough, and she can't swim, anyway. Unlike any other assignment she's been on, there's no way to abscond here. Unless she gets friendly with one of them that delivers rations and convinces them to take her away. Olivia doesn't like her chances.

What annoys her most is that Micky's words and the magistrate's words keep echoing in her head, even though she knows there's no hope of freedom. Their voices keep telling her there is. So, what if she tries? What if she tries to stay out of trouble, stay quiet, do as she's told? Olivia shudders. That's not as easy as it sounds.

Olivia is unpinning washing from the line out back of the hut when Brick approaches her. There are no trees here, no shade, so the linens dry well if the sun comes out from the clouds and a breeze blows across the rocks. Pity if there is a strong wind, though, then sea spray covers the linens.

Brick must have recently woken from his sleep. Olivia glances at the sun, which is sinking toward the horizon beside Mt Wellington. He will need to be at his station in the lighthouse soon, for the night shift. Now that winter approaches, the days grow shorter and the men work longer hours at the lights. That means that there's less daylight for them to bother her, but still too much apparently.

'Mornin' sweet face.'

Olivia supposes he thinks he's funny, but that leer curving his mouth takes all the humour out of it.

'Brick.' She gives him a curt nod. The last thing she wants to do is encourage him.

'Well, here we are, all alone.' He steps closer. Too close. She can see water dripping from his beard, where he has just rinsed his face.

Olivia takes a step back, making it look like she's focused on the next piece of laundry to remove from the line. Usually she prefers to be alone, but not at this moment.

'Where are the other fellas?'

'Still coming off shift, and Paddy is still snoring,' he scoffs, 'but that leaves more time for you and me.'

He moves closer again and runs a finger along her arm. Olivia tries not to shudder and backs away again, unpinning the linen as she goes.

'Now why would ya wanna spend time with a girl like me?' she attempts drollery. 'Ya know why they call me The Shank, don't ya?'

'Can't say as I do.'

He's followed her around the lines, so it's easy to eye him straight and fierce. 'I stabbed a fella in the eye with a broken lamb shank. Waste of a tasty piece of meat, that.'

Biggest. Lie. Ever.

But Olivia hopes he buys it.

He backs off for a moment, but then he chuckles.

'Good thing we got no lamb over here then, eh?' He turns serious and closes in again, forcing her back and back, until she is against the wall. 'Don't you try threatening me, lassie.'

Yeah, that might have been a mistake. Olivia doesn't know what crime he's here for, either. Maybe he's the violent one. But now she is pressed up against the wall and he leans over her with one arm on each side of her shoulders. Nowhere to go. Olivia tries to keep her breathing slow. She doesn't want him to see how much he scares her.

'Aww, I didn't mean to threaten ya,' she says, using a light voice. 'Just a bit o' banter, ya know?'

He brings one hand over and strokes her throat. But it's in a way that tells her he could add a little more pressure and choke her if he wanted to. He slides his fingers along her braid, all the way to the end, the back of his hand brushing over her chest. Olivia hopes he can't hear her heart pounding. In the seconds that pass, she runs over her options. She could bring her knee up hard into his groin. Or she could smash him in the face, like she did to Ellen. Either would work. And either would land her in more trouble again. Is that what she wants? But can she let this brute threaten and manipulate her, which will probably be worse for her in the end?

'What's going on here?'

It's Mrs Douglas. Just when Olivia was about to swing her elbow up into his nose. Brick backs off immediately, giving her relief like she can't explain.

'Nothing at all, ma'am,' Brick puts on an innocent smile. 'I was just saying hello to Miss Cruikshank, here.'

Mrs Douglas looks from him to Olivia. 'Is this true?'

Olivia could tell Mrs Douglas she fears Brick's intentions toward her are harmful. But one look at his face and Olivia can read a warning there. On a rock island with nowhere to go, there aren't many options. She pastes on her brightest smile and straightens her dress.

'Yeah. Just sayin' hello.'

Mrs Douglas eyes them both for a moment and then calls her husband. 'Go and get yerself ready for work, Brick,' she dismisses the convict.

Olivia returns to unpegging the linen where Mrs Douglas joins her.

'You should watch your behaviour, Miss.'

That's right. She's read the situation as Olivia trying to seduce Brick. Of course she has.

'What do you need, Sarah?' Mr Douglas comes around the corner.

'I need you to lock Miss Cruikshank in the tower during the day. She is a temptress and will lead the men astray.'

He looks dumbfounded for a moment.

'She's not—don't you need help with your work?'

Olivia presses her lips together. Mr Douglas must have thought the better of defending her. After all, he is a man.

'I can manage.'

Mr Douglas looks uneasy, but he shrugs. 'All right, then.' He turns to Olivia. 'I guess you will spend your days cleaning the lighthouse.'

Please no, not up there. Olivia feels sick already. But what can she say? This is her prison. This is her punishment. She nods.

'And cut her braid off, will you? Maybe she won't look so enticing then.'

***

Mick

'It's a veritable crush in here,' Mick says to Dad as they enter the public hall in Hobart, squeezing past dozens of people to find a place to sit or stand.

'Didn't you realise how big the transportation issue is?' Dad laughs.

'No, I guess not.' Here he thought he was one of a handful of people interested in seeing the end to transportation. Serves himself right for not reading the newspaper enough. Mick scans the crowd. 'I don't know how I'm going to find Raff, though.'

'Yeah, that could be a challenge.'

There are no seats left. They should have arrived earlier. They find a spot where they can lean against a wall. Mick wonders if there is unity in the crowd, or are there people who want the convicts to keep coming?

Soon enough, the hall quietens down as the meeting gets underway. One gent welcomes everyone, thanking them for their time and support, then he hands over to the key speaker, Reverend John West, who's come down from Launceston. It shows much dedication to travel over a hundred miles. He begins his lecture, sharing a vision of their future civilisation without convict labour or transportation. He is very eloquent and is obviously passionate about what he says. Mick's impressed. He is convinced the reverend cares about the people and what they suffer at the hands of the penal system. He gives them the mission to spread the word, convince people of the atrocities being committed in the name of justice, and recruit them to the cause.

Throughout his speech, there are voices of assent here and there, a hand clap or two. Even Dad gives a 'yeah, good' at one point. Mick studies the faces of those around him. Mostly, they seem to agree, but he notices one or two with their arms folded across their chest who don't look happy with the proceedings.

When the time comes for questions, there is a clamour for the floor. The chairman calls for quiet and then points to one at a time to air their concerns. And even then, voices pile on top of each other.

'What about the farmers who rely on convict labour? How will they survive if they must pay others to work for them?'

'Put the prices of produce up.'

'So, we all have to pay the costs of no transportation?'

'But isn't that better than seeing more people tortured for petty crimes? I'd pay that extra cost!'

'We don't want our society poisoned by more criminals. Stop the transportation!'

As the people become more impassioned, the chairman finds it more and more difficult to keep control of the meeting. Dad raises his eyebrows to Mick and gestures toward the door. Mick nods and they press through the crowd again and out into the crisp evening air.

'See what I mean? A bit of a hotbed.' Dad's words come out like vapour in the cold air.

'Yes. But it's good to know there is an increasing number of people wanting to see the end of this.'

'And for different reasons.'

'Yeah.'

'Well, I suppose we should head to our lodgings.'

'I guess. I was going to meet Raff, but I didn't see him.'

'What do you mean, you didn't see me?'

Mick turns around to find Raff coming down the steps of the hall.

'I saw you.' He laughs. 'How about we go across the road, here, to the Drunken Duck? I hear they have a nice hot cider.'

'Lead the way, mate,' Mick says after Dad gives him the nod.

The warm cider staves off the cold of the late autumn evening, as does the welcoming fire in the grate, which is where they sit. They share a few laughs and old stories, and it is good to reminisce, but Mick only has one thing on his mind.

'Have you heard how Miss Cruikshank is going out at the Iron Pot?'

Raff stares at him over the rim of his mug for a moment, then puts it down.

'I only hear of them if there is trouble, so I assume all is well. Have you heard something?'

Mick is about to answer when Dad puts a hand on him arm, gesturing across the tavern.

'I'm gonna go 'ave a yarn with Dave over there.'

'Righto.' Mick turns back to Raff as Dad moves away. 'No, I've not heard anything, but I can't stop thinking about her.'

Raff's mouth curves into a big grin, and his eyebrows rise, creasing his forehead.

Mick half-grins at himself when he realises what Raff is thinking.

'Not like that,' Mick says.

'Sure.' Raff nods but doesn't look convinced as he takes another chug from his cider.

'It's just that I thought I was making headway with her. I hope she has the strength to change her life, but I got the sense that she is quite vulnerable.'

'Her record makes her appear to have plenty of strength.' Raff looks thoughtful.

'What do you mean?'

'She's been before the bench on several counts of assault. This last one was the first time anyone claimed it was self-defence. Most times, she refuses to give her own testimony, or she just agrees with whatever the other party says.'

Mick draws his brows together.

'She doesn't come across as violent or even aggressive. Not like others—Ellen Smith, for example, who is openly hostile.'

'Yeah, well, sometimes the quiet ones are the most dangerous.'

Mick is silent for a moment. Raff's words don't sit well with him.

'I really can't see it.'

'Listen, Reeve. Don't take this the wrong way, but maybe her pretty face has turned your head. I mean, it's only natural. And part of me hopes you're right about her. I would like to see her reform and live a peaceful life. But you can't ignore the facts, either.'

Mick studies his face. Raff is genuinely concerned. Miss Cruikshank is attractive and amusing, for sure, but Mick has never considered her romantically. His desire to see her change stems only from compassion. At least, he thinks so. Another thought strikes him.

'Raff, do you know why they sent her here, to Van Diemen's Land?'

'Petty theft,' he shrugs.

Mick sits back, surprised. 'So, with all this talk of violence, that's not what imprisoned her in the first place?'

'No, but prison can change people. You've seen that as much as I have.'

'True.' He cannot deny that fact.

Raff tosses back the last of his cider. Mick's hardly touched his, too caught up in his thoughts and the conversation.

'You know, Reeve, I'm not saying all this because I disagree with you. I think there is more to Cruikshank's story than meets the eye, and I also think she has a real chance at change. I just wanted to make sure your intentions were sound before I make any suggestions. You follow?'

Raff is eying him intently. Reading him. He's been testing him. This intrigues Mick, because now he wants to know what is going on in that head of his. Mick nods.

'Yeah, I follow.'

'Well, how about joining me on a fishing trip?'

'What?' Just when Raff piqued Mick's interest, he jumps topic completely. Mick shakes his head, confused.

'Have you never heard of fishing, mate?' He grins at Mick, teasing.

'Of course, I've heard of fishing, numbskull. But what has that to do with Miss Cruikshank?'

'You really cannot think of anything else, can you, Reeve?' He is laughing now and slaps Mick on the shoulder.

Mick glares at Raff, exasperated. What has gotten into him?

'You see,' he says, like a teacher explaining one plus one to an infant. 'We get into a boat and go down the Derwent, throwing a few lines in as we go, and maybe, just maybe, we might happen to pass the Iron Pot.'

Mick's eyes widen as the realisation hits him. Raff is offering to take him to visit Miss Cruikshank!

'Now who's the numbskull?' His laughter echoes in Mick's head for a long time.

CHAPTER
Eight

Olivia

A week has passed since Mr Douglas locked her in the tower. He only allows others in during the day if they are not alone—two at a time or none—and that is only if there is maintenance to be done on the light. In the same way, he only allows Olivia out of the tower if Mrs Douglas is free to supervise her. Mrs Douglas tries to tell her it is for her own good, but Olivia knows better. Mrs Douglas doesn't trust Olivia, and she doesn't trust her husband.

Olivia's legs ache from the constant up and down in the lighthouse and she has lost most of her appetite from the constant dizziness up there. She has counted the spiral wooden steps—there are fifty-three—and she named every one of them as she polished them the other day. It gives her something to do as she climbs, something to take her mind off the spiral dropping away below her. 'Hello John, hello Mary, hello William …' At least she knows Mr Douglas, Brick, and Paddy don't have it any easier in that sense. They must go up and down every few hours at night to refill the oil in the burners.

Every morning, Olivia cleans and polishes all nine reflectors, removing soot and grease that might impair the bright reflection. She must clean everything in the light room, including the walls and floor. This is the hardest part of her day. She finds it hard to breathe, especially when she's outside cleaning the glass reflectors. There are only a few steps between her and the railing, and she can see the churning ocean below. Sometimes the floor is slick from oil spills and that makes it scarier than ever. Olivia is required to make sure the water buckets are all full. They keep these on hand in case of fire.

The one good thing up in the tower, so far from everyone, is Olivia can sing. She sings to the nine lanterns and to the seagulls flying outside. Sometimes, when she's had enough of cleaning, she sings to the ships passing, though they can't hear her. It helps her forget where she is, but only for a moment. She would rather be outside singing her arias to the deep blue ocean, the mountains in the distance, the billowing clouds. Nature is worthy of her song.

As much as Olivia is constantly busy, she is also constantly alone. Not lonely as in she needs company, but lonely as in she needs a friendly face. That would be nice. Back at the Factory she had Ann, and even some of the other girls were pleasant enough. But here—Mrs Douglas watches her with suspicious eyes, even when she peels potatoes. Mr Douglas is Olivia's overseer and has much to say about her lack and nothing to her gain. Paddy either glares at her or ignores her and Brick pays too much attention, always suggestive if he can get away with not being seen or heard.

They bring her food in the middle of the day and deposit it inside the door at the bottom. Olivia must ring a bell if she needs to relieve herself, but if she does it too often, she is scolded by Mr Douglas for idleness. And he cut her hair. Just as Mrs Douglas told him to. One tug at her braid and some sawing of his knife and it was gone, burned in the fire. Now Olivia wears the shame of short hair, which makes her look like a boy. The only consolation she has is knowing it will grow back quickly.

The worst thing is, she can't get Micky out of her head. Those last moments when he spoke to her continue to play over and over in her head.

You are more valuable than you know. The way his Adam's apple moved as though he swallowed past emotion. Is it possible he actually cared? No, he followed his self-imposed mission, telling her that God cares, which Olivia still doesn't believe. If only she could see Micky again, to ask him what he meant. Not because he is handsome or anything, but because she enjoyed his banter. He kept it light and humourous, well, most of the time. He is the strangest prison officer she ever met, and she'll probably never see him again.

'So, Abraham,' Olivia says to the step she polishes. 'What music do ya like to hear?'

Singing will stop her from thinking about—about everything—and it is imperative she stops thinking. Constant rumination only leads to one place, and she can't afford to go there again. Not now. Not if she wants to stay on top of everything and keep out of trouble.

So, Olivia sings to the stairs. She sings to the walls. She sings to the ocean beyond. She sings to her silent audiences and appreciates their acceptance, and lets her mind wander to images of theatre stages, bright lights and cheering crowds.

She is so lost in her song, she doesn't hear the key grating in the lock at the bottom of the stairs. She remains unaware until boots appear on the stair below the one she polishes. With a gasp, Olivia shuts her mouth. Who heard her sing? She clenches her teeth as she raises her head slowly. She wants to close her eyes, dreading that it's Brick who's snuck in, but she needs to know.

Her eyes keep going up and up. This person is tall. Olivia's breath catches in her throat.

'Micky?'

'Miss Cruikshank.' He smiles down at her, but his smile is a little uneasy.

She clambers to her feet, realising she is a mess. But there is little she can do about it. She tries to tuck the short strands of her hair up into her mobcap.

'What are ya doin' here?'

He glances down and kicks at the stair, awkward.

'I, er, came to see how you are doing?'

'Oh. But, how …'

'A friend brought me by boat.'

Olivia is tongue-tied. Wasn't she just wishing she could see Micky? And now here he is in front of her. But she finds it hard to believe he would come here for her. There must be some other reason.

'Are ya bringin' provisions for the crew?'

'No.'

'Deliverin' mail?'

'No.'

'Did Mr Douglas send for help? Complain 'bout me?'

'No.' He narrows his eyes a little. 'Did he have cause to?'

Olivia shakes her head quickly. Why should she tell him about Brick? She wracks her brain, trying to think of another reason that might have brought Micky out here.

He stops her racing thoughts with a gentle laugh, then drags a hand through his hair.

'I came here to see if you are all right.'

But he still looks unsure of himself, which Olivia never saw at the Cascades. Not once. He must be hiding something. Then it dawns on her.

'Ya told them 'bout the knife, didn't ya? You're here to arrest me an' take me back to court.'

He shakes his head and laughs properly now, the awkwardness melting away.

'Stop being a goose. I came here to check on you, honestly.' He puts his hand on his heart to emphasise the point. 'Is there somewhere more comfortable we can talk, rather than here on the stairs?'

Has he not seen this island? There is nowhere to go. Nowhere that's comfortable anyhow.

'Here's as good a place as any, ya know. The house has two rooms but there's people in there. We could go outside on the rocks.' Olivia shrugs.

'How about up?' He jerks his chin toward the light. 'I'd wager there's a fantastic view from up there.'

Olivia's not about to tell him the view terrifies her. She can't argue with him, so she turns and climbs the stairs with her stomach in a knot, still confounded at why this one officer thinks he needs to check on her. Olivia shivers at his proximity to her, but she doesn't know why. Micky has never given her cause to fear him.

At the top of the stairs, she stands well away from the glass and lets him take in the view full circle. His face fills with delight as he stares out over the blue sea at the mountains, as he watches the gulls circling, as he studies the size and shape of this rock island.

'Not the worst place to live,' he says as he returns to the top of the staircase, where he leans against the wall opposite her, crossing his arms and ankles in a casual stance.

'Speak fer yerself.' She can think of plenty of places she'd rather be.

Now they stare at each other again, and the uneasiness about him returns. What is going on in that addle-pated head of his? Addle-pated, yes, because he must be unhinged if he thinks it is anything but a waste of time to visit a worthless prisoner.

***

Mick

He cannot believe how discomfited he is. All the way here he knew what he wanted to say, but when he saw her lovely face, his heart did a somersault. Confound it all. Maybe Raff was right. Perhaps he feels more than compassion for this girl. That thought alone has swept his head clear of purpose. He cannot think of anything more than the mundane to say. And she stares at him like he has a secret motive that will be her undoing. Suspicion oozes from her.

And fool that he is, Mick just trivialised her incarceration here. Of course she doesn't want to be locked in a tower on a tiny island, no matter how inspiring the view might be.

'Sorry about that. But how do you find it here?' He manages to find his tongue again.

She purses her lips, folds her arms, and he figures she doesn't want to talk about it. But then she puts her hands on her hips in her characteristic, saucy manner.

'I'm surprised they let ya in here, knowin' how dangerous I am an' all.'

Yes, Mick had noticed the lock on the door, and he did question Douglas on the matter. He told Mick she is an evil temptress. He wonders what she did to earn that label. But he will not question her about that.

'I assured Mr Douglas I was a prison guard and quite capable of taking care of myself—well aware of the menace you are.' He tries not to grin, but he is sure she sees it.

Silence hangs between them again. Miss Cruikshank pokes some loose strands of hair into her cap. Dear God, they have cut her hair.

'I still don't see why you're here. Unless yer takin' me away from this rock, I can't see the point. I'm just a damned prisoner.'

Strangely, he doesn't have an answer for that. Mick thought he knew what he was here for, but what can he say to her that he hasn't already said? Is it really something else that draws him to her? One thing she said strikes him.

'You may be a prisoner, but you are still a human like me, and I think you are worth a visit.'

She blinks at him. Do her eyes seem a little glassy? And then it is gone again, replaced by a smirk.

'You're human, are ya, Micky?'

She might make light of it, but he can feel he's close. Perhaps he can get through those tough scales she holds up like a shield.

'You think me a monster, is that it? You think I have some ulterior motive to destroy whatever is left of your soul? Tell me truthfully, Miss Cruikshank, have I done anything to support that belief?'

Mick stares her straight in the eye. He will not back down in humour or banter this time. Her mouth opens and closes a few times, and she scratches her arms.

'Why should you care when nobody ever has?'

The question is almost fierce, like a challenge.

He breathes out a long breath. 'Listen, can I tell you a story?'

Miss Cruikshank frowns and shrugs, sliding down the wall to sit on the stair. He supposes she has resigned herself to his presence here. He joins her on the stairs and clears his throat.

'My father was born in England, in poor circumstances. As a young man, he stole some goods—a piece of meat to begin with. Sure, he did it to help his family, but it was still theft. After a few crimes of that nature, they sentenced him to Norfolk Island for seven years. My mother had a similar story. They met soon after being released from gaol. They were shipped to New Norfolk here in Van Diemen's Land, given a selection of land and made a life together, a life that is much better than they would have had back in England. Now, the time Dad spent at Norfolk sounds like a living nightmare, and he bears several scars from that time. But as bad as it was, good has come of it.'

'Why are ya tellin' me this?' Miss Cruikshank wears a bored expression.

'You asked why I would care. I can see from the other side what your future could be like. All you need to do is serve your time in the best way you can.'

'Ya don't understand.' She blinks her eyes and bites down on her lip as well. She even gets up and paces around the light, although she stays close to the centre. At that moment Mick realises she is afraid of heights, but refuses to let him know it, and Mick doesn't want to interrupt this conversation by moving.

'I do understand. My parents have told me their stories over and over. And I've seen it repeatedly in Hobart Town. Former prisoners who have made a genuine success —'

'I were innocent!' Miss Cruikshank covers her face with her hands, and she shakes her head. Somehow, he thinks she didn't mean to let that out.

He stands up and goes to her, reaching out to touch her shoulder, but she recoils.

'It's all right.'

'It's not alri'.' She glares at him, although she is almost gulping down her emotions. 'You talk of your parents, your family, and their families as though they are full of love and care. My mother made me carry her stolen goods and then left me to rot in prison, and my father did nothing to stop her. She was the thief, and she stole my life from me. I have nothing left.'

Mick is shocked by the level of anguish in her voice and the anger on her face. He doesn't know what he expected, but it certainly wasn't this. His heart aches for her even more than he thought possible, and moisture pricks at his eyes. How he wishes he could take that pain away from her, but only God can do that.

'Miss Cruikshank, I —'

'Just go, please. Go.' She turns her back to him. 'Before I commit another one of them crimes fer which I'm known.'

She tries to rally her courage and banter with him again, and his heart swells further with compassion and admiration. Truth be told, he is at a loss for words right now. He doesn't want to say anything that sounds trite, or that might hurt her further.

'All right,' Mick says. 'I'll go. But I will be back. And I will keep you in my prayers.' His prayers and every living, waking thought.

She gives a slight nod but doesn't turn around.

He descends the stairs and walks out onto the rocks, leaving Douglas to lock her in again, the idea of which troubles Mick more than he can say.

Twenty minutes later he is back on the dory with Raff, who has caught several salmon in the hour they were apart.

'Well, and how did it go?' He asks as soon as they pull away from the island and settle into a good rowing rhythm.

'You were right on two counts, my friend.'

'Aye? And what are they?'

'My feelings may run deeper than my occupation demands.'

At this, he chortles. 'I knew it.'

'Yes, you are very insightful.' Mick rolls his eyes. 'But I don't see how anything can come of it as things stand.'

'Things can change.' He shrugs, but there is a glint in his eye as he pulls his oars.

Match maker.

'You should hear her sing. And she is so courageous when you consider her circumstances. You know they've locked her in the tower. For what I don't really know, but Douglas—the keeper—hinted that she tried to seduce the men.'

'And you don't believe that?'

'I've never seen that kind of behaviour in her. Mocking flirtation perhaps, but not outright intent to make a conquest.'

Raff looks thoughtful.

'Didn't Miss Smith accuse her of seducing her own lover?'

Mick pulls hard at his oars, not happy to be reminded of this. He doesn't want to believe any of it. And yet, he cannot afford to be narrow-minded—let attraction cloud his judgment.

'It's hard to know where the truth lies.'

'And that is the difficulty we face. What is the other thing I'm right about?'

'There is a lot more to her story than we thought.'

'Yes?' He raises his eyebrows.

'She claims she was innocent of theft back in England. That her mother

68

was the one who stole but left Miss Cruikshank to bear the punishment.'

'If that's true, then she has suffered much injustice.'

'And still so young, too. I can see why she feels so bereft.'

'So, you believe her story, then?'

'I suspect it's not something she's told many others. She's kept it like a secret, locked up tight, and let everyone think of her what they wish. She opened up to me today. It was brief, but I saw raw pain in that moment. Something tells me that anguish is her true self, and the tough, devil-may-care attitude is the pretence.'

'It's very possible. Many prisoners need to develop a thick exterior to survive.'

'Well, if Miss Cruikshank can let her guard down for me, then perhaps I can get others to as well.'

'You've some hard work ahead of you, Reeve.'

'I don't doubt it. But moments like today make it worthwhile.'

'And that's not just because you like her?'

Raff grins at Mick, jiggling his eyebrows. If Mick could cuff him around the head, he would. With the oar he is dragging through the water. Instead, he laughs at Raff's ribbing. He's not likely heard the end of it.

'I like her enough to ask you if you would mind taking me fishing again next week.'

Raff laughs out loud this time.

'Fishing? What kind of fishing?'

Mick makes a face at his drollery.

'Very funny. So, is that a yes?'

'Sure Reeve. I'll take you *fishing*.'

CHAPTER
Nine

Mick

Several of the prisoners are responding better to Mick now. They don't react with fear or aversion when he approaches them and will speak to him in a less guarded fashion than they used to. Of course, it's easier to work with the prisoners in classes one and two. They are the least troublesome and will soon be out in the community. The Super has sent Mick to inspect the Class Two prisoners several times, while he inspects the hospital or third class. Mick is to check the yard is tidy, their sleeping quarters are clean, and that the other turnkeys keep them in order. Class Two spend their hours picking, carding, and spinning wool, and it is good to hear their plans for the future and to hear their hopes.

Today Mick is back in the wash yard with the crime class. He managed a brief conversation with Miss Ann Finnegan, whom he believes is a friend to Miss Cruikshank. It quickly became obvious she wanted information. After listening to Mick politely for a few minutes, nodding and generally agreeable, she changed the subject.

''Ave ya heard any news of Livvie?'

Several years older than Miss Cruikshank and not half as pretty, she nevertheless showed genuine concern in her eyes.

'Yes, indeed I have,' Mick replied, though he ought not to tell her he's been to visit that prisoner. 'She is on assignment at the Iron Pot Lighthouse and from what I understand, she endures with formidable courage.' He grins at his description of her.

'I do hope so. She's the youngest of what I've seen sent here. Just thirteen she were when she arrived. Too young to see such troubles.'

'So, you were here when she was first transported?'

'Aye, that I were. No more than a child, she were. Thin, an' small. Reminded me of me kid sister who died 'round that age, rest 'er soul.' Miss Finnegan crossed herself. 'But she's tough. I'll give 'er that.'

'I'm sorry you suffered the loss of a sister.'

Miss Finnegan shrugged.

'It's all water under the bridge now. Can't be helped. I s'pose I took Livvie under me wing to replace sweet Catherine, now that I think on it.'

'I'm sure Miss Cruikshank appreciates your friendship.'

'It goes both ways, sir.'

Mick is still thinking about the truth of her words when he comes across Miss Smith and he braces himself for impact. Not physical impact, the force of her manipulation. What will she try today?

She steps toward him with a swing of her hips, while twirling a loose strand of her hair coquettishly.

'Hello, handsome,' she says.

She has been more and more flirtatious with him of late, and he suspects she wants something, but the only way to find out is to play along a little. Maybe it's a dangerous game he plays, and he won't let it go too far, but he needs to figure out where her true character lies.

'Hello yourself,' Mick offers her a smile and tries to ignore the way she arches her back to draw his attention to her body.

She leans in closer and whispers.

'Meet me 'round the corner in five minutes.'

With a gesture of her head to the corner she means, she swaggers away. Mick is curious enough to heed her request, thus five minutes later, he sneaks around the corner to discover what may unfold. She is there waiting for him in the shadows. They are out of sight here, a definite sign her intentions are underhanded.

True enough, she comes close, too close, playing the coquette again, laying her open hand on his chest.

'Anyone ever told ya how gorgeous you are, Reeve?'

He gently grasps her by the shoulders and pushes her back to arm's length.

'My mother perhaps,' he gives her a dry answer. He doesn't want to lend her any license.

Miss Smith forms a pout but then gives a flirtatious smile.

'Yer mother is a lucky woman.'

'Or maybe I'm the lucky one—she is an excellent mother.'

Her dark brows close together in consternation for a moment. He is not responding the way she wants him to.

'Ya care about us girls, don't ya, Reeve?'

'You know I do.' But maybe not in the way she hopes.

She reaches her fingers down inside the bodice of her dress, suggestively, of course, and withdraws a few silver coins.

'Got me a few shillin's saved up. I need me some whiskey. It helps cope with bein' separated from me boy most o' the time. Ya know what I'm sayin'?'

Miss Smith presses those coins into Mick's hand and looks up at him with wide eyes.

'Ya can get me some whiskey, can't ya, Reeve?'

Mick stares at the coins in his hand. Does she really think he's that soft?

'I could, but I won't.' He turns her hand over and drops the coins into her palm.

She presses her lips together and he thinks he detects a flash of defiance in her eyes, but then she develops a pout again and her eyes become glassy.

'I thought ya said ya cared about me.'

'I did and I do.'

'But not enough to help me.'

'I'll not help you make things worse for yourself, no.'

She wipes at her eyes and shoves her coins back into her dress.

'What would ya know 'bout better or worse?' Miss Smith throws the words at Mick through angry tears. 'Do me a favour though, will ya, Reeve? If ya find I've got me whiskey another way, turn a blind eye.'

He opens his mouth to protest, but she cuts in.

'Or I can make yer life 'ere very hard. Then we'll see what ya really care about.'

With that thinly veiled threat, she flounces away, wiping at her eyes again. Ellen Smith has just set the challenge. Will Mick bow to her wishes, or face whatever manipulation she has in mind? One thing he knows, capitulating to her demands is not an option.

A few days later and the immediacy of the decision is out of Mick's hands, although not happily. Fred—a harsh man who will show her no mercy—caught Miss Smith with the whiskey. Mick remained unaware of her quick success in procuring the drink.

Miss Ann Finnegan is happy to relay the details to him when next he enters crime class. Mick winces as she tells him Fred wrenched the flask from Miss Smith and took his baton to her. Fred hit her half a dozen times or more before he stopped. And from what Mick knows of Fred, he strikes hard. She will be badly bruised for a few days.

'Not that she don't deserve it,' Miss Finnegan added. 'Always trouble that one.'

'I don't know that anyone deserves to be beaten, Miss Finnegan,' Mick mumbles.

'What's that?'

'Never mind.' He probably shouldn't admit his sympathies aloud to the prisoners.

'I'll give 'er credit, though. She took it well. Never gave much more than a whimper.'

He nods. This doesn't surprise him.

'An' now she's in the dark cells for a couple o' days.'

This doesn't surprise Mick either. Since he also works in the yard, he goes over to Fred for his version of events.

Fred spits on the ground. 'Filthy whore. Thinkin' she can pull one over on me.' He pats the baton at his waist. 'Well, it's my whiskey now.'

Mick frowns at him, but there's not much he can say. 'Does she need a nurse?'

'She'll be right. Plenty of fight left in 'er yet.'

Mick grunts at him. Fred's callousness shouldn't astonish him. And there's not much use in appealing to the Super or Matron. Matron's given birth in the last week and the news is they do not expect the little one to live. They've lost so many children, the Hutchinsons, indeed many women who birth children here lose them. It is a tragic, but common occurrence.

With a heavy sigh, Mick makes his way to the dark cells to see how bad Miss Smith is. As he approaches, he hears faint whimpering, but it ceases as soon as he unlocks the door. She cradles one hand, and he suspects she collected a blow on her fingers in trying to deflect the baton away from her face. He will provide medical treatment for her himself, since no-one else will.

**

Olivia
July 1845

Olivia is busy polishing the lenses—her arms are used to it now—but she can't stop herself looking down from the lighthouse to see if Micky has arrived, even though the action makes her head spin. There must be something wrong with her, or she's become too stupid to be sensible. She shouldn't expect him. Sooner or later, he will stop coming—when he realises she is not worth it.

At first, he came every Sabbath, but now the winter has set in, and the weather is less predictable, he only makes it every few weeks. Today, although clouds clutter the sky and the sea is choppy, it might be possible. But Olivia shouldn't be hopeful.

He is always so attentive to her, asking how she does, not that anything has changed. She's still locked in the tower, most of the time, which keeps her safe from Brick, most of the time. But Brick seems determined to get to her. He often stands at the bottom of the lighthouse and calls Olivia to throw down a rope so he can climb up. Certainly, there are ropes coiled, hanging at the top of the stairwell, but just as certainly Olivia will not throw them down to him.

Whenever she is out of this lighthouse, he tries to find her alone. Therefore, Olivia endeavours to stay near Mrs Douglas or another of the convicts. Yet there are moments he discovers her alone, and he presses his suit—if you can call it that. She usually tries to make a loud jovial noise, which has Mrs Douglas running to see what she is up to. She never strays too far from the hut.

But Olivia can't tell Micky any of that. He will probably assume she is the cause, just as everyone else does. Thankfully, he doesn't probe her too hard on her current circumstance. Instead, he tries to get her to think about what she will do when her sentence is over, but she avoids his probing questions with a witty comeback. She regrets telling him as much as she did. It makes her too uncomfortable, even though part of her wants to tell him more. But that would really prove her stupid.

When Olivia doesn't answer his endless questions, he ends up telling her things about himself. She has learnt he is a carpenter; he attends church services every Sunday, and he is good friends with a man in the law offices. He tells her he has two brothers and two sisters, all older than him and married with their own families. Apart from that, as she listens to him talk, she's noticed he taps or drums his fingers almost constantly and he is left-handed.

Olivia likes the sound of his voice. It is calming, so she is content to listen to him tell her whatever he likes. Except when he speaks of the Cascades. Although she likes to hear about Ann and several of the other girls, she doesn't want to hear about Ellen and the trouble she causes. Especially the trouble she causes Micky. Why it bothers her so much, she cannot say, other than she's hated Ellen as long as she's known her.

Micky says on one hand the Super and Matron push him to be more severe with the prisoners, and on the other hand Ellen goads him to bend all the rules. So far, he has avoided disappointing either of them, but it is only a matter of time until they force his hand. Olivia wonders what he will do then.

Another glance from the window reveals a dory pulling up to the island and her heart leaps suddenly, fluttering. Olivia drops her rag and descends the stairs as fast, but as carefully as she can, arriving at the bottom slightly breathless. The key already grates in the lock, and she quickly brushes off her skirts and straightens her cap. She doesn't know why she does because there is no way a girl can look good in a drab grey dress and cap—even if it is dyed pink—and why would Micky notice, anyway? Why does she even want him to notice?

The door opens, and his tall shadow fills the space. Olivia bobs a raffish curtsy.

'G'day guvna.' Her usual impertinent greeting, even though her heart still races in an unruly manner.

He takes Olivia up on her humour and bows low over her hand, which he takes and kisses. *Oh Lordy, he kissed my hand!* For a second, she wonders what she would do if that kiss were higher up, like on her mouth. Would she fight him off? It scares her to realise she wouldn't. Shaking with that realisation, she looks up at him as he straightens, and he offers her an impudent wink. Does he know what he just did to her?

'Hello Songbird.'

They turn and climb the stairs and all the while she wonders what he's thinking. She knows where her own mind wanders, and she wishes those thoughts were on the other side of the ocean. Why does this prison officer have to be so good-looking and friendly?

He gazes over the view for a while, as he always does, drumming his fingers on the glass, leaving fingerprints she will have to polish away after he is gone.

'Have you ever been up the mountain?' He nods toward Mt Wellington, although it's barely visible today beneath the clouds.

'Now there's an 'airbrained question if ever I heard one.'

'Of course.' He shuffles his feet, looking sheepish.

'What about you?'

'I did once when I was about seventeen. Took most of a day to get up there and back.'

'What was it like?'

'If you think the view from here is good, up there, it's like standing on top of the world. Hobart Town seems so small.'

Olivia can't think of anything worse than standing on a mountain top, with all that air between her and the ground, but she's not about to admit that.

'And 'ere? The Iron Pot?'

'I suppose one could see it at night from up there, but during the day, I doubt you could make it out.'

'It's like I don't exist,' she shrugs. For some reason, those words hurt. She is invisible to everyone.

'Oh, but you do.'

Micky looks earnestly at her again. He does that often. She has never fully believed he is genuine. But he keeps coming back, so maybe he is.

'For you, maybe,' she mumbles, even though voicing that terrifies her.

'For me definitely,' he grins, 'and for God, too. And that's what matters most.'

Her heart runs away again, making her breath come quickly. Why do these conversations scare her so much? She tries to laugh, but it comes out as a nervous giggle. She swallows, trying to calm herself. There must be something funny to say, something diverting, but nothing forms in her mind. The only thing that pops into her head is the piece of paper she has hidden in her bodice.

If Micky talks about God, same as that lady way back in Newgate, maybe he can explain the writing to her. But can she trust him? Dare she trust him? He might laugh at her. What if he tears up her treasure and throws it from the window? He might lie to her about the words. Plenty of things could go wrong. But Olivia very much wants to know what is on that scrap.

With trembling fingers, she reaches for it. This will be the test of him.

'M-Micky,' she can hardly breathe. You would think she is standing on the edge of a cliff the way she quakes. 'Can ya … can ya … tell m-me … what this s-says?'

And yet she cannot hold it out to him. She still clutches it to her chest, even though he puts out his hand to receive it.

'It's all right, Olivia,' he says with a gentle smile.

This is the first time he has used her Christian name, and strangely, it helps a little. With much hesitation, she hands it over and his large hand envelops hers for a moment before he takes it. She looks up into his concerned brown eyes.

'I can see this is important to you. I will do my best not to let you down.'

She nods.

He reaches into the pocket of his shirt, pulls out some spectacles, and slips them onto his nose. Olivia's breath catches. He looks even more gentle and kind with those on and, of course, he must smile at her, making her stomach feel like it's filled with melted butter. He carefully unfolds her treasure and reads in silence, squinting a little. Some of the writing has smudged and faded. Soon, though, I see a sad smile in his eyes. Why would he be sorry for this?

'How long have you had this?' he asks, his Adam's apple bobbing as he swallows.

'Since Newgate afore I came 'ere. Six years.'

'I take it you never learnt to read?'

Olivia shakes her head, ashamed. He must think her an imbecile now.

'And no-one has ever read this to you?'

She shakes her head again.

His brown eyes are filled with … pity?

'Why … why are y-ya upset? Am I in t-trouble?' She wraps her arms around her chest, suddenly cold.

He shakes his head this time and sighs.

'These are precious words, and I am so sad for you that you have never heard them.' His lip trembles a little.

'Wh-what does it say?' Olivia feels as though a band squeezes her chest.

He scoots across the floor, so he is right next to her. She can feel the warmth of his shoulder against hers. He takes a deep breath, and his hand shakes as much as hers as he points to the words and reads.

'Proverbs twenty-three, eighteen. For surely there is an end, and thine expectation shall not be cut off. Psalm nine, eighteen. For the needy shall not always be forgotten; the expectation of the poor shall not perish forever. Jeremiah twenty-nine, thirteen. And ye shall seek me, and find me, when ye shall search for me with all your heart. And I will be found of you, saith the LORD; and I will turn away your captivity.'

Micky looks at her with shining eyes. 'These are verses from the Bible, and they say exactly what I've been trying to tell you. God cares about you and your future.'

CHAPTER
Ten

Mick

Mick stands on the shore after Raff leaves, facing south as the sun sets behind him, wishing he can see the light that will soon grace the horizon. The light that represents Olivia Cruikshank. He marvels at how the Lord has worked, even when he is unaware. How could he know someone gave her those words of encouragement so many years ago? And she treasured them, even though she remained ignorant of what that note contained. She linked the value of that paper to the woman who gave it to her, and Mick is thankful for that person, whoever they may be.

If only Miss Cruikshank believed those words as easily as it was to read them out to her.

For now, he must be content that she trusted him with the knowledge of the paper's existence and to read it to her. That trust was hard won, but it is a breakthrough that brings him much joy. His visits with her are like a sunburst amid a shower. She grows dearer to him each time he sees her.

When he read those verses to her, it was all he could do not to take her in his arms to show her how much he cares.

She had been scratching at her arms, but after Mick read the verses, she stopped and looked at him, dumbfounded. He wanted to kiss those trembling lips, heaven help him.

'The Bible says those things? About me?'

'Yes, it does.'

She scrambled up and stood with her back to him, shaking her head.

'I deserve to be here.'

It sounded as though she spoke the words through gritted teeth. Her statement surprised Mick. Has she lied to him all this time?

'I thought you said you were innocent of the charges?'

She swivelled and glared at him.

'I was … *then*. My mother stole me innocence.' She pressed her lips together.

'And now?'

Olivia shook her head again and swung her arms out in exasperation. 'Now I'm just another worthless prisoner. The things I've done to survive.' She put her hands over her face and groaned. 'God might've offered me freedom once, back then, but not now.'

'God doesn't change his mind.'

'How can ya know that? You've seen what I done to Ellen.'

'That was self-defence.'

She gave a mirthless laugh.

Mick remembers the incident. Ellen attacked Olivia, not the other way around, but the look on Olivia's face makes him doubt. Had she been waiting for an opportunity?

'It ain't the first time I broke 'er nose.'

What? Did he hear right? 'I beg pardon?'

Olivia's gaze dropped to the floor. 'Back at the beginning. She wouldn't take no for an answer. Ann had taught me how to fight, so, well, I did.'

Mick sighed. Things were becoming a little clearer. But now he needed to know more. 'And what of her accusation that you seduced her lover?'

Her chin jerked up, eyes lighting with disdain. 'I told ya she'd blame me for the impossible.'

And the Super had said something similar.

'I were sent on assignment, but nowhere near this lover of 'ers. I don't even know who 'e is. My guess is 'e figured what a lunatic she is and ran off with someone else. And good for 'im. She deserves it.'

Strangely, relief flooded Mick. Not at her vitriol, at the fact she wasn't a seductress.

'The point is, I'm not worth it, Micky. Not worth yer care an' concern. God won't forgive me now.'

'That's where you're wrong. So very wrong.' He got up and went to her. The desire to wrap his arms around her was so strong. Instead, he gripped her upper arms and gazed into her eyes. She needed to believe him. 'He always forgives.'

Her eyes were wide, searching. And then her gaze dropped to his lips. She would have let him kiss her then. He knew it, heaven help him, but he took a step back. It was more than enough to realise she felt the same pull to him as he did to her. He refused to take advantage of her vulnerability and brand new trust.

And now he stands here, praying she will think on the words of those Scriptures, praying she will believe the promises in them. More than anything, he wants to see her free, and not just free from prison.

A few weeks later and he attends another anti-transportation meeting with Dad and Raff. They are all encouraged to write letters to important people in the community to raise awareness and ask them to join their cause. And not just to those in Hobart Town or the rest of Van Diemen's Land, but to the colonies in Melbourne and Adelaide where there are no penal settlements. People in those regions do not want their society infected by the after-effects of the prison system—poisoned by corrupt ex-convicts.

As Mick listens to the discussions, he is disturbed by this ongoing negative view of prisoners—that they are a burden to society and a malignancy to their civilisation. Where is the fight against injustice? Where is the battle for the life and future of unfairly treated men and women? In the end, he can no longer sit quietly while this goes on around him, although his nerves race and images of being whipped flash through his mind. With his father's brows raised in question, Mick stands up and clears his throat.

'Fellow anti-transportationists, you are all concerned for the state of our society, and that is commendable, but would it not serve the community's future by reforming the prisoners properly, rather than making them more corrupt through unjust treatment?'

'What are you talking about, man?'

Several voices rise in question, and Mick puts his hands out in a gesture to quiet them.

'I would ask you to think about your own childhood. No doubt most of you have felt the sting of the strap or the lash of the switch at least once in your life. But did you ever feel like that discipline was unwarranted, too severe for your alleged disobedience? And where your punishment was unfair, what did it arouse in you? Feelings of gratitude for your parents' thoughtfulness?'

A few laughs scatter through the room.

'No. Of course not. You felt angry, didn't you? Perhaps resentful. And maybe it even incited you to do something that your parents wouldn't like in reality—or at the very least, wish you could.'

Several men nod at him now, and Mick can see they understand.

'Now, take a grown man who has stolen, let's say, a pair of shoes. The judge sends him here for seven years of imprisonment, and during that time he is very likely flogged till his back is shredded for the merest infraction. Or locked in a dark cell for a week and fed on bread and water.' Mick looks around at the gathering, making eye contact to make sure he has their attention. 'Do you really think this kind of punishment will make him a better person?'

Silence reigns for a long moment.

'What are you saying? We should let them all go free?'

'Not at all,' he hastens to subdue this protest. 'What I mean is that the punishment should befit the crime. Petty theft should not result in being sent across the ocean for years on end. Simple insubordination should not result in being flogged with the cat-o'-nine-tails. We create prisoners who resent the society that sent them there. Our system corrupts them further, rather than reforming them. Of course, not every convict becomes corrupt and I daresay some of you here have experienced what I am talking about. Some of you bear the scars on your person. There must be a better way.'

With that Mick sits down again, amidst a few 'hear hears.'

Dad slaps him on the back. 'Well said, Son.'

'Agreed.' Raff nods at him.

'Yeah, well. It annoys me how they call prisoners a blight on civilisation when they create that blight to begin with. And plenty of you are *not* a blight.'

He squeezes Dad's arm with affection. His father is the opposite of a scourge. He has taken his time of trial and turned it for good, and that is what Mick wants to help other prisoners do. It's what he wants to see in Olivia Cruikshank and the others, even Ellen Smith.

Ellen Smith and Olivia Cruikshank are as opposite as ice and fire. Where Olivia continues to relax more with Mick, even opening up, he suspects Miss Smith has ulterior motives. She continually behaves in a flirtatious manner when other guards watch, but if they are not in the turnkeys' line of sight, she practically spits on the ground at his feet in contempt.

Mick is uncertain where the end of her game lies, but he does endeavour to treat her with the same deference as everyone else, despite her strange and sometimes offensive behaviour. There is little else he can do. Except pray. He prays she will change her ways before it is too late.

***

Olivia
September 1845

The weather is bad today. Ferocious, even. Olivia finds it hard to concentrate on her work when the whole tower shudders with each howling gust of wind. She looks from the window, but only once. The waves are like wild animals, attacking this small rock and spraying water fifty feet into the air. Occasionally, she even feels the spray come inside. All she wants to do is stay at the bottom of the stairs and grip onto anything that will hold her, should the lighthouse fall. And it is so cold. Her hands are numb, so numb she can't feel the scrubbing brush she holds. What she would give for a warm cape and a bowl of hot soup. And some company to pass the time while the wind screeches, the timbers groan, and the ocean roars.

But she is on her own. It can't even be the middle of the day, though she couldn't find the sun even if she looked for it. The men will all be fast asleep—though how they sleep in this noise, she cannot say—and Mrs Douglas no doubt sits quietly, sewing and mending.

If only Micky were here with his warm presence. Olivia wouldn't care if he asked for her deepest held secrets right now, she just wishes he was here. She can trust him. He has shown her that. She never thought she could ever believe someone again, but there it is. And him a prison worker and everything. She smiles to herself despite the raging storm.

He has read to Olivia more from the Scriptures of late, even explaining to her what different letters look like and how they make the words. Who ever thought she would learn to read from the Bible?

Not to say she believes all Micky's earnest assurances about God, but she likes to listen to him. She likes to have him here. He makes her laugh and forget her situation. She especially likes his kind eyes and handsome jawline which is softened by a fashionable beard. She wonders if his beard is soft, but she dares not touch it. He is only five years older than her, which surprised her when he told her, because he is mature for someone just past their youth.

Olivia's heart flaps about just thinking about him. Not that she will ever tell him how he makes her feel. Oh how she wishes he were here now. He would be someone who could hold her in a storm, make it less scary. Maybe if she just imagines his arms around her, that might help.

A foreign sound pricks her ears of a sudden. Someone calling, perhaps? No, the men should be asleep. Olivia goes back to scrubbing the stairs.

But there it is again, a voice, faint, but calling. She runs up the stairs and creeps to the glass to peer through the heavy rain and spray. Slowly and hesitantly, she does the full circuit of the lighthouse twice before she sees it, and a chill runs the full length of her spine. There is a man out there, clinging to the rocks. No, make that two men. The crashing waves could wash them out to sea at any moment. They need help. Trembling, she opens the door to the narrow platform that runs around the light. She holds tight to the thin railing, believing the wind could toss her small frame over the edge.

'Mr Douglas!' Olivia yells as loud as she can from the tower, raising an arm to protect her face from the slicing rain. She watches the hut for several moments while she keeps yelling, but no-one appears. Either they are all asleep, or they can't hear her. And they can't hear the men crying out either, as the lighthouse stands between the hut and where they are.

Olivia's brain scrambles for a way to help, but there's not much she can do while she's locked in. She remembers the ropes, several coils of them, hanging at the top of the stairway. Her stomach turns over at the thought. The one thing she thought she could never do, and it is the only option. If she doesn't try to help, will she be able to live with herself? Who knows, but it might even be Micky and his friend out there?

That thought drives Olivia to move, and heads back inside to collect the ropes. They are heavy. She will need more than one, but she can't carry them at once. She grinds her teeth, knowing the smallness of her frame will mean she loses precious time while she goes back and forth.

Minutes later, she has two ropes out on the landing. This one thing she can thank her father for, he taught her how to tie a knot. She drops one coil of rope from the window and prays the waves don't wash it away. She ties one end of the other rope around the railing and hopes it will hold her weight, little of her though there is. Olivia looks down at her skirts and knows they will be a problem. Without another thought, she removes the dress, leaving her in her drawers.

She looks out at the two men struggling to hang on as waves lash at them. How much longer can their fingers grip those rocks? She looks down at the ground and is sick. The island seems to spin. She takes several deep breaths. She must do this. Olivia tosses the rest of the coil over the rail and lifts one leg over, twisting the rope around her wrist. It is her life or theirs, and hers is not worth much. She swings the other leg over and it hits her that there is now nothing between her and the ground but the rope she clings to. Panic threatens to rise. She reaches one hand out to grasp the rail again. Maybe she can scramble back inside to safety. But already it is out of reach. She hugs the rope tight and closes her eyes. She can't do this. Heck, she can't even breathe.

But what if it's Micky down there? There is no choice. Olivia holds her breath and makes her way slowly down the rope. She trembles so hard, every movement is that much harder. She'll never make it. But she will die trying.

'I'm coming for you Micky,' she mumbles.

How did they come to be there? Why would they be out in this weather? Micky is smarter than that, and his friend is an experienced boatman, so she thought.

The rain lashes at her face and makes the rope slick, not to mention the deluge has drenched her. *Please, just let me get to the bottom.* She can't look down or else she'll swoon. A vice clenches her stomach, her arms burn, and her hands are numb. But inch by inch she keeps going, though terror makes it hard to breathe.

'Mr Douglas! Brick! Paddy!'

Olivia calls them over and over, till her voice grows hoarse.

'Hold on Micky! I'm coming.'

The rain is like ice needles, and it becomes harder to move, she is that stiff with cold.

Mercifully, her feet finally touch the ground, and she gasps for air, falling to her knees. She has never been more grateful for this rock island. And grateful that the other rope has not entirely washed away.

There is no time to rest. She takes the rope, ties it to a boulder at the base of the lighthouse, and hopes it is long enough to reach the men. With salt spray and rain flying in her face, it is hard to find her direction, but she twists the rope around her wrist and starts moving in the direction she thinks they are. Olivia yells all the while, and soon she hears a reply. The men are still there, and they know she's coming. After forty feet, she comes to a small cliff and must go down again.

She can see the men now. It is a wonder they have held on for so long, despite the waves. Those breakers are relentless. Once again, she swallows her fears and eases herself over the ledge. *You can do this. Not far to go now.*

Once she is on the lower level of rock, she carefully makes her way toward the closest man.

'Here I am,' she calls to him.

Just when she is about to reach him, a wave knocks her off balance and she hits the hard rock with her right knee. She cries out in pain, but she clings to the rope with all her might and pulls herself to her feet again.

Olivia glances back to see if the same wave that threw her has swept him away, but he is still there.

A few more steps and she kneels beside him.

'Micky. Micky. I'm here.' Olivia has to shout because the roar of the wind and waves is so loud.

The man squints up at her, eyes filled with terror. But they are a stranger's eyes, not Micky's.

'Take the rope.'

She grabs his arm with one hand while she kicks the end of the rope to him. He gets the rope, but he's still lying on the rocks.

'Can ya walk?'

If he can't, they're going to have a big problem, because there's no way she can carry him.

In answer, he drags himself out of the water and sways to his feet. She notices a tear in his shirt and there is a wash of blood around the gash. Olivia motions for him to pass her on the rope and then she follows. A few times he stumbles, and she hears groaning, but with much effort they get to the base of the ledge.

Olivia thinks she might have to climb up and then pull him up. But she's not even sure she has enough strength to pull herself up, let alone him. Sure, she's exercised for years in the cells to keep her arms strong, but her energy is waning fast. Still, she must try.

'Wait here,' she tells him amidst another spray of ocean wave.

Olivia hasn't gotten very far when, mercifully, she hears a voice above her. She looks up. It's Mr Douglas, covered with a hat and oilskin coat.

'Hang on. I'm pulling you up.'

Olivia clings to the rope and allows him to do the work.

Moments later, she is back to relative safety, and Mr Douglas pulls the stranger up. Olivia lies there on her back, eyes closed, too tired to worry that she's still being deluged with rain and spray. But she is conscious of pain in her right knee and every burning muscle in her body.

Mr Douglas drags the stranger to the base of the lighthouse and Olivia climbs to her feet and staggers behind him.

'There is another one,' she tells him.

'Yes, I saw. I'll go after him. You rest here.'

With those words, he is off.

Olivia rolls to her knees, keeping the weight off her right knee, to check on the stranger. Is this Micky's friend? Is Micky the one still out there? There is a big rip in his shirt, the one she noticed before. She leans over him and moves his shirt aside to see how bad his wounds are. There is a deep gash in his side. Without thinking, she reaches out her hand to touch it and he gasps and then groans.

'I think I've cracked a few ribs,' he grinds out between teeth clenched in pain.

'I'm sorry.'

He also has a cut near his brow which leaks blood. Olivia tears a piece of cloth from the cuff of her drawers and dabs at the wound.

At that moment, Brick comes around the corner of the lighthouse. He takes one look at Olivia and his face changes.

Rage.

That is about the only thing she has time to acknowledge before he throws her away from the stranger. Despite her weariness, she scrambles to her feet. But he is already coming at her. She has seconds to act. Her years of practice kick in and as he closes in, she brings the heel of her palm up into his nose.

He shouts, but it sounds more like anger than pain. He presses his hands to his face for a moment, but seconds later turns on Olivia again. She goes to knee him in the groin, but too late remembers her own injury and she is ineffective. Catching her off guard, he shoves her hard, and she falls back to the ground. Her head meets rock with a sick thud and the sky, the rain, the waves and Brick all start spinning.

But she is conscious of Brick on her, straddling her, his hands sliding around her neck. He is cursing, using the filthiest words she's ever heard.

'Slut! Whore! You are going to regret this.'

His fingers press harder, his face mottled with crazed fury. It's hard to breathe. He will kill her.

But Olivia doesn't want to die. She wants to finish her sentence and be free. And she wants to see Micky again.

CHAPTER
Eleven

Mick
New Norfolk

The Sabbath is a good day and not just because it is the day for church services. It is a family day. It is Sunday roast dinner day. Mum left the lamb leg, potatoes, and other vegetables in the stove while they walked together down to the church for the service. It is the one day of the week Mick sees all his sisters and brothers in the one place. After church, they all return to the farm together to eat, the house filled with the savoury aromas of their family meal.

They fill these Sunday gatherings with ladles of laughter, a sprinkle of silliness, and lashings of love—just like the gravy Mum pours over the steaming meat. One by one, Mick's siblings have all married in the last several years and he had to build Mum a bigger table to fit them all. And now they're adding to the number with children. He might have to start on a second table.

Mick's older brother Tom shows off his newborn son, whose puckered mouth shows signs of intent to bawl.

'He's hungry, I think.' Tom says.

'Who wouldn't be with the smell of that lamb?' Dad quips.

'I think he's more interested in the smell of milk at this point,' Mum returns, pinching Dad on the arm.

With flushed cheeks, Tom's wife Ellenor, gathers up the wailing bundle and disappears into another room, but then pokes her head back around.

'Don't wait for me.'

A picture flashes into Mick's mind of Olivia carrying an infant like that, and his heart does a leap. He takes a breath and tucks into his food. He can't think like that. But it would be nice if she were here, sitting around the table with them.

They are in the middle of dessert, and a long round of banter, when there is a knock at the door. They only just hear it beneath the bellowing laughter. Dad scrapes his chair back and goes to the front of the house.

Soon he is back with Raff beside him. The lawyer greets everyone in short, then turns to Mick. 'Can I speak with you? It's about the, er, lighthouse.'

Frowning, Mick wipes his mouth with the napkin and rises to follow him out.

A round of whoops rises from the table.

'Going to see your girl, eh?' Tom winks.

The heat of discomfit burns on Mick's cheeks. Tom can read him too well. It's all Mick wishes for, and they know Raff has taken him to see her regularly.

'Mum, feed him some more apple pie,' Mick retorts. 'Give him some indigestion.'

'What are you sayin' about my bakin' Son?' She's got her hands on her hips.

'Oh,' everyone is gasping and laughing, like he's in big trouble.

He scoots over and gives her a big kiss on the cheek.

'Love you, Mum.'

He hurries out of the room with Raff. His family doesn't seem to have noticed what Mick has. That Raff has ridden hard to get here. Something is wrong. As soon as they are out of the dining room, Mick stops him. 'What's happened?'

Raff shakes his head, and he looks grave. 'There's been an incident out at the lighthouse.'

'What do you mean, incident?'

Raff shoves his hands in his pockets and looks down at the floorboards.

'Not sure exactly. From what I can gather, Old Jim Drummond went out on his fishing boat just before the storm hit yesterday morning. He's getting old and doesn't always make the best decisions. Sadly, no-one stopped him either—perhaps because he has always been a belligerent coot. From what I've learnt, he had two or three others with him, and —'

'I don't understand. What has this to do with the lighthouse?'

'The news is that they never came back.'

This is terrible news, Mick gets that, but he still doesn't see how it links to the Iron Pot. He sits down in an armchair, trying not to appear impatient, although he cannot stop tapping his fingers on the armrest.

'Wrecked, you think?'

'That is the news that's filtering in. They wrecked out somewhere near South Arm.'

And South Arm is near the lighthouse. Oh.

'Now,' Raff takes a big breath, 'the other news drifting in is that a convict from the Iron Pot absconded after reporting a request for urgent help down on South Arm. I suppose they sent for help soon after the storm abated. Why Douglas sent a convict, I'm not sure, and what has happened out there is anyone's guess, but I suspect it's connected with Drummond's missing boat. All I know is they've sent police to hunt down the fugitive and sent a boat out to the island at the first change of tide this morning.'

He pulls a fob from his pocket and checks the time.

'I'm guessing they should be just about due to return.'

Mick quits tapping the arm of the chair and grips it hard instead. Raff has not told him anything. The one name on his lips, the only one he wants to know about, hovers in the room like an elephant. Mick wants to ask him, but he doesn't want to seem insensitive to the possible tragedy that has occurred.

'How do we find out what's happened?'

Raff stares at him like he's queer in the attic.

'We're going back to Town, that's how.'

Feathers for brains, that's why he's here. Mick jumps up from his chair.

'Let's go then.'

'Perhaps I can get a bite to eat first?' Raff looks embarrassed to ask.

Mick should be the one ashamed. Raff's just ridden for hours without a break to get here. Mick apologises, and they head back to the dining room to fill a plate.

Three hours later, they have travelled the twenty miles into Hobart Town, pressing their horses to run as much as possible without wearing them out. They go straight to the wharf, but there is no sign of a boat they can see. After asking around, they discover the boat landed two hours earlier.

'Where did they go, may I ask?' Raff questions harbour master.

'Can't rightly say, sir. They took one bloke away in chains, and they carted two fellas and a woman off in stretchers. Three different carriages or carts, there were.'

At the word 'woman', Mick's heart has stilled. Every other word comes slowly and muted. A woman? There were only two on the island. Is it Olivia? And why would she need to be carried? Blood surges to his head in a rush. He needs to know, and he needs to know now.

'We need to go, Raff,' he yanks on his friend's arm. 'To Cascades.'

While Raff thanks the man, Mick is already mounting his horse. They have another four miles to travel, and he nudges his horse into a canter, leaning forward to apologise in her ear. If something has happened to Olivia …

Mick's heartbeat matches the pounding of the horse's hooves on the road. He cannot keep thoughts of dread from seeping into his head. Raff is close on his heels but doesn't try to slow him. Raff understands the urgency.

Finally, they rein in outside the gates of the Female Factory, and Mick dismounts before the horse has fully stopped. Leaving Raff to tether the horses, he races to the iron door.

'Have officers brought a sick prisoner here recently?' he asks the guard.

The warden looks at Mick with a smirk. He knows who Mick is, and he is one of them who calls him soft. So, he takes his time to answer Mick, spitting on the ground and having a good look around.

'Well, yeah,' he drawls. 'They brought The Shank in, not an hour ago.' An icy glint flashes in his eyes as he slices the dagger home. 'Looks like she finally got the beating she deserved.'

Mick clenches his fists, fire building in his gut, but Raff grips his arms, bringing him back to a semblance of sanity. There is no point questioning the turnkey further since he is just out to cause trouble.

'Open the door.' Mick grits out between teeth that want to shout and bite.

The guard grins at him. He enjoys Mick's feverish impatience. For a second, Mick thinks he will toy with him further, but Raff gives the guard a stern look, and he relents.

They find Olivia in the infirmary, where the men who brought her in still stand about.

'What happened out there?' Raff asks before Mick can say anything. He knows Mick is likely to say something stupid or reckless.

'Douglas says two men from a wreck washed up on the island and Olivia Cruikshank tried to help them. He is unsure of what happened after that, as he was occupied with assisting one of the wreck victims.'

Every fibre in Mick's body is tight. All he wants to do is see her, but he is not supposed to entangle himself with a prisoner, and so he holds it all in as best he can.

'The other prisoner involved says Cruikshank attacked him. He has a broken nose to show for it. But Cruikshank has not yet spoken of the incident. One of the washed-up sailors has been mostly unconscious, so unable to give witness yet, and the other is the one Douglas worked with.'

'So, we don't have the full story, then?' Raff clarifies.

'Until the injured parties make some recovery, we cannot make a full assessment.'

Recovery. That word sits in Mick's belly like a lump of clay. Olivia is injured. He needs to be with her.

'May I see Miss Cruikshank?' He forces his voice to sound calm.

'We are waiting for a doctor to inspect her wounds, but I see no harm in you attending her for the moment. She certainly is not dangerous in her current condition.' The man nods at Mick like that would assuage his fears, even though he doesn't have any. Not a single one.

'Where?'

He points to a door, and without hesitation, Mick heads to it.

'I'll wait here,' Raff tells Mick's retreating form.

There are several beds in the infirmary, and they all contain patients with either fever or dysentery—the common maladies of Cascades. Mick eventually finds Olivia at the far end and his stomach turns at the sight of her. Face pale, so pale, with smudges of dried blood on her white skin. Her mob cap is gone, and a bandage circles her head, while salt crystals matt her hair. Has no-one taken the time to bathe her? Lurid welts stand out on her neck like the red cross on a medic flag. She is unconscious, or asleep, and would look serene apart from the obvious injuries. But she is alive, and he breathes out some relief.

'Olivia?'

She doesn't respond.

He drags a chair over and sits by her bed. He wants to stroke the side of her face, kiss her ashen forehead, cradle her damaged head in his arms. The yearning is so strong it aches. Instead, he hooks his fingers around the pinky of her limp hand. Her hand twitches, and he looks up, but she is still out. He notices, as he turns her hand in his, that her palm is raw and blistered, and a fresh rush of pain surges through him.

'What happened to you out there, Olivia?'

***

Olivia

Micky is here. Olivia knows his voice. She doesn't want to open her eyes and let him know she is awake, because he holds her hand, and she doesn't want him to let go. It is comfort; it is warmth; it is safety. Never has she found that with another person, except perhaps Papa, before … before everything. He used to hold her hand when they walked through crowded markets so she wouldn't get lost.

And she's felt lost for the last seven years and more since Papa left her.

But Micky is here. She wants to grip his hand in return, beg him to stay. Olivia needs him. She never thought she needed anyone, but right now, she doesn't want to be alone.

Olivia can still feel Brick's hands around her neck, still see the wild rage in his eyes, still recall the feeling of impending death. Like he seared the image into her mind, a still frame that won't move forward, and she can't look away.

94

Micky's voice stirs her attention. He is praying—for her. His thumb caresses her knuckles, sending warmth to her toes, while his voice gently murmurs his supplications. Doesn't he know those prayers are wasted? God has not listened to her yet. But it shows that Micky cares.

He cares. About Olivia.

About me.

Emotion wells up in her like a fresh spring of water bursting to the surface. She cannot hold this in. And Micky is the iron pick that has cracked the rocks open.

With a rush, his hand leaves hers and his chair scrapes as he stands. No, no, no. He can't leave.

'Micky!' But her voice doesn't work, only a whisper escapes. Her throat is closed and swollen and sore.

Her body shakes with the tears that rise with volcanic force and already she feels them leaking from the corners of her eyes.

And her head hurts.

She opens her eyes, but his back is to her, one hand rubbing his face. She tries again.

'Micky!'

This time he turns, but she can't be sure if it was her voiceless call or her choking sobs that he hears. With one stride he is back in the chair, his eyes wide with worry, but he stops short of taking her hand again.

'Do you need the nurse? Are you in pain?'

Olivia shakes her head a little, but every movement hurts. She just wants him.

He stares at her for a few seconds, searching.

'You're crying.'

She wants to make a smart quip about his intelligence, but very little sound passes through her damaged throat. Brick has murdered her voice even if he failed to murder her body. *I'll never sing again.* The convulsions of grief wrack her body even more.

The next thing, Micky pulls his chair right up close to the bed, takes one of her hands in both of his and leans forward so that his forehead is resting on his forearms. His grip is so tight it hurts, but she doesn't care. She turns her face to the pillow and lets the tears come. It has been too long. She has held this pain locked down tight forever, and now it all comes out at once. Mother's heartless manipulation, Father's abandonment, false imprisonment, injustice, lies, abuse, neglect—it is all rolled into one big torrent of anguish.

'It's all right, Olivia. It's all over now.'

Does she imagine it, or does he press his lips against the back of her hand momentarily? His breath is warm on her skin.

He holds her hand until at long last the flood has waned and the sobs fade.

But then the surgeon appears and asks Micky to leave. She grabs onto his sleeve as he stands.

'No. Please.'

No audible sound again, but Micky gets her meaning anyway and smiles that gentle smile of his.

'I'm not going anywhere. Just giving the doctor some space.'

He turns his back, though, to lend them some privacy.

'Can you tell me what happened, Miss Cruikshank?' The doctor asks as he starts with the obvious, unravelling the bandage around her head.

'Brick tried to kill me,' she tells him, though she doubts he can understand anything. And the mention of it makes her want to cry again, so she swallows hard, which also hurts.

He straightens a bit, then looks at her neck, then back in her eyes.

'Something was around your throat? Tight?'

Olivia nods, though the movement makes her head spin. She lifts her hands and tries to make a strangulation gesture with them towards his own neck.

'I see.' He looks grim. 'And your head?'

'On the rocks,' she rasps. Again, she makes a gesture with her hands, one fist banging onto the other flat palm.

'Any other injuries?'

Olivia points to her knee and he draws the covers back to examine what she knows is stiff and swollen. Then she shows him her hands, which still burn like she's been too close to the stove.

After a few more minutes of poking and prodding, he steps over to Micky, who turns to face him.

'It is hard to know exactly what happened without her story, but it seems she has been the victim of a violent assault—strangulation. It may be several days until the swelling in her throat goes down enough for her to speak. Indeed, the damage to her voice may be permanent. Only time will tell.'

I knew it. Olivia knew she would never sing again. Fresh grief wells up.

'The other injuries are not too serious but keep an eye on her over the coming days. If there is any turn for the worse—she becomes disoriented, nauseous, loses consciousness—send for me at once. I'll send a nurse shortly to bathe her.'

'Thank you, doctor.' Micky nods, but his expression is a mask. Olivia can't tell what he's thinking.

As soon as the doctor leaves, he comes back to sit on the chair and looks into her eyes. Does she mistake it, or do his eyes reflect her own pain? Why is he so good to her?

'I'm so sorry you have suffered like this. I don't understand how …' He swallows and clears his throat. He glances away, but not before she sees a flash of fury in his expression. 'The other prisoner says you attacked him.'

Olivia shakes her head, anger taking place of sadness. She guesses Micky can tell she is uptight because he takes her hand again.

'It's all right. I don't believe him. I doubt anyone does. But you did break his nose.' He grins at her this time, like he's proud of her or something.

'Good,' she nods.

'Where did you learn to fight like that?'

It's not the first time he's seen her do damage. Olivia wishes she could tell him the story, but weariness overtakes her. All the emotion, all the examination, it's all sucked her energy away. She lets her eyelids close even while Micky gives her permission to sleep, and the memories swirl in her mind.

Olivia kept mostly to herself on the transportation ship. On arriving in Van Diemen's Land, she shrunk into herself even more. They stepped off the ship into what seemed like a fire pit. Hot sun glaring down, hot wind buffeting her. So dry and sapping. This was to be her seven-year punishment.

She was terrified more than she would even admit to herself. She was still a child and petite and oh so vulnerable, just knowing it would all be bad.

One other prisoner—Ann, who has become her ally—must have read her true, though she never spoke a word to her. Something akin to sympathy lit in her eyes as she spoke to Olivia.

'What ya need, pet, is to learn how to defend yerself. 'Tain't that hard, ya know. I, meself, was once a tiny thing like you.'

In truth, Ann was not much taller than Olivia, although much more rotund. A feather could knock Olivia over given the chance, half starved as she was.

'I can look after myself.' She tried to sound braver than she felt.

'Sure ya can. Just like I ain't chained here next to ya.'

Well, she could look after herself, to a certain extent. But next thing Ann had knocked Olivia to the floor and pinned her there, holding a fist threateningly over her face while pressing down on her chest. Olivia fought against her, wriggled, clawed at her arms, to no avail. Then, abruptly, Ann let go before she drew too much attention from the others.

'See. Ya need to know how to fight.'

'All right.' Olivia had no further argument. But it was a frightening way to learn a lesson. In truth, she thought she was going to die for a moment.

That day, and for the next weeks, Ann regularly gave her lessons on how to wriggle free in that kind of situation, how to find a man's weak points and do damage. She taught Olivia how to strengthen her arms and shoulders and legs. Olivia felt as though she had a new power. She felt less vulnerable.

Until her first assignment post.

The Super sent Olivia, soon after arrival in the penal colony, to a farm to work as a domestic. That didn't seem so bad. Cleaning, washing, cooking. None of that seemed as terrible as she had expected.

But another assigned convict started paying her too much attention. He must have been around nineteen years old, she guessed. But he would often corner her, say things that gave her to understand he wanted her, and that she would have no say in the matter. The fact she was only thirteen did nothing to stop him. One day, he trapped Olivia in the woodshed. Started putting his hands on her, forced his mouth on hers. Fear stuck in her throat.

She couldn't even scream. But then, then, she remembered Ann's lessons. She watched for the right moment, then brought a knee up into his groin, hearing his agony as he fell back. For a moment, he doubled over in pain and stared at her in shock. Olivia could not help but grin at her success. She had power; she had control; she had freedom.

For a moment.

But then he came at her with the horsewhip.

The landowner pulled him off her soon after, and the end of it was he sent Olivia back to the Cascades where the Super put her in solitary confinement for a week. So much for justice. The other convict avoided any punishment whatsoever.

She would never be truly free. Never.

CHAPTER
Twelve

Mick

Mick's duties monitoring the wash yard are little more than an annoyance to him today. He cannot focus when his thoughts are with Olivia in the infirmary. If only he could sit by her bed all day long. She looks so fragile, lying there. A knot twists in his gut as he remembers her desperate sobbing yesterday. What must she have gone through to tear her so deeply? It took all his power not to take her in his arms and hold her tight.

More of the story about the Iron Pot has filtered through now. The damage to Olivia's hands is rope burn, from climbing out of the tower and rescuing one of Drummond's crew. That brave, darling girl risked her life to save a stranger. And that despite her terror of heights. She never went near those windows when Mick visited her, instead almost clinging to the opposite wall. So that makes her risk even greater. He knew it from the beginning—that she wasn't the person everyone made her out to be. Pride swells in his chest. More than ever, he wants to see her embrace the freedom at her fingertips. More than ever, he wants to hold her in his arms. More than ever, he wants her to know how he really feels about her.

Truth be told, he is more in love with her every time he sees her. Yes, in love. He knew it for a certainty the moment Raff mentioned trouble at the lighthouse. He couldn't lose her. Not then, not now, not when there is still so much to discover. A lifetime of getting to know her is all he wants.

But how does he tell her? When does he tell her? Should he wait until she finishes her sentence? He's not sure he can wait that long. But how does he know if or when she is ready to hear it?

Heavens, but this yearning is far too distracting. He pulls his fob from his pocket. It is still several hours until he can be with her.

Mick looks over at Miss Smith as he walks through crime class and tries to focus on his responsibilities. Why is it he cannot find any compassion when he looks at her? Mayhap because she represents the very thing that delivered Olivia to the infirmary. An unwillingness to change. The prisoner, Brick, has obviously shown no sign of reformation. Raff discovered he is serving fourteen years for violent assault. Mick would like to throttle *him*, given the chance.

He taps his fingers against his baton. Why is he thinking this way? This is not who he is.

'Itching to give her a hidin' are ya?' Fred has wandered over and smirks at Mick. 'Figured you'd come around eventually.'

'Who?'

'Smith. She needs a good beatin'.'

Mick shakes his head. He hadn't even realised he still stared at her.

'I'm not set on beating anybody.' *Except you if you don't be quiet.* Or Brick, if he can get his hands on him.

'Well, ya sure look like y'are. Flamin' nemmos. All need to be knocked around if ya ask me.'

'I didn't ask you, Fred.' The words hiss through his teeth.

Mick is that close to knocking Fred around, he clenches and unclenches his fists. But he takes a deep breath and lets it out slowly. This is not him. This is not who he is.

Fred laughs, a mirthless grating sound.

'Touchy!'

Thankfully, Fred moves away, but minutes later Miss Smith sways over.

'Hey, lover boy.'

Mick grits his teeth.

'I'm not your lover boy.'

She pouts at him.

'Someone's in a sour mood.' She runs a finger along Mick's forearm. 'Does it have to do with that poor little Shank in the sickroom?'

So, the news has travelled.

'I gotta say I'm upset too,' she croons. But then her face twists into a mask of unrestrained hatred and she spits her words at him. 'Upset she's not dead.'

Mick's whole body jerks forward to grab her, shake her, shut her mouth. He wants to yell at her, to make her understand. But he can't do it. This is not who he is. He holds himself back, but not before she sees the fleeting moment of insanity in his face.

She throws back her head and laughs, mockery in every chortle.

'You're no different from the rest of us.' Her eyes glint with malice. 'You think you're so good, being all kind to these girls, but deep down you know they don't deserve it.'

Strangely, with those words, the anger washes out of him, like water flowing from a drain when the plug is pulled.

It is not about deserving. It is about grace and mercy.

Whether the women deserve their punishments, or whether they don't. Whether Brick deserves retribution or whether Olivia didn't deserve the attack she received. It is all irrelevant. The only thing that matters is offering people grace and mercy despite what they deserve. Mick must operate in that mercy and forgiveness, or he will become as heartless and vengeful as every other officer in this prison. It's not who he wants to be.

He looks Miss Smith in the eye, calm as the sea on a windless day, and even manages a smile.

'What about you, Miss Smith? Do you deserve kindness? Or do you deserve to be here?'

Her grin vanishes. There is no safe answer, and she knows it. She doesn't deserve compassion, but neither will she admit to her guilt. She opens her mouth and closes it again, saying nothing.

'Perhaps you just deserve another chance, eh?' Mick leaves her with that thought and strolls away to see what the other prisoners are doing around the wash tubs.

Peace has found its place in his heart again. Mick doesn't know whether

Miss Smith will think on his words, or will remain antagonistic, but he hopes she will realise her need for grace.

Ann watches him approach, so he crouches down beside where she scrubs the linens. Her eyes are wide and filled with concern.

'What happened to that poor lamb?' she whispers.

Mick is not prepared to tell her everything, but he will tell her the best of it.

'She saved a man's life, but suffered several injuries in the process. She will mend, though. All is well.'

Ann is content with that. She is as proud of their girl as he is. He can tell.

He walks away, though, before she sees his uncertainty. For he is not sure that all is well. Will Olivia heal from this? And not just the external, physical wounds. If only he could erase it all for her.

***

Olivia

It is six days since the storm. She can speak now, though her voice remains broken. She cannot sing for the trying. Her head, hands, and knee are all much better and the Hutchinsons decide she should leave the infirmary. But, her first stop is the Magistrate's court, that familiar place where justice is rarely served. Well, not in Olivia's case, anyway.

Her future is uncertain at this point. Will they send her back to the lighthouse? Or somewhere else? Micky tells her not to worry. Sweet, caring Micky who has visited her every day when his work in the prison is over. How she looks forward to those warm, brown eyes that are filled with tenderness. Every day, he sits by her and tells her all will be well, and every day he says goodbye with a kiss on the back of her hand. And every day he leaves her wanting more of him.

But how could she expect more? Olivia is a prisoner, and just one of his projects, one of those he hopes to reform by his acts of kindness. And for his sake, Olivia wants to reform. She now sees and understands what he means. If she can get past this court case without making things worse for

103

herself, she will do her best for the rest of her sentence.

Unfortunately, Brick wants her charged for attacking him and she doubts they will believe her story, even if she tells it. Is there any point in trying? Who will believe a female convict with a history of breaking noses?

Mercifully, they bring the prison cart around, so she doesn't have to walk, but it is Fred, the turnkey, who escorts her out.

'Time to get yer comeuppance, eh Shank?' He laughs.

Olivia would like to accidentally step on his toes right now, but she has made a promise to herself to behave. Where is Micky? She had hoped he'd be the one by her side for this. Apprehension swirls in her stomach like so much rotting garbage in the sewer. But she pastes on a smile and gives Fred a pert wink.

'I'll be back to haunt ya. Better keep yer eyes open.'

He leaves her alone for the rest of the trip and she doesn't know whether to be grateful or not. Though he is bent on insulting her, it is a distraction from her dread thoughts. Olivia scratches at her arms, creating wounds where there were none.

Her hopes sink further when she sees the magistrate is not the same as last time. This will be bad. This will be all bad.

When the proceedings start, and Brick reels off lie after lie, Olivia switches off. She closes her eyes and goes to the only place she has ever found a mite of happiness. When she was four and Papa used to hold her on his lap and read stories to her. Stories of magic and adventure, always with happy endings. Then he would tuck her into bed, kiss each of her hands, each of her cheeks and then her forehead, calling her his little cherub, before he left her for the night. Which reminds Olivia of Micky holding and kissing her hand and making her feel valued. Seen. He is someone she never wants to lose.

'Olivia.'

She can hear his whisper in her ear, so close, it is as though her memories have come to life. She opens her eyes and turns to her left. It is him. He is here. Relief washes over her and her emotions surge, but she can't show that here. She needs to be in control, so she takes a deep breath and nods at him. Glancing past him, she sees his friend, the one who works in the law offices.

Micky gives her a quick wink and stands. The magistrate has just asked for witnesses.

After they swear him in, he gives his account of Olivia's character as he sees it. She keeps her eyes downcast. If she looks at him, it will be obvious how she feels about him and his words. She'll be lucky if the magistrate doesn't think he's biased. He's making her sound like a saint.

When Micky finishes, his friend takes the stand.

'Rafaello Cardamone,' he states his name, then swears on the Bible.

'I have a statement here from Mr Henry Douglas, who cannot be here today due to his duties at the Iron Pot Lighthouse, and one from Mr Selwyn Drummond who also cannot be here due to injuries sustained during a shipwreck. Both are witnesses, sir.'

Olivia's ears prick up at that. Did Mr Cardamone go in search of these statements on her behalf? She watches him as he reads, half in disbelief.

'"My name is Henry Douglas, Lighthouse Keeper at the Iron Pot. The Superintendent of the Cascades Female Factory assigned Olivia Cruikshank to assist me and my wife in domestic duties at the lighthouse. It became apparent early on that she would be a hindrance to the male convicts in my service because of her handsome features, so I enforced separation between them. The convict Seth Brooks, otherwise known as Brick, seemed especially keen and often sought her out. I did not see her respond to his advances at all, though Brick claims she was his girl. On the day of the storm, I woke from my daytime sleep and soon heard distant and urgent voices calling. I immediately went out to the lighthouse to see what was amiss. When I left the hut, Brick was still on his cot.

'"Upon rounding the tower, I saw a rope hanging from the upper windows, and another extending from the base towards the rocks. My first thought was Cruikshank had tried to escape. However, when I followed the rope, I quickly found her halfway up a small cliff, with Selwyn Drummond on the rocks below her. I quickly helped her up and then Mr Drummond. I left the two of them at the base of the tower and went after the other stranded crew member. When I returned with him several minutes later, I found the three of them, Brick, Mr Drummond, and Cruikshank, all

105

unconscious, while my other assigned convict, Patrick McIntire, stood over them in utter confusion. Neither of us saw what happened between Cruikshank and Brick, but I can attest to the singular courage and sacrifice Cruikshank showed in her rescue of Mr Drummond. I recommend leniency, if not a full pardon for Miss Cruikshank."'

The court is silent as Mr Cardamone finishes the statement and passes it to the magistrate. Olivia doesn't know what to think. Mr Douglas reckons they should pardon her? She is beyond surprised. Before she has a chance to process this properly, Mr Cardamone reads the other statement.

'This is the statement of Mr Selwyn Drummond, son of the late James Drummond who perished in the storm that wrecked his fishing boat. "My father did not think the storm too severe to go out fishing that day, and none of us, my brothers nor I, could convince him otherwise. I chose to accompany him, against my better judgement, to look after him should he get into trouble. As is now known, the storm capsized our boat and it broke apart on the rocks. I stayed afloat long enough to be thrown onto the outlying rocks of the Iron Pot island. Although already injured, I managed a strong grip around a rock and held on for dear life. My strength had waned when Miss Cruikshank appeared and helped me to safety. I remember being laid at the base of the lighthouse, and Miss Cruikshank, although she must have been exhausted, examined my wounds, trying to stop my head from bleeding.

"The convict known as Brick rounded the corner and upon seeing her, immediately attacked. He threw her away from me, yelling obscenities at her. Miss Cruikshank tried to defend herself, breaking his nose, but before she could disable him, he threw her to the ground again, then proceeded to choke her. I knew if I did nothing at that point, he would kill her. So, I gathered all of my remaining energy, got myself off the ground, and went over. I knew I didn't have the strength to pull him off, so I took the nearest piece of rock and hit him on the head as hard as I could. Then I blacked out. The next thing I recall is being carried to the hut.

"I cannot fault Miss Cruikshank's actions. I am unaware of the history between her and Brick, but my impression of his actions and words was that he flew into a jealous rage upon seeing her with me. My thanks go to Miss

Cruikshank, who saved my life. I am truly indebted to her.""

'That's not what happened!' Brick yelled from the other side of the courtroom. 'She attacked me, I tell you!'

His eyes are still black from the broken nose Olivia gave him. At least that is something. But her stomach crawls at the sight and sound of him. Her breath comes quickly, and she digs her nails into her arms. Brick struggles against several guards who try to hold him back. He still wants to kill her.

'Remove that man from the court,' the magistrate says with a frown.

Olivia feels a steadying hand on her shoulder and she turns to Micky.

'It's all right, Olivia. There is no-one here to accuse you now. Not one.'

How can that be true? It's always been one accusation after another, with never a soul on her side.

'Miss Cruikshank, do you wish to make a statement?' The magistrate is looking at her.

She turns to Micky again, unsure.

'You can do this,' he winks at her again. 'Just tell him the truth.'

On unsteady legs, she takes the stand, swearing to tell the whole truth. For several moments, she cannot even open her mouth. Is this what stage fright would feel like? She has no casual remarks, no nonchalant jokes, no witty defence. Just her. Just the truth.

'It … it's … just as Mr Drummond wrote.' Her voice is so patchy still, she hopes the magistrate can understand her. 'Brick made his intentions clear from the moment I landed on the island. He assumed I liked his advances, an' his version of romance were to pin me against the wall an' threaten me. Mr Douglas "separating us" is truly what kept me safe, rather than keepin' the male convicts safe from me. I were locked in the tower as usual on the day of the storm, but I heard the men shoutin' for help. It were my life or theirs, an' since I'm just a convict …

'Anyway, I climbed down the rope an' ya know the rest. Brick saw me leanin' close to Mr Drummond. He would 'ave seen Mr Drummond were practically shirtless an' I'd removed me skirt to climb the rope, so he must 'ave assumed the worst, an' since he decided I belonged to him ...'

Olivia shrugged. What else was there to say?

The magistrate flicked through papers on his desk, then looked back at her. 'It seems you have broken several noses over the past six years.'

'Yes, sir. I find that bein' a convict somehow makes men treat me as though I'm an easy woman. The men I've been assigned to, their sons, other assigned convicts, think they can make whatever demands they like. Yet, I don't reckon they would treat a free woman that way. I've just let 'em know they can't treat me that way neither.'

The magistrate flicks through his papers again, then sits back in his chair.

'Given that Seth Brooks has a history of violent assault against women, and Miss Cruikshank has many witnesses in her defence, I am inclined to rule in favour of the defendant. However, as Miss Cruikshank has previously shown her own violent streak, I will assign her to Class Two imprisonment at the Cascades Female Factory, to see out her sentence.' He turns to Olivia. 'Be on your best behaviour now, Miss Cruikshank, you only have seven months to go.'

He raps his gavel on the desk and it is over.

CHAPTER
Thirteen

Olivia
October 1841

It's been a while since she's been in with the Class Two girls. With seven months to go to serve, she can almost taste freedom, and it scares the rhubarb out of her. What is she supposed to do outside these walls? She can no longer sing, so even that dream, as slim as it might have been, is gone. She will have to work—probably domestic service—to support herself. Find somewhere to live. Make new friends. Stay out of trouble. Her stomach churns at the thought of it.

But she doesn't want to stay here. At least, she doesn't think she does. That was the thought that struck her when Brick had his hands around her neck. She wants a life, a proper life. All she must do is keep her head down for the next half year. Maybe she can do this. Maybe.

The only thing that worries her is that in Class Two, she is open for assignment. And if she gets sent out again, depending on who it is, might be her undoing. *Please God, let me stay here.* Just for a little longer.

Micky has influenced her more than she realised. Here she is praying. But maybe, just maybe, he is right. Maybe God cares after all. The thought brings a lump to her throat. Ever since the storm, her emotions don't want to stay down anymore, no matter how she tries. Maybe that's a good thing. And maybe it's not.

It was strange the day they brought her back here. The girls in Class

Two all stopped and stared, like she amazed them or something. Like they saw a ghost. Like she was some kind of hero. Olivia isn't sure which. But after a moment of eerie silence, one of them started tapping their tools on the bench. One by one they joined in until they had the rhythm going and next their voices added to the noise. 'Shank. Shank. Shank.'

The welcome was like a balm on her ears. She grinned at them and offered a playful curtsy. But Olivia couldn't sing.

She couldn't sing.

She couldn't sing.

Pain slices through her every time she realises it. Singing was the one thing she enjoyed, that gave her solace. And she can never comfort herself in that way again. *God in heaven, if ya love me, can ya please give me voice back?*

The girls welcomed her back into the fold with open arms. She joined with them in picking wool, a simple though mundane task. Olivia knew more about growing fruit and vegetables than working with wool before she came here. She has learnt to pick and card, but she's not so good at spinning. Or sewing or knitting. Her mother never taught her—well, nothing but the basics. Some of these ladies are excellent with the needle and can create delicate embroidery and tat lace. Some of them knit, some of them crochet, but Olivia's one skill is gone.

Then again. If she could just get herself re-assigned to Class One, then they might let her cook or mind the children or nurse the sick in the infirmary. Those things Olivia reckons she could do rather well. She supposes that would be a good thing to aim for. *Exemplary behaviour, here I come.*

She is going to take a leaf out of Micky's book and be kind. She can help the new prisoners adjust. Surely, she can befriend other prisoners— properly, not just because she has use of them. And she can show respect to the guards, even if they don't deserve it. It won't be easy, Olivia is sure, but she feels lighter just in the consideration.

Micky has just walked into the workroom. He will pretend like he's checking on all the girls, and maybe he is, but Olivia likes to pretend he's just here for her. Lordy, she could look at that man all day long, but she doesn't want to make it obvious. She fakes serious concentration on her wool, though she is conscious of his every movement.

A nudge in her ribs jerks her upright. It's Nancy, the woman sitting next to her.

'Oi, that officer is a bit of all ri', ain't he?' she whispers, leaning close enough Olivia can smell her breath.

Olivia shrugs, but all her nerves go tight. She wishes Nancy would take her rotten eyes off him.

'I wouldn't mind meetin' him in a dark alley, if ya know what I mean.' She nudges Olivia again and chuckles. Olivia clenches her teeth.

She wouldn't mind sticking Nancy with a needle. But she is an exemplary prisoner now, and that means no retaliation. Except …

'I don't reckon he's the type to wander into dark alleys. Looks like one of 'em churchy types.' Olivia keeps her voice light, jocular even, and nudges Nancy back.

'True, ya reckon?'

'Yeah. They say he's incorruptible. I've heard he wears a big fat cross 'round his neck. Might as well be a priest.' Now Olivia is going overboard, but she doesn't care if it means Nancy loses interest.

Nancy stares at Olivia, trying to read her genuineness, so Olivia nods to her earnestly.

''Struth.'

'Nah. He's too pretty. What a waste o' good looks.'

Olivia clucks her tongue and shakes her head in agreement, going back to her work.

He's getting closer. Olivia's heart cranks up a notch. She has missed him for two whole days since he last came in. He seems to spend longer in here than he should. In truth, she doesn't know why he's in here at all. Isn't his duty in the wash yard, crime class? But Olivia's imagination might have run wild. Maybe it's silly wishful thinking to believe he's here to see her, and she needs to get a hold of reality. She is a prisoner. End of story.

'Good afternoon, Mrs Thorne, Miss Cruikshank.'

He stands right behind them now. Olivia's fingers shake as she tugs the wool fibres apart.

'Afternoon, laddie,' Nancy grins up at him, while Olivia merely nods and tries to focus on her picking.

'Shank here tells me you've got a big cross 'round yer neck. Mind if I see it?'

Oh dear, let the floor give way beneath me now. Heat rushes up from Olivia's feet to her neck to the hairs on her head. She squints even closer at her fleece, as if there is a tiny speck of dirt she needs to remove.

'Did she now?'

He sounds amused, but Olivia can't look. Heaven's sakes, she can't even swallow.

'Well, I don't like to disappoint, but it's not so big, and it's not around my neck. However,' and Olivia turns a little to see him thrust a hand into his pocket, 'I have a small one connected to my fob.'

Olivia thinks he hands it to Nancy, but she is busy analysing this wool and hoping her face isn't as red as it feels.

'It's very nice, but why would ya carry it 'round everywhere with ya?'

'Well, you see, whenever I check the time, I am reminded that Christ died for one and all. It reminds me to be patient with people, despite who they are or what they might have done.'

Another nudge in Olivia's ribcage makes her drop the wool she's working on, and she sucks her breath in.

'Hey Shank, ya wanna see it?' Nancy is handing the fob and chain over.

'Sure.' Olivia tries to sound disinterested, leaning down to collect the fibres from the floor, but anything connected to Micky is exactly the opposite.

Olivia takes the watch, which she has seen many times, but never examined. She turns it over in her hand. There is an inscription engraved on the back and she runs her thumb over the uneven surface. She can't quite read it, but it looks similar to those writings on her piece of paper.

'What does that say?' Nancy is the one who asks.

'It is a Bible verse from Ecclesiastes,' he says, putting his hand out to receive his watch back. 'He hath made every thing beautiful in his time.'

Is Olivia imagining things, or did he emphasise the word beautiful? She chances a glance up at him and sees that gentle smile of his as he looks directly into her eyes. Olivia places the fob in his hand, and he closes his fingers over hers, just for an instant, but it is enough. Maybe she is not imagining things.

Heat rushes through Olivia again, and she turns her attention to her work again. Oh saints, but she likes him so much. Too much? She shouldn't hope for anything with Micky, but she can't fathom never seeing him again. What will she do without him when she is free?

'Does poking your tongue out like that help you pick the wool better, Miss Cruikshank?'

He is laughing at her. He has no clue what he does to her. That her insides are all jumbled up in his presence. Olivia turns around to him again, trying to look fierce, with a smart retort on her tongue. But his face, although laughing, is filled with something that melts all her angst away. There is warmth and light in his eyes—delight?

Olivia breaks out laughing. 'Why yes, Micky Reeve, it does.'

***

Mick

How he wishes he could spend more time with Olivia, tell her what is in his heart. By the pink flush to her cheeks just now, he feels hope of acceptance. He is sure she is not averse to his attentions. However, he has already lingered by her table for too long. He must move on, but it is hard to convince his feet to co-operate.

'I will see you ladies next week.' He'd better make it known, otherwise he'll never move.

'See ya, laddie,' Mrs Thorne winks. Mick wonders how she justifies her flirtations. Perhaps she left her husband behind in England when she went to prison. That must be a painful separation.

'Bye.' Miss Cruikshank doesn't shift her focus from her wool picking. But Mick wants her to look up. He needs to see into those brown eyes one more time before he goes. He stands there and waits until it looks questionable at best, willing her to look. Ah, finally she lifts her chin and

113

gives him the smile that will feed him until he sees her again.

He will carry the warmth of that smile all the way home, though the night is chill, and all the way back again on Monday morning. To call her his own, that would be better than a wagonload of perfect logs for turning. Only imagine how it would be to take her home with him, rather than leave her here.

Mick's smile is still in place when he walks onto the family property in New Norfolk. A few hours of future dreaming on the mail coach makes it easy. And nothing at home disrupts his happy state. He sleeps like fallen trees in the forest, still and peaceful, and wakes in the same objective mood as when he lay down. Mum laughs at him, whistling as he bathes and dresses.

'You better hurry up an' marry that girl, Son.'

Mick kisses her on the cheek.

'I intend to. Don't you worry about that.'

She giggles, but then her face turns serious.

'Is she goin' to be all right? I remember some prisoners were—'

'She'll be fine, Mum,' he pats her cheek and steals a piece of toast from her hand. 'She's not one of those.'

Back at the Cascades Female Factory the next week, Mick's day starts as usual. He does the rounds, seeing the crime class prisoners have their cells in order, sending them out to the yard for their hard labour. All the while, he knows Miss Cruikshank is only a few yards away.

'Oi! Reeve,' Fred calls Mick over from where he is inspecting the wash yard.

'What's happening?'

'We got another load of Nemmos comin'. Gotta go out front.' He jerks his chin toward the exit.

'When did the ship arrive?'

'Yesterday, I think. They been checkin' 'em over an' such, makin' sure there's no fever on board or what not.'

'Fair enough.' Mick follows Fred outside.

There are several lines of women prisoners being herded up the street. Matron directs Fred and Mick to those destined for crime class, few in number. The ones who have committed violent or serious crimes, or if they have shown unacceptable behaviour on the voyage from England. One by one, women file past, still wobbly with their sea legs, and most of them wearing apprehension like a blanket. Mick tries to smile and welcome them, although it probably sounds trite to be welcomed to a prison.

He remembers the day he first saw Miss Cruikshank arrive on foot, though she only came from the courthouse. She had him captivated from that moment. He knows that now.

He focuses back on his work, and it is as though he has a moment of déjà vu. A petite woman with a long blonde braid and large brown eyes shuffles past in one of the other lines. For a moment he swears it is Miss Cruikshank, but then he shakes his head, knowing Olivia is busy picking wool in the Class Two section. The woman, along with her train of fellow prisoners, files past him and he cannot help but stare.

'What are ya doin'?' Fred nudges him. 'Pay attention.'

Mick drags his eyes away from the apparition and focuses on Fred. 'Sorry, where are we up to?' But he can't help glancing back at the woman who now disappears inside the prison. She turns her head in his direction at the last moment and smiles at him. Oh Lord in Heaven, it's the same smile.

An uneasy feeling swirls in Mick's stomach. He needs to get these new prisoners settled so he can go back and find out who that woman is. Before she enters the yards.

Never has he been so brusque with the women. Never has he bluntly told them the way of things and then left them be. He cannot afford the time for introductions and light conversation. As soon as possible, he makes his excuses for needing a break, and makes haste to the Matron's office. Knocking on the door, he tries to slow his breathing. Please, please, please let it be his imagination.

'Come in,' she answers with dull tones.

'Sorry to bother you Matron,' Mick stands by her desk. 'But I wondered if you could check the manifest of the new arrivals for any familiar names.'

She stares at him, her jowls sagging more than usual. 'Why?'

'I thought I recognised someone.'

'And what difference would that make?'

'Very little, I suppose, but I should like to know if I am correct.'

She lets out a heavy sigh.

'Very well. But do you know how many Smiths there are? It's not likely that there will be a standout name. Let me see.' She runs her finger down a list that is several pages long. There must be more than a hundred names on there.

'Like I said. Smith, Smith, Smith. Then there's Johnson. Is that familiar?'

She looks at Mick with dull eyes. All right, he gets her point, but he just nods for her to continue. It's there, he knows it is. His churning stomach tells him it is. His shaking breath tells him it is. And his fingers drumming on the edge of her desk tell him it is.

'Ah, is this what you're looking for?' She looks up and there is a faint spark in her eyes this time. 'Mary Cruikshank.'

Mick supposes a small part of him hoped she wouldn't say that name. But there it is. Olivia's mother. Is here. In Cascades Female Factory. He gulps.

'What class is she?'

'Two.' Matron flicks the list closed.

Mick draws in a deep breath, unsure how she will respond to his next request.

'Is there any way we can warn Olivia Cruikshank that her mother is here before she walks in?'

'Why should I allow that?'

'Do you remember the day Ellen Smith saw Olivia Cruikshank walk into the crime class yard?'

'Yes.'

'I'm afraid this might be a repeat of that reaction.'

Another heavy sigh leaves her chest, and she shakes her head.

'I'll see what I can do.' Then she frowns at Mick and wags a finger at him. 'But it would be better for you if you cared less about these women. They are criminals. Sometimes you seem to forget that.'

'Yes, ma'am.' He nods. Not yes that he should stop caring about them, but yes that he tries to forget they are prisoners.

Mick steps out of her office, relaxing a little, now that she will try to make Miss Cruikshank aware before she suffers a rude shock. How will Olivia take this news? It might be all right. But then again, it might ruin everything.

116

CHAPTER
Fourteen

Olivia

It feels good to laugh. Olivia has not felt so relaxed in a very long time. Picking and carding wool is a hundred times easier on the back and shoulders than scrubbing and wringing, or even the work that she did at the lighthouse. And the girls in here don't fill the room with anywhere near as much tension. Maybe it's Ellen's absence. Since she's not nearby, Olivia doesn't have to feel on edge all the time.

Nancy and Olivia have swapped their stories. Well, Nancy does more of the talking than Olivia. She doesn't want to think about those years in England. She'll talk about anything since then, but not home, not them.

Turns out Nancy had a rotten husband who wasted all their dosh on ale, leaving nothing for her to feed her sweet bairns with. She knew she did wrong, but the law caught her trying to fence some ribbon she'd stolen from a milliner whilst he was busy speaking with another customer. She doesn't miss 'that drunken sod', but her eyes rapidly spill over with tears at the mention of her children. Nancy does not know what might have happened to them. Guessing their father would neglect them, and their relatives being too poor to give them aid, she fears they may be in an orphanage or the workhouse, or worse.

Strangely, Olivia now sees what Micky sees. A prison yard full of women who've made mistakes and now suffer the consequences of their choices. Not evil people as such, but many who made poor decisions born out of dire circumstances. She would that her story held more of that. She'd suffered no dire circumstances, and she had no choice.

If only she could sing. Right now, she might even soothe them with one of her secret arias. Her stomach quivers at the thought. Would she? Would she dare share that gift with others? Make herself open to ridicule and criticism? It is a confronting thought, but one Olivia doesn't have to act on, as she has no singing voice, anyway.

As she collects a fresh piece of fleece, she notices several of the girls putting their heads together, one after the other. Like a chain. News is coming around the yard. Olivia cannot help but wonder what causes the hushed exchange of words from one to the next. But she will know soon enough.

'Freshies.'

Nancy whispers the word into her ear, passing the news on. Freshies. A new transportation ship must have landed, and they will receive more prisoners into the fold. It's time to set up a warm welcome. Olivia grins to herself at memories of jovial song they have heralded the freshies with in the past. Alas, she cannot do that today. But then, on second thoughts …

'Let's give 'em a Cascades welcome, eh.' Olivia leans closer to Nancy and gives her a nudge.

Nancy looks at Olivia in doubt for a second and then passes the word along. They all no doubt wonder how they will do this, seeing as Olivia can't sing. She can tell by the looks she's getting from all around the room. What she reckons is that they've all heard Olivia's little ditty plenty enough times to remember it for themselves.

So, they wait. And when the door finally opens and the first unfamiliar face appears into the Class Two yard, Olivia bangs her fist on the table in the good old rhythm. The other girls all join in, despite the calls for silence from the turnkeys.

'All ri' Nancy. I need ya to sing nice an' loud with me.'

Nancy looks at Olivia like she's crazy, but one doesn't need to be too tuneful to carry this off. Olivia squeaks out the lyrics as best she can, which would probably hurt a deaf person's ears.

Welcome to this grand hotel, not so very far from hell.

They lock the doors and ring the bell, but we can dance all night.
Welcome to our palace hall, where we dine on bread and gall.
The whip is large, and bed is small, but we still dance all night.

Olivia stands up and twirls around, swishing her grey serge skirts as though she is in a ball gown, clapping her hands. The ladies' volume has taken over now. Olivia only needs to mouth the words and let them do the singing. They all smile and laugh and the freshies don't really know what to make of it. One by one they file in, dumbfounded, staring.

And then Olivia sees a face that makes the whole world stop. Her feet stop, her hands stop, her breath stops, even her heart stops. Just for a moment. But it starts again with a pounding that knocks loud in her ears. So loud, she can't hear the girls singing anymore, just the thump, thump, thump of her blood in a panicked frenzy. A scream freezes in her throat. What is *she* doing here?

In that moment, a thousand voices in her head rush at Olivia. There are raging screams of hate, questioning cries of 'why,' terrified wails of 'not again,' accusers, complainers, and the ever-present child's voice begging not to be abandoned. Olivia puts her hands over her ears as if that could stop them. She can't deal with this.

I can't. I can't. I can't.

Olivia turns to the nearest turnkey and grabs him by the arms. 'Get me out of here.'

He looks at her like some piece of filth and shakes her off.

'Sit down Shank.'

His voice echoes back from the opposite wall and Olivia realises everyone has gone dead silent. And still. Every eye on her. Her legs are quickly liquefying beneath her. She needs to leave. The quickest way to get herself locked in a cell, maybe even solitary, is to start a fight. One punch will do. Olivia pulls back her arm to show the turnkey how serious she is, when two things happen. One, Nancy grabs her arm to stop her swinging, and two, the Matron walks in.

'Who caused this disturbance?' She growls, her brows drawn together so low Olivia can hardly see her eyes.

'The Shank,' the guard spits, pointing his baton at Olivia. He's probably disappointed he didn't get to use it.

'Take her to the dark cells.' Matron doesn't wait for any further explanation.

The turnkey wrenches Olivia's arms behind her and cuffs her with the shackles they always carry on their belt. Olivia turns to Nancy and forces a grin, then shares it with the other prisoners—except for *her*. ''Twas just a bit o' fun, Matron,' Olivia says, forcing herself to sound loud and carefree, while the guard shoves her forward towards the door. 'Gotta welcome the freshies. Give 'em some good ol' Cascades hospitality, eh what?'

Olivia tries whistling the tune as she walks, but everything is shaking, and it gets worse as she passes *that* woman. Olivia can feel her staring at her, and she guesses some of the other girls have figured it out. But Olivia refuses to look. She holds her chin high and nods to the Matron.

'Olivia?'

The rage rises in her again and it is all she can do not to fly at her mother. Good thing the turnkey has a firm hold on her. Just before they reach the door, Olivia turns her way. 'Never. Speak. To me.' Olivia hisses each word with all the venom these years have leached into her soul. 'Never.'

***

Olivia

'Pull yourself together, girl,' Matron growls as the turnkey shoves her in a dim cell. The familiar comfort of solitary confinement. Olivia could almost thank her. 'I'll not have you attacking other prisoners. Is that clear?'

'She's not just another prisoner,' Olivia grinds out between clenched teeth as her mother's face appears in her mind's eye again.

'I don't care who she is. The goodwill you have received from this institution will quickly cease if you stir up trouble.'

Goodwill. It's almost laughable, but Matron's eyes have that unbending, resolute stare, and Olivia swivels away from her. She'll not be showing Matron any gratitude today.

'All ri',' Olivia hisses in frustration.

'Prepare yourself. You *will* join the others again on the morrow.'

A shudder sweeps through her at the words. She never wants to go out there again.

As the door clunks behind her, the lock sliding into place, Olivia collapses against the wall. Her stone-wall audience, who are now the only friends she has. She leans on them, the hard, uneven surface against her cheek like a soothing embrace she'll never get, and she lets the tears come.

Just when she thought her life might have promise, it all crashes down with a splintering scream, like a thousand pieces of shattered glass around her feet. And she dares not take a step, lest she cut herself.

Why? Why? Why is she here?

Well now, that's obvious, really. She was always the thief, not Olivia. Without a namby-pamby coward to assist her, she must have finally done the job herself—one too many times. Serves her right then. Olivia only hopes that her mother must serve longer and harder than herself. Now there is an idea—Olivia wonders if she can set her mother up to find herself in solitary or in crime class.

She spends the next few hours plotting her mother's downfall. Further downfall, that is. It will be easy to do. The other girls will do whatever Olivia asks of them. Shall she make sure officers catch Mother with contraband? Cause her to embroil herself in a fight? There are plenty of options. Olivia only needs to decide which will hurt her the most.

Olivia has devised several plans by the time she hears the lock rattle again. Supper, no doubt. And look who has brought it to her.

'Micky Reeve.' She squints into the sudden light.

She doesn't move from her spot on the floor. Why him? Why now? One look at his face and she feels the gulf of contrast between him and all he stands for, and Olivia's darkened thoughts of the past few hours. Why did she ever imagine she could try to be like that?

'Tough day?' He has his head cocked to the side, like he endeavours to read her.

She lets out a short, sarcastic laugh and rubs her face.

121

'Wanna talk about it?'

Olivia sucks in a deep breath, summoning whatever control she can find. She is not in the mood for this, but she doesn't want to upset him. Not Micky. She scratches at her arms.

'Nothin' to talk about.' She even attempts a light-hearted shrug.

Without comment, he places her tray of food on the floor and then steps back to the door. But he doesn't leave, the stubborn mule.

'Once, I would have accepted that and let it be. But now I know you well enough to know when you're full of bluff.'

He lets that hang in the air for a moment and she knows he watches her, waiting for an answer. A response she's not giving him.

'I also know your mother arrived today.'

You'd think he'd just flung a knife into her chest, the way those words stung. And made her bleed, her pain pooling on the floor beneath her.

'You shut up about 'er. Not another word.'

So much for not hurting Micky.

'But she's—'

'Not another word!'

Olivia scrambles from the floor and flings herself at him, screaming, swinging her arms. Not her usual carefully placed punches, but wild, frantic hits.

'I hate her! I hate her! I hate her!'

Micky doesn't react in anger as she expects. He doesn't react at all. Not in the slightest.

'Shh,' is all he says, his strength doing the rest. He encircles her wrists in each of his large hands and holds them still until she stops trying to swing and even until she stops trying to wriggle free. But most of the force has gone out of her now, and instead overwhelming grief takes over and she sobs. Again.

'Shh,' he repeats over and over, still holding her wrists but gently now, his thumbs stroking her skin.

'I hate her,' Olivia moans.

'I know.'

'Why'd she 'ave to come here?'

'That, I cannot answer.'

'I don't wanna see her.'

'I know.'

He just lets her carry on venting her spleen until, in exhaustion, she pulls away from him and lays down on the cot. She stares at the wall in dejection.

'Things was just startin' to get better, Micky.'

'They were.' He nods and sighs and leans up against the wall nearest her, crossing his long legs at the ankles.

'She's gonna ruin everythin'.'

He leans down and pulls a loose thread from the blanket that's tossed at the end of the cot.

'Only if you let her, songbird.'

'What do ya mean?' Olivia turns so she can look at him. She must look a fright after all that crying, but he doesn't comment.

'She may have controlled you in the past, but you're a grown woman now. You have your own choices. You can let her ruin your remaining time here, or you can rise above it.'

Olivia frowns at him. 'But how?'

'By letting it go.' He twists the thread around his finger. 'It is one of the hardest things to do, but forgiving her is the only way to be free of her.'

'She don't deserve it.' Olivia's insides twist like that string on his finger. How could he suggest such a thing?

'In the end, it doesn't matter whether she deserves it or not.' He shrugs. 'Forgiving her will not change her or even affect her unless she seeks it. But it will change you. When you don't forgive, you hold on to your anger, which makes you bitter and ties you up.'

Wait. What? Did he just read her mind?

'Olivia, you are one of the bravest people I know. I believe you can do this.' He reaches down and squeezes her shoulder ever so gently. His eyes are so warm and genuine, he almost makes Olivia believe she can forgive her mother.

Almost.

'I'll try,' she murmurs. And she will.

'That's my songbird.' With that, he straightens to leave.

Perhaps she should have argued some more. Would that make him stay?

'Micky?'

'Yes.'

'Thanks.'

He gives a half smile and scuffs his shoe on the floor.

'I saw her before you did. Recognised the similarity to you. I tried to get a warning to you, but I guess Matron wasn't there in time.'

'She got me outta there quick smart. I shoulda' known you was behind it. Always lookin' after me.' In a moment of emotion, she gushes her appreciation. 'How am I ever gonna make it up to ya, Micky?'

'Don't you worry, little songbird. I'll find a way.' He wiggles his eyebrows and winks at her before ducking out of the cell and locking it.

And there it is. Suddenly Olivia feels deflated again. He isn't as selfless as she thought he was. He is going to exact some kind of payment out of her. Olivia will be a prisoner forever.

CHAPTER
Fifteen

Olivia

She can't sleep. Her mother's face and what she did circle around her head along with Micky's words. One thing he is right about—this is going to be hard, if it's even doable. Olivia's life might have been vastly different if her mother had never handed her those olives. What has her life been instead? Punishment, injustice, degradation, and such aloneness. Her mother abandoned her. It's all her mother's fault. And now Olivia's supposed to forgive her? Forget it.

After tossing and turning for what must be hours, she gives up and wriggles off the uncomfortable cot. She wishes there were a window through which she could look at the moon and stars, but there is only darkness. She can't even see her hand in front of her face.

Olivia goes over to the wall, running her hands over the familiar stones, reciting their names as she remembers them, though she can't see them to know if she's touching the right one for the right name. They have been so steadfast; they deserve a song. Olivia knows it will sound terrible, but she can at least try.

Expecting the sound to come out squeaky or raspy at best, she launches into her favourite aria. The first few notes are rough, but then, strangely, her voice improves, strengthens. With each rising note, she sounds more like she remembers. Her voice squeaks a few times on the very highest of notes, but within a few minutes, even that is gone.

I can sing again! With tears streaming down her cheeks, she gives her

125

audience wall the aria of a lifetime. She doesn't hold back, not in volume, not in passion, not in gratitude. *Thank you, God.* The singing gives her presence of mind, calms her. In this moment, she can see clearly. She knows what she must do.

When morning comes, Olivia is impatient to join the girls in the yard. She will face her mother. Even though her stomach feels like it wants to rise into her throat. Even though her hands shake, and she needs to scratch her arms to still them. Even though her heart flutters like a hummingbird's wings. A turnkey brings her food, but she can't eat it. She just needs to get this over with.

Finally, they come and fetch Olivia to the yard. Her legs feel as weak as an uncooked egg as she walks, and it seems her breath has deserted her. Why does she feel like that child in the marketplace again? Part of her wants to turn around and run back to the cell. On her own, at least she knows what to expect.

And then there she is. In front of her. Olivia can either succumb to this crazy weakness or pull out her expert fun side. She glances at her mother briefly and then gazes around the room.

'Mornin' ladies,' she crows. 'Lovely day for a parade 'round the park, don't ya think? Show them fellas how posh we look in these mob caps. Eh, what?' Olivia struts to her place like a lady of the ton, flicking her head about ludicrously. Laughter greets her inane act on the one hand, but on the other, a harsh 'silence' from the guard.

She pouts at him. 'Ain't ya havin' a good day, there guvna?'

He frowns at her and puts his hand on his baton in warning. 'Get to work.'

'I'm workin'. I'm workin'. Don't get yer knickers all twisted up now.'

All the girls snicker, and Olivia sneaks a glance at her mother to see her response. Her mother is looking wide-eyed at everyone around her. Hopefully, she sees Olivia is not someone she can lord it over anymore.

'Yer daft, ya know?' Nancy whispers when Olivia sits down, although she is grinning, showing the gaps where she is missing teeth.

'Just a bit o' fun.' Olivia shrugs.

'One o' these days, yer gonna get yerself flogged.'

'If I were a bloke, maybe,' Olivia winks. They don't seem to take the cat to the women anymore. She picks up her fleece and starts picking. There's plenty of wool today. It's going to keep her busy.

After a few minutes of silent picking, Nancy nudges Olivia. 'So, what was that about yesterday?'

'What do ya mean?' Olivia pretends ignorance.

'I mean, one minute you was all up an' dandy, an' the next you was pickin' a fight.'

Olivia is not ready to tell the girls the truth yet. Not that Nancy will shout it out to everyone. She's not game enough to make a big noise like Olivia is. But until Olivia has spoken to her mother, none of them are going to know who she is. Unless they, like Micky, are smart enough to recognise their likeness.

'Ah, nothin'. That guard looked at me the wrong way. Just moody, I guess.'

Olivia's not sure if Nancy believes her. She looks doubtful. But she goes back to her carding just the same.

After their lunch break, the officers lead them out into the open yard to walk and see the sun—if it has made an appearance. In Class Two, the girls often pair off or gather in small groups to circle the yard, taking their exercise. A couple of them do a toffy walk, showing Olivia they haven't forgotten this morning's lark.

This is where her mother will approach her. She is sure of it. Olivia will not look for her and she will not go to her. Olivia is the one in control here. Sure enough, it only takes her mother a minute to sidle up to her.

'Ya didn't mean that, did ya? About me never speakin' to ya?'

Olivia shrugs but doesn't answer her.

'I can't tell ya how happy I am to find meself in the same place as you.'

And suddenly Olivia wants to spit and rage at her. Olivia shouldn't have been here in the first place. Is her mother happy she got Olivia put in prison and sent to the other side of the world? *Freakin' cow!* But she holds her tongue. With every ounce of strength Olivia has, she clamps her teeth together.

'I've missed ya, lovey.'

How dare she? How can she assume some kind of affection for Olivia?

'Please don't,' Olivia grinds out, her voice sounding guttural even in her own ears.

'Don't what?'

'Don't pretend ya care.'

Her mother opens her mouth and then closes it again. Olivia keeps walking.

'I gotta say I'm impressed.' Her mother's tone sounds light, but Olivia's not sure of her intent.

'About what?'

'These women look up to ya. Ya have them eatin' outta yer hand.'

Olivia's mouth goes dry and her stomach churns. Is this meant to be a compliment? Admiration? In an instant, she is that little girl again, hoping for a positive word from her mother. But isn't this what Olivia had wanted—her mother to see she was the one in control? She doesn't know what to say, so she shrugs again.

'Just think, Livvie.' She turns this way and that, Olivia can see her from the corner of her eye, making sure no-one is in earshot. 'Now that I'm 'ere, we can be a team again. With the respect you 'ave from these girls, we could make ourselves a tidy sum.'

Olivia stops walking and faces her, barely taking note that she can actually look down at her now. She's too angry to take pleasure in the small things.

'Team? We was never a team.' Olivia's chest is heaving, and it's all she can do not to scream at her. 'An' what, you've been here less than a day an' ya think ya know how to run things? Ya got no idea what I've been through to get here, an' if ya think I'm gonna share it with ya, you've got rocks in yer head.'

When her mother's lips curl and her eyes narrow, Olivia is surprised, although she doesn't know why she should be.

'Why, you ungrateful—I am your mother!'

Olivia glances around, pretty sure they all heard that and now they all know.

'You ain't nothin',' Olivia raises her voice enough so they'll hear her as well. 'Mother's don't make their children into criminals an' leave them to rot in gaol.'

Olivia stalks away from her then. She can't look at the other girls either. Hopefully, their yard-time is almost over, and she must only wait at the gate for a few minutes. Micky was right. Her mother is controlling her—not by physically telling her what to do, but she controls every emotion Olivia has, just with a word. *Blast you Micky. Why do ya have to be so right an' so wrong at the same time?*

And now Olivia owes him for the privilege.

***

Mick

The day drags on. Mick is impatient to know what has transpired between Olivia and her mother. Alas, he must fulfill his duties first. Two camps have developed in crime class. One group responds well to him, listens to his advice, and seems to try their best. The other group, which includes Ellen Smith, still looks at him with suspicion. Miss Smith continues her pretence of coquetry with him from time to time and he is not sure exactly where her intention lies.

Mind you, she does the same with the other guards, and he wonders how far she takes those flirtations. There are moments he thinks she may exchange her favours for forbidden time with her son, or for common vices such as tobacco or rum. She is not the only one who trades in this fashion, and there is more than one turnkey willing to take such bribes. It is a sad state Mick sees inside this factory. He makes a mental note to prepare a speech on this situation for the next anti-transportation meeting. The way society is governed means they corrupt people and then punish them for it.

Finally, in the late afternoon, it is time for Mick to end his shift and he makes his way to the Class Two section. His heart swells with the memory of Olivia opening up even more yesterday. She carries such deep agony. He wishes he could take it away from her, but there is naught he can do but give her the best advice he knows. But his heart aches for her. He cannot hold back his feelings for her much longer. He must declare himself to her soon, or he will burst.

He steps into the picking and carding room and scans the tables. Mary Cruikshank is over to the side, working quietly, but often glancing over her shoulder at Olivia, who is up near the back at a table with Mrs Thorne as usual. Olivia does not return those furtive glances but keeps her head down.

So as not to be obvious, Mick wanders through the sea of mobcaps, exchanging greetings with different ladies as he goes. But he aims for Mrs Cruikshank first. He is curious.

'Good afternoon, ma'am. You're new here, I see.' He pretends he doesn't know who she is.

'Yes, sir.' She glances up at him, unsure of his friendly greeting. It is a common reaction.

'I am Michael Reeve, and you are?'

'Mary. Mary Cruikshank.'

'Cruikshank? I recognise that name. Any relation to—?'

'Olivia Cruikshank. I'm 'er mum.' No hesitation at all.

Mick glances over at Olivia. She stares daggers at him now. So much for keeping her head down. He offers her a conciliatory smile before he turns back to Mrs Cruikshank.

'Her mum? It must be nice to see her again.' Mick needs to show himself unbiased. He cannot let Olivia's feelings affect the way he treats someone else.

'Yeah. But I don't think it's mutual,' she whispers.

'Well, give her time. It must be a shock, after all.'

'O' course. I'm probably the last person she expected to see.' She shakes her head and turns her attention back to her work.

'I daresay.' There is much more he could tell her, but he won't betray Olivia's confidence. 'I hope you settle in quickly.'

Mrs Cruikshank nods but doesn't look up again, so Mick continues his way around the room until he gets to Olivia's table.

'Hello, laddie.' Nancy, of course, is the first to speak.

'Good afternoon, ladies.'

Olivia won't look at him. She fiercely tugs at the wool in her hands like it is made of tough reed fibres.

'I seen ya talkin' to the Shank's mama over there. What's she like?'

Olivia's shoulders stiffen even more.

'Like the rest of you, I suppose. A prisoner, a person suffering the consequences of her own mistakes and bad choices.'

'Ain't that ri'? Only thing is I think we suffer a mite more than we should.'

'And I won't argue that point with you.'

Nancy chortles at me. 'Well then, hows about breakin' us outta here?'

'Somehow I don't think adding poor decisions to the ones we've already made will help, do you?'

'No, I s'pose not,' she sighs.

And all the while Olivia remains stiff and silent, her only movement the frequent tugs on the fleece. An obvious message she is not happy that he spoke with her mother. He will have to find another way to talk to her.

'See you later.' He walks away, watching Olivia as he does. Not a single movement in his direction. She must really be fuming at him. He sighs as well.

Later, Mick swings it so he can be the one to escort Olivia back to the dormitories for the night. It will cost him a few extra hours of work, but she is worth it. When he collects her, she rolls her eyes in disdain.

'What are you still doin' 'ere?'

'Waiting for you, of course.' He attempts to take her arm, but she shakes him off.

'Why? So ya can gloat?'

'What do I have to gloat about?' They head for the dorms, but he walks as slow as he can.

'That yer right about me mother. That yer now mates with her, too.'

'So, I take it you don't appreciate me speaking with her?' Stating the obvious now.

Olivia opens her mouth, closes it, then opens it again.

'Ya can do whatever ya like.' She shrugs like she doesn't care. All the walls are going up again.

'Come on. This is me you're talking to. Say what you really think.'

She is silent for several moments.

'Why would ya even want to talk to her, knowin' how I feel about her?'

'You think I've betrayed you?' Mick keeps his eyes ahead. He doesn't think he can take the hurt that must be showing in her eyes.

'You *have* betrayed me. I thought ya was doin' all this because …'

She doesn't finish. They are close to the dorms, but he needs to hear what she wants to say.

'Because why, Olivia? Say it.'

She bites down on her lip and shakes her head.

'It don't matter.'

'It does matter. It matters more than you can imagine.'

Mick sees a room off to the side that he knows is empty, and with a quick glance around them, he draws her inside and shuts the door. He turns to face her and give her a direct look.

'Tell me what you were going to say. Please.'

Her eyes are glassy with unshed tears. She takes a deep breath and lets it out slowly, shaking her hands.

'I thought ya was doin' all this because ya cared, like maybe we was friends or somethin'. But now ya tell me yer gonna make me pay. An' I can see how. By bein' all friendly with the mother I hate.' The tears spill over. 'Why'd ya make me believe, Micky? Why?'

'Oh, my darling Olivia. You have it all wrong.' He can't believe how wrong. This is it now, there's no way he's waiting another minute. Mick reaches out to brush the tear from her cheek. 'I am head over heels in love with you, goose.'

'What? But you've never ...'

'No, I never did. You are worth far more than some cheap tryst. I refused to take advantage of your trust, so I have held back for a long time. But I can't wait any longer.' He moves closer to her.

'I am befriending your mother because I believe, and assuming my hopes are not misguided, that she will soon be my mother-in-law, likeable or not.'

She wrinkles her face up like he has just spoken in another language.

'What? How? I don't under—'

'Understand this.' He drops to one knee. 'I love you, Olivia Cruikshank. Will you give me the honour of your hand in marriage?'

Olivia stares at him like he is half crazed. Maybe he is. But then as his words sink in, her eyes widen and light up as though they have candles burning behind them.

'Oh Micky, yes. If only I'd known—Yes! I've been hopin' for the longest time ... Oh, yes.'

She is crying happy tears now as he fervently kisses each of her hands and then stands to his feet.

'You have just made me the happiest man alive.'

He cups her face in his hands and then does the thing he has wanted to do for months now. He kisses her. Oh, the delight of her embrace as she returns his kiss with a fervour that makes him never want to stop. But stop they must, and he draws back from her, gazing into her brown eyes.

'And now, my love, you must endeavour to stop glowing.'

CHAPTER
Sixteen

Olivia
November 1841 – five months remaining

He wants to marry her! Saints alive, but she must be dreaming. Of course, she'd hoped, dreamed of such a day, and she believed he liked her, but never really expected as much as a marriage proposal. And now she has to keep it a secret. Olivia understands he's already labelled as soft towards prisoners, and it is partly for her safety, but oh, how hard it is to keep the smile from her face and the laughter from her mouth. Olivia sits and picks and cards wool in endless repetition, doing her best to look as bored as everyone else, while inside she is all dance and song.

And she can't stop thinking about his kiss. So tender. So warm. So full of promise. Olivia carries it with her all day long, always wondering when she will see him next. Soon she will be his forever. She must wait for him to apply to the governor, however. She must keep her head down until then, even though she still has five months left of her sentence. Five months as Micky's prisoner, captive in his arms. Olivia cannot believe the way her fortunes have changed so dramatically over the past half year. She never thought she could look to the future with excitement, and now she can barely wait for it.

It's been nine days since he dragged her into that room and made his declaration. He comes to see Olivia every day if possible and tries to squeeze her hand or touch her shoulder—some slight gesture of affection—without being seen to do it. Meanwhile, Olivia makes every effort to appear as though his presence is nothing special, nothing out of the ordinary, as though she doesn't care a whit about her gorgeous fiancé at all. So far, Nancy, who always sits next to Olivia, doesn't seem to suspect anything. She glances at her now, while tying off a thread. It appears her thoughts are afar, perhaps with her children in the motherland. And if she doesn't suspect Olivia's joy, then she doubts the others have either.

Not even Mary. That's what Olivia's calling her now, as she isn't fit to be called Mama. Although, every time Olivia calls her that, Micky's words echo in her head. *Forgiving her is the only way to be free.* And Mary won't leave Olivia alone. Every time they are out, taking the air, she must come and walk with Olivia. Mary has tried many angles to get Olivia on side. She has tried to arouse her pity. Then she tried to stir guilt within her. She has even tried to come down all authoritarian on her. But Olivia will not have an ounce of it. Olivia will not bend to her wishes.

Why, then, does she feel mixed up every time she walks away? As though a pudding was beaten inside her, and now sits to rise and ferment like a toxic lump in her gut. How dare Mary rob her of happiness? Olivia must not think about her. Only about Micky.

Therein lies the problem. Two opposing feelings at war within her. Hateful thoughts about her mother only serve to stain her happy thoughts of Micky, and her tender feelings toward Micky have no balm to offer the pain of what Mary has done. And so again Micky's words roll around Olivia's head. How she wishes he wasn't right.

The bell rings and Olivia's stomach responds, not with hunger, but with the knowledge Mary will soon try to coerce her again. The midday meal is served, which is nothing to speak of. It is as colourless as their garments.

'How I should love a duck's wing right now,' Olivia quips to Nancy.

'Aye, and a pint of sweet ale to go with it.'

'One can only take so much of oats an' potatoes an' bread.'

'I don't reckon I'll ever eat 'em again when I'm out.'

Olivia laughs. 'When I get out, I'm gonna find me a pleasant inn an' get some juicy meat covered with gravy.'

'Here's to that,' she lifts her tin cup of water and salutes.

Nancy looks thoughtful for a while.

'Ya know, Sally, over in crime class, knows how to get hold of some good meat. Jerky's the best, but sometimes she can wrangle a bit of fresh cooked knuckle or somethin'. What do ya reckon?'

Olivia nods while she swallows a mouthful of potato, which is crying out for some salt and lashings of butter.

'Yeah, she's got me some before. But to be honest, Nancy, I'm not in the smugglin' trade no more. I got five months to go, an' I don't wanna risk extending' me time if ya know what I mean.'

'Good fer you,' she sighs. 'I guess I'd be like that too, if I were you.'

'But don't let that stop ya from gettin' some meat if ya want. I won't say nothin'.' Olivia pats her on the shoulder.

Soon, the officers lead them out into the yard for their daily exercise. Olivia glances over her shoulder. *And here she comes.*

'Mary,' Olivia nods, giving her as brief acknowledgement as she can.

'Why do ya insist on callin' me that?' She sounds frustrated. 'Can't we put the past behind us?'

'But the past ain't behind us, is it? You haven't changed. Ya still think ya can have me at yer beck an' call, an' I'd wager you'd throw me into the iron jaw of the law again in a heartbeat.'

'I wouldn't.' Her voice is pleading, but Olivia doesn't believe it.

'Yeah, ya would.'

She huffs and puffs for a few steps. Olivia's not sure if she's as offended as she's making out.

'Listen,' she says. 'I need yer help. No-one knows me here yet, an' I need to get me somethin' from outside. I know ya can do it, or ya know the people what can. You're like the queen bee 'round here. One of them flash mob, eh? Do this one thing for yer mother, eh? It would mean the world to me, an' I'd be eternally grateful.'

Here we go again. Just like that, Mary has Olivia's stomach churning and her heart fluttering like a handkerchief in the wind. More than anything, she just wishes she had that affection Mary offers, but why must it come with a price? Anger and longing fill Olivia at the same time.

'I ain't in that business no more, Mary.' Olivia shakes her head, even while her heart thumps with fear of rejection again.

Her eyes narrow and her lips curl. 'Ya think these women care about ya? That they'll still give ya respect when ya won't provide what they want no more? No. They'll turn on ya like a bunch of hungry dogs an' tear ya to shreds.'

Olivia's breath comes quick now. It can't be true. She lies. The girls like Olivia, for *her*. They do.

'I'm the only one who'll stick by ya through thick an' thin. So, ya'd best show some good sense an' look after me.'

With her head still reeling from Mary's last onslaught of words, it takes several seconds for her to find a response, but anger rises.

'Yeah, just like ya stuck by me back in England. Why would I believe a word ya say? I'm not smugglin' for ya.'

But can she stick to that? What if she's right? What if everyone hates her now?

Mary lets out a scornful snort.

'I s'pose ya think that pretty boy's gonna look after ya.'

Olivia turns sharply to look at Mary.

'What? Ya think I wouldn't notice you all blushin' like every time he comes near? Livvie, ya need to grow up an' stop thinkin' like a child. No wholesome lad like that is gonna look yer way. Yer just a prisoner. An' I'm only sayin' this 'cause I don't wanna see ya get yer heart broke.'

She reaches out and strokes Olivia's head like Micky has done so many times, but it feels more like she's taken a whip to Olivia. Forget breathing fast. Now she can hardly breathe at all, like she's going to choke on the dread Mary's words stir up. Olivia recoils from her touch. And she can't tell her, she can't give away her secret.

'Ya best get in touch with Ann Finnegan in crime class. She can help ya,' Olivia mumbles and stalks away without looking back.

***

'It's been a while, Reeve. Where've you been?' Raff sits down with Mick in the pub, both with ciders in their hands.

'Sorry mate,' Mick says, with a grin that doesn't convey much apology. 'Been too busy courting.'

'Of course,' Raff winks. 'It's always a woman that comes between good friends.'

Mick laughs, because he knows Raff's not serious, and then takes a drink from his cider.

'How are things with you?'

He looks past Mick and jerks his chin toward someone behind them.

'That fellow looks a bit lonely. Mind if we invite him over?'

Mick checks over his shoulder to see a man who seems to be deep in his cups, gazing into the amber liquid of his tankard.

'Sure.'

Raff rises and goes behind Mick, bringing the man back moments later.

'This is Michael Reeve, and I am Rafaello Cardamone,' he introduces them as he takes his seat again.

Mick nods a greeting and puts out a hand to shake.

'Trevor Stanthorpe,' the fellow slurs a bit as he clasps hands with Mick.

'We couldn't leave you over there by yourself,' Raff says. 'Seeing as you're on your own.'

'I appreciate it,' Mr Stanthorpe rubs a hand over his face. He glances at each of them in turn, as if deciding whether to say more. 'My wife died recently.'

Raff and Mick exchange concerned looks.

'Sorry to hear that, sir.' Mick gives him a pat on the shoulder. He definitely shouldn't be drinking alone.

'Aye, it was childbearing that took her. And the little one along with her.' Mr Stanthorpe takes a deep swig of his ale.

'That is a tragedy, and I am sorry for it.' Raff seems as sympathetic as Mick feels.

The poor gent.

'It's hard to know how to go on,' Mr Stanthorpe continues. His burden must weigh heavily on him.

'What do you do for a living?' Mick asks. Perhaps they can help him focus on the future.

'I run an entertainment troupe,' he hiccups.

'Entertainment?'

'Singing, dancing, that kind of thing.'

'Oh,' Mick's ears prick up with interest. 'That must be an intriguing line of work.'

'Have you had much success?' Raff asks.

'Aye. Usually have a full house wherever we go.'

'So, you travel a lot then?' Mick asks.

'Continually. My family—brothers and sisters—live near Sydney Town, but I haven't been there in a long while. Perhaps it's time to go home for a visit.'

'Sounds like a good idea.'

'Except that I have good people relying on me for work.' Mr Stanthorpe tips his tankard up again and drains it.

'Ah, I see your difficulty,' Raff nods.

How hard that must be to lose a wife and then not really have the time to grieve due to the responsibilities of providing for others. Mick can see why the poor chap is so burdened.

'How many do you have?' Mick wants to know.

'We are a small troupe. Just a magician, a trio of musicians, and then there was my wife, who sang.'

At the mention of singing, Mick is distracted by thoughts of Olivia.

'Oh, Raff, did I tell you Miss Cruikshank has her voice back?'

'No. Do you mean she can sing again?' He raises his eyebrows.

'Yes, like an angel. She sang to me the other night to let me hear.'

'Who is this Miss Cruikshank?' Mr Stanthorpe's gaze flicks between them.

'Oh, yes, sorry, old chap. She is a prisoner in the Female Factory where Reeve here works.'

'Yes, and I've not heard the like of her before. She could be one of those opera singers, she is that good.'

Mr Stanthorpe looks at Mick with keen interest, even though his eyelids droop with the effects of alcohol.

'She sounds very gifted.'

'Most decidedly,' Mick nods. 'Sorry, but you were saying about your troupe, and I interrupted.'

'It matters not. When all is said and done, I have half a dozen mouths to feed, and without my dear Maggie to help me, I feel rather lost.'

'Understandably,' Raff draws his brows together. Mick can tell he is trying to think of a way to help, not that there is much one can do for a grieving heart except offer a willing ear. 'I wish there was aught we could do.'

'You fine gents have done enough. Your hospitality alone is a balm to me, but you also remind me of the joy people receive when hearing a beautiful song. I fear I must press on. And so, I bid you good night.' He pushes his stool back and stands up, giving them a nod of respect before putting his hat on.

Raff and Mick bid him farewell and watch him walk away, his steps lilting and swaying.

'Probably a good thing,' Raff mutters. 'He's had more than enough tonight.'

'He is certainly a man in pain.'

'That he is,' he sighs.

'I can't imagine losing Miss Cruikshank. My heart would break. I suppose Mr Stanthorpe feels like that. He must have loved his wife very much.'

'It seems so.' Raff sips from his cider. 'So, you've been courting her, then?'

Mick grins. 'As much as one can court a prisoner.'

'And she is receptive?'

'More than that, my friend.' Mick slaps him on the shoulder. 'She has agreed to marry me.'

Raff stares at him with his mouth open for a long while, but his eyes are alight.

'You old scoundrel. You really have been busy. Congratulations.'

Mick nods, feeling like a giddy schoolboy, and drains his drink to the bottom.

'But now I'm thinking—what if she gets assigned? I don't want her to go anywhere except with me.'

'She only has a few months left, doesn't she?'

'Yes, but there is a possibility, isn't there?'

'Of course there is.'

'I've applied to the governor for a special license, but I can't help worrying she'll be taken away before it comes through.'

'Well, believe it or not, our government likes to see convicts married off, so I don't think you'll have a problem obtaining the license. They think it is a good way to build society—especially if you marry her properly.'

'Properly?'

'Plenty of prisoners just shack up together, and if they don't stay together, then society labels those women as whores. But I know that's not the kind of man you are.'

'Most sincerely not,' Mick agrees. He wants to marry Olivia before God, with a clergyman present.

'So then?' Raff wiggles his thick eyebrows. 'You'd better start planning a wedding.'

Mick laughs. Of course. That will keep him occupied while he waits. 'Will you stand up with me as my witness?'

'I'd be honoured.'

A list of tasks fills Mick's head. He needs to procure a dress for Olivia, a clergyman to marry them. He needs to pick a day and have his family at the ceremony. Some flowers for his bride. A ring—heavens, he needs a ring.

'What's wrong Reeve? You've gone a trifle pale.' Raff laughs at Mick, though his words sound caring. He slaps Mick on the shoulder. 'C'mon. It'll be fine. You'll see.'

CHAPTER
Seventeen

Olivia

She hasn't seen Micky in three days. She doesn't know why or what he's doing, but her mother's words won't stay out of her head, even though there can't be an ounce of truth in them. He'd asked Olivia to marry him, and he'd kissed her. Surely that's as good as a vow. Surely, he wasn't in jest. Surely, he will be back, and not be having second thoughts.

Mary has taken up with Ellen Smith. Olivia doesn't know if her mother tried to speak to Ann at all, but the other day, after sneaking her way into crime class, Mary came back with a dark light in her eyes.

'I met a girl called Ellen,' she told Olivia at her earliest chance, with a significant lift to her eyebrows.

Olivia grunted. She wasn't about to give Mary the satisfaction of a reaction. 'I'm glad yer findin' new friends.'

'Well, an' she told me some stories about ya.'

No surprises there. Ellen will say anything to paint Olivia with dark shadows. 'I'm sure she did.'

'You've got yerself quite the reputation, my girl.'

If it came from Ellen, then it was the false reputation, but Mary won't care about that. 'Have I now?'

'Yeah, but unlike you, Ellen is willin' to help me get what I need.'

'Ya didn't ask Ann, then?'

'I ain't met Ann. Ellen came to me. Such a friendly lass.'

Sounds like they're made for each other. Olivia knows how Ellen works, though. She'd be trying to find an angle to get to Olivia. Mary likely had a big whine to Ellen about the failings of her daughter, and Ellen would add to the poison. Mary would, no doubt, believe every word of it. And this is the person who wants to call Olivia 'my girl.' She rolls her eyes before pasting on a grin.

'I'm happy for ya,' Olivia told her with a bright smile.

'Ya really should make it up to her, ya know.'

Olivia frowns at her, confused. 'What do ya mean?'

'She told me how ya used to be close, but then ya got all hoity-toity an' left her behind. Especially since they say ya saved a fella, an' now ya think yer too good fer anybody.'

Olivia let out a snort of laughter. Ellen would paint it like that.

'Mary, ya don't know what yer talkin' about. But here's what I think. You go an' enjoy yer new friendship with Ellen, an' leave me be. Like she said, an' like you've already guessed, I've got me sights set on greener pastures now.'

And that's it. With those words, Olivia decides to stop striving for Mary's acceptance or approval. She must let it go. She doesn't know if she can forgive Mary yet, but she's sure she doesn't want to have these feelings clawing at her for the rest of her life. As scary as it is, Olivia wants to hang on to the hope of her freedom, a future with Micky and peace. Peace would be good.

She must admit, she feels a little lighter having made that decision. She'll just focus on picking and carding, do the best she can, and treat others as nicely as she can, no matter what they think of her in return.

The next morning, when the light has just dawned, the turnkey comes to let them out of the dorms as usual, so they can wash and eat their measly breakfast. On this occasion, however, a turnkey grabs her by the arm just as she finishes her last mouthful, and leads her in a different direction. They're not going to the picking and carding yard, that's for sure.

'Hey, where ya takin' me?' Alarm sweeps through Olivia. Plenty of terrifying things happen in this place. But when she glances at the guard, he looks bored, not like he's planned something sinister.

'You're goin' outside today.'

'Outside? But I haven't done anythin'.' Olivia's going before the Principal Superintendent? What on earth for? Panic still rises, even though the turnkey doesn't seem malicious.

'Just followin' orders, wench.'

Confused and a little scared, Olivia has no choice but to stumble on beside him, with her heart floating up near her mouth.

They stop at the doors and the turnkey uncuffs her. Then he shoves her outside and closes the door behind her. This is highly irregular and Olivia stares at the closed gate of Cascades in shock. She is outside on her own. Or is she? She swivels around to see if anyone is behind her and lifts her eyes to the full height of the man who stands there. The sight of him washes all fear away as joy takes its place.

'Micky!'

Olivia runs into his arms, and he swings her around in a circle before setting her back on her feet.

'What's all this about?'

He looks sheepish, but grins.

'It's taken a bit of organisation, and I must work several extra shifts to make up for it, but this is our wedding day.'

'What?'

He wraps a large hand around each of Olivia's upper arms and smiles down at her with those warm eyes.

'I don't want to wait until your sentence is over. I want us to be married right away. What do you say? Shall we start our life together outside these walls today?'

Olivia can't believe what she's heard. Just when she started doubting again, Micky surprises her all over. 'But how?'

'I made plans in the hope the governor would approve our license soon. And he did.' He looks like a cat that just ate a whole jug of cream.

That's why Olivia hasn't seen him. It makes sense now. They're getting married today! Her stomach starts to jump up and down like a baby mouse has taken up residence.

'Where's the minister?'

He chuckles softly and links her arm through his, leading her down the street toward Hobart Town. 'I'll take you to him now. Reverend Thompson and my good friend Raff are waiting for us at the church. Along with my family.'

Olivia doesn't know what to say. She is flabbergasted. But there's no way she'd say no to this.

Glancing sideways at him, she sees he is wearing a fine suit, and he's oiled his hair. Her stomach sinks. 'Micky, I don't got a pretty dress to wear for ya.'

His face lights up in that big grin she loves and pats her hand. 'Don't worry, songbird. I have a few surprises for you.'

Olivia feels like she's floating down the street next to him. She wonders if she should pinch herself. *Am I dreaming?* Another realisation smacks her in the face like icy water on a frosty morning. 'Micky, does this mean I don't have to go back there?'

He laughs out loud this time, and the sound rings with genuine joy. 'Never again, my darling. You are mine from this moment on.'

This can't be real. Olivia feels dizzy with delight. Or shock.

But it is real. When they arrive at the church, one of Micky's sisters takes her into a side room and helps her change out of her prison clothes into a simple white dress. A lump wells in Olivia's throat as she hands her a small posy of flowers and smiles at her with genuine warmth in her eyes. Olivia doesn't deserve any of this. Part of her wants to run and hide in a corner, too scared to believe this much good could come her way.

Over the next half hour, Micky and Olivia swap vows and promise to love each other until death. And she can't stop the tears leaking down her cheeks. She tells herself to toughen up, but that hasn't worked for weeks now. And it doesn't help that Micky's eyes are glassy too. They both sign some papers, even though Olivia's never learnt to write. Her mark is on there and she will testify to anyone who doesn't know an X from a real name.

Even so, she still has trouble believing it's real. Micky's family engulfs them with congratulations, embracing her, a convict, and smiling at her like she's one of them. Surrounded by their merry chatter, they all walk toward the river where large picnic rugs cover the grass and Micky's mum has laid out platters of sandwiches, cakes and cold meats. *Oh, my heavens!* She can't take it all in.

One minute a cold, dark cell and the next a picnic in the sunshine with her new husband. *Husband!*

They spend the afternoon between laughter and grateful tears, although to be honest, it's only Olivia who cries. Every now and then she is overwhelmed, and happy tears escape her again. As the sun dips toward the horizon Micky's family drift away until it's just her and Micky left.

'What now?' Olivia asks. It still niggles at her—this feeling that she might go right back to the Factory.

Micky grins as he slips his arms around her waist. 'Back to my lodgings.'

'Your lodgings?'

'I stay in a local inn during the week. Like I said, I have a couple of shifts to make up for the last few days, so we'll stay there for now. But in a few days, I will take you home to the family farm in New Norfolk.' He sticks out his elbow for her to take, and she entwines her arm tightly about his. No-one can come between them now, not while he walks her to his inn. Not ever.

It's a small room in a small hotel, and it's not got much besides a bed and a stand with water to wash, but it's a darn sight better than the cells. Olivia's barely had the chance to take it in before he wraps her in his arms and kisses her. Gently at first, but then deeper and stronger until there is no thought in her head except for him. Over the next few hours, he shows her about love in a whole new way and she knows she will never be the same. It is a night she will remember for the rest of her life.

Early in the morning, when the birds begin their wake up chorus, Olivia feels Micky's gentle fingers stroke her hair. She's still in his arms. What a perfect way to greet a new day. The first day as a free woman and a new wife.

He draws his arm from beneath her and climbs out of bed. 'I have to leave you now, my lovely songbird wife, as much as I wish I could stay.' He leans down and kisses her even while he tucks his shirt into his pants, and his lips burn on hers just the same as they did last night.

'When will I see ya?' Olivia doesn't want to be parted from him, not even for a workday. He will take her heart with him when he walks out that door.

He brushes a thumb over her cheek and gives her a soft smile.

'Very soon. You have naught to do today but rest from all your labours.

Before you know it, I'll be back again.'

Olivia yawns as she watches him tie his shoes, and he chuckles.

'I'll let you get some more sleep now, songbird.'

Olivia pulls the blanket around her but shakes her head. 'I don't think I want to sleep.'

He leans down and kisses her again, then caresses her cheek, staring at her like he drinks in her face. That look of adoration warms Olivia to her toes.

'I love you, Olivia.'

'I love ya, too, Micky.'

They kiss once more and then he is gone, leaving her with just the memories of last night, which are more than enough to keep her company until she sees him again, and a couple shillings for food when she gets hungry. She is married. Olivia squeals and jiggles her whole body with happiness. She is Mrs Reeve. The Shank is gone—gone forever.

***

Mick

He has just had the best day of his life. If he were a wealthy man married in a church with marble floors and high cathedral ceilings, it couldn't have been better. He doesn't know how he's supposed to keep the smile from his face today. And now that he has married her and shared her bed, he is impatient to be back with her again. Is it possible to love her even more?

Right now, Mick is on the way to Matron's office as she has summoned him. He figures she has learnt of his marriage, but whether she approves is another matter. His nerves are on edge as he knocks on her door.

On the muffled command to enter, he opens the door and steps inside. This office does not receive much more light than the prison cells, and several lanterns flicker to enable her to see her work.

Matron's slack mouth hangs in an expression one could only call unhappy. She doesn't even look at Mick as she shuffles papers on her desk. He suspects the loss of her babe still weighs on her deeply. That doesn't bode well for any infraction he may have committed, small thought it may be.

'I've heard too many reports of your friendliness with the prisoners. That you are not willing to discipline them. The other guards call you soft.'

Mick clasps his hands behind his back. No doubt marrying a prisoner has not helped that opinion. This will be difficult.

'I try to treat the women with fairness and some compassion. It is my belief the misconduct must warrant the punishment they receive.'

Now she looks up at him and studies his face.

'It is not for you to decide who deserves what. These women are criminals, and we employed you to keep them in order, not be their friend.'

'Aren't we here to reform them? How can they change if they keep meeting injustice?'

'Dare you question the methods of this institution? You have worked here, how long?'

'A few months.' This is not going well.

'And already you know better than everyone else.'

Mick is tongue-tied. He only knows one thing. The prisoners are women who are precious, despite what they may have or have not done. He remembers the moment he knew he needed to help these prisoners.

It was after a tiring day at the lathe crank. He went with the master carpenter to the pub for a drink. Mick was sixteen, apprenticing at carpentry and eager to learn. Wood working quickly became his passion. The smell of sawdust. The smoothness of freshly sanded wood beneath his fingers. They had worked on the legs for a grand dining table all day long and his arms ached. But it felt good to have achieved beautiful work. His work impressed his master, he thought.

They sat and enjoyed their ale, discussing plans for the morrow, when some turnkeys from one of the local prisons came in to quench their thirst. Mick remembers them being rather loud as they spoke of the 'pig convicts,' looks of disgust written across their faces. He ceased to hear what his master said to him.

They each bragged and boasted about ways they had punished, ill-treated, mocked, or humiliated different convicts. All intended to keep them on their knees, servile, humble. The things they said, the insults they brandished about, sickened Mick. It was as though they spoke about his parents.

Did these men have no respect for the humanity of these prisoners? Did they not care about what injustices, hardships, or desperation had resulted in their presence here? Granted, some prisoners were guilty of terrible crimes, but that number was in the minority.

To treat a petty thief as though they were a cold-blooded murderer was too much. To make someone sit in their own filth for a day, just to humiliate them, was inhumane.

Inhumane.

That is what those turnkeys were.

Something needed to be done about the treatment of prisoners. Someone must take a stand for them. Mick had already suffered enough for standing against injustice when he tried to defend Raff in school. Back then, he was too scared to do anything, but eventually his convictions grew, and he could no longer be complacent.

But as he gazes unwaveringly back at Matron, he wonders if he will suffer as he did fighting for Raff.

'I do not pretend to know better, ma'am. I merely want to help these women look to the future, to find some peace and hope.'

'We have chaplains for that.' With a dismissive air, she went back to her paperwork.

'With respect, ma'am, the chaplains only come once a week and remind them over and over that they are terrible sinners and condemn them. Shouldn't we show them some grace if they've served their time?'

The Matron thumps her hands on the desk and glares at Mick.

'And now you know better than the ordained. Your arrogance is astounding, Mr Reeve. For the next week, you will oversee the wash yard. Not standing by, *running* it. If those women step out of line so much as to speak when they shouldn't, you will deal with them severely. If you do not, your time here will be over. Do you understand?'

'I understand ma'am.' Mick nods his obedience, although his heart wages war within him. No matter what in the week to come, he knows he will not mistreat those women.

Matron's eyes narrow a little. 'I understand you favoured Olivia Cruikshank to the point of uniting yourself with her.'

Mick clears his throat and shuffles his feet, but can't hide his joy. 'Yes, ma'am.'

'I understand,' she says, although she looks more frustrated than understanding. 'I have seen guards often become attracted to one or another of the girls. It's a dangerous entanglement. You're a fool to think there is any future there. At any moment, she could turn your attachment against you, be aware. She was born into felony, and if she turns, it will be you who suffers.'

Mick almost laughs. A happy fool. He believes Olivia is beyond turning their love into a means of manipulation. But, to think Matron would turn a blind eye to liaisons between prisoners and guards, that she would allow men to take advantage of the women locked in here. It is not right. She is, at the very least, misguided, and at the worst, no better than a madam. She allows the corruption to breed right beneath her nose, and yet blind to it at the same time.

'Thank you for your words of advice, ma'am.' What else is he going to say? He's already seen her hackles raised this morning. There is no need to provoke her again. She has laid down the gauntlet and Mick has a challenge on his hands. To manage the crime class labour yard. He swallows his rising gall as he leaves her office. What will he do?

CHAPTER
Eighteen

Olivia

Wouldn't you know it? Mary has made her way to crime class. Well, so Micky tells her. Olivia has seen little of him these last couple days, since he's paying his dues in crime class. A few hours together in the evening where they've shared their news interrupted by intense kisses. Well, mainly his news, since Olivia has little to talk about sitting in a hotel room. How she loves that man! She cannot wait for him to take her west. Ugh. She must learn to be patient now.

So, apparently, the turnkeys caught Mary with contraband. Since it was her first offence inside the prison, they gave her one week's hard labour in the wash yard. It won't be the last. It is her pattern. Just like it was Olivia's pattern. A pattern she probably learnt from Mary. But it is a pattern Olivia has learnt can be broken. And strangely, part of her hopes Mary can break it too, even though the other part of her thinks she deserves it.

Olivia can't help but think Ellen is behind all this. Ellen has several people, guards even, in her pocket. It would be a simple thing for her to organise some smuggled whiskey or such to Mary and then have Mary caught with it. And it would be just like Ellen to orchestrate all that to get even with Olivia. She's held a grudge against her for far too long.

Micky doubts the truth of Olivia's words. He always believes the best of people, which is one of his characteristics she loves so much. But where

Ellen is concerned, Olivia insists.

'Ellen is bent on revenge against me,' she told him. 'An' she is usin' me mother to do it.'

He strokes Olivia's cheek and shakes his head.

'But they have teamed up like long-lost friends.'

'That makes me even more suspicious.'

Micky shrugs.

'Perhaps it is one of those "enemy of my enemy is my friend" type scenarios. Perhaps they related on the grounds of their animosity toward you. Sounds harsh, I know.' He adds this last bit when he sees her eyes widen.

'Harsh? I wouldn't 'ave called Mary me enemy.'

Again, he strokes her cheek. 'That is because deep down you still care about her.'

What is she supposed to say when those brown eyes are brimming with tenderness? She cannot deny him, but she does not want to agree either. So, she kisses him. And she has no guilt. He is her husband.

'Besides, there are other things on Ellen's mind right now.' Micky says between kisses.

'Like what?' Olivia is not really interested.

'Her son died. So, she's been subdued of late.'

That stops Olivia. The death of a child is not something she wishes on anyone, not even Ellen. And too many children die at the Factory.

'Somethin' needs to be done about that,' she murmurs.

'I agree.'

They sit in silence for a while, considering this sobering news.

''Ave ya found it necessary to punish anyone yet?' A change of subject will help.

'Not so far. The women have been on their best behaviour. Of course,' and he gives Olivia an impertinent wink, 'they have no Shank to stir them up.'

She gives him an affectionate shove.

'Be off with ya then, afore I stir you up.'

Micky wiggles his eyebrows. 'Maybe I'd like that.'

Olivia swipes at him again, but he ducks out of reach with a laugh and goes off to the Factory.

But he's left Olivia thinking. Does she indeed care about Mary? Or does Micky just want to believe it? Hoping for love and then being disappointed repeatedly wears at your soul like the pounding surf wears down the rocks on the shore. It is easier to build a barricade of anger than to suffer that kind of endless torture. But now she is tired of all the anger as well.

And Ellen.

What is that woman up to? Buddying up with Mary like that. She must have something planned. And a grieving Ellen would be even more dangerous. Would Mary have told Ellen about Olivia and Micky? Or at least what she believes about Olivia and Micky? A sick feeling spreads in Olivia's stomach. That would put Micky directly in Ellen's line of sight as a target. Ellen would do anything to get at Olivia. She needs to warn her husband.

It is another whole day before she sees him again, and they only have the nighttime. Of course, he wants to kiss and be all romantic, but Olivia has one thing on her mind.

'What if Ellen's makin' plans to get ya?' Olivia asks, while he is nuzzling her neck.

'I've suspected her of nefarious scheming for a long time,' he answers between feathery kisses on her jawline.

'Ya have? Why didn't ya say?' She pulls away from him. She needs to look him in the eye.

Micky sighs, sounding a little impatient, as though Olivia is a pestery child.

'Because I'd rather not spend these precious moments always talking of the unpleasant. I'd rather focus on us.'

'But what if she hurts ya?' He might not think it matters, but Olivia does. She needs to discuss the unpleasant to rid herself of the unpleasant feelings Ellen arouses. She scratches at her arms beneath her sleeve, while her stomach slowly twists into knots.

He runs a hand over her hair, then down her arms until he holds her hands and looks into her face with an earnest gaze.

153

'She won't hurt me. I've got my eye on her. And like I said, she is caught up in grief at the moment.'

The knots loosen a little. Olivia is glad to know he does not naively assume Ellen will do nothing.

'All right?' He tucks a loose strand of her hair behind her ear.

Olivia nods and leans into his chest while he wraps those loving arms around her tight.

But later, when she lays there beside him trying to sleep, the knots are back. What if Micky has missed something? In all his optimism, is it possible he has overlooked an important detail? Ugh. If Olivia were still in crime class, then she could keep watch on Ellen herself. Could warn Mary of her duplicitous nature. Could even prevent Ellen from doing something they will all regret.

Olivia's not in crime class, though. She's not even a prisoner, and she must try to trust her dear husband to take care of things. Trust him, and perhaps God. She prays a tentative prayer, not sure if God will even listen to someone like her. But hey, it's worth a try, right? Anything is worth a try at this point. As much as she doesn't like her mother, she would not see her hurt by the likes of Ellen Smith. *Please God, protect her and Micky.*

***

Mick

Mick has marched up and down this yard all day, and it is another day of non-event. The women all do what they must without noise and without complaint. All is in order. He smiles to himself, remembering Olivia's worries. She will rest soon enough. One more day and his trial at the helm of this yard will be over. One more day and he can make good on his promises to his wife to take her home. *One more day, Lord, give me one more day of peace.*

The worst Mick has had to deal with this week was an argument between two of the women, which he mediated without it becoming worse, whereupon he would have been required to mete out discipline. Gratitude swells in his heart. He has not had to make the difficult choice Matron wanted of him.

Even Ellen Smith has been on her best behaviour, mostly working in silence. Olivia would probably say it is the calm before the storm, but Mick prefers to believe it is the hand of grace. Today, she smiles at him each time he passes. Sometimes those smiles are saucy, granted, but it is better than the glares he usually receives.

And Mrs Cruikshank is pleasant enough. Most days she asks Mick how Olivia is and most days he tells her she is well. There's not much else he can say. One day perhaps. In his heart, he would desire to see them truly reconciled, but it will take significant change on both sides, he is sure. Olivia is on the edge of such a change, but Mrs Cruikshank is far from it.

It nears the end of Mick's shift when he notices Miss Smith huddled with another of the women. He knows not what they are engaged in, but it is his duty to separate them, else Matron be confirmed in her belief that he is soft. He approaches the two from the opposite end of the yard, calling out a greeting as he nears them.

'Come Miss Smith, you know you are not to interact with … '

Before he can finish his sentence, she swings around and what happens next seems to slow down in his vision, even as his whole body goes rigid. Mick notes the sparking gleam in her eyes, the malicious intent as clear as the flagellation scars on his father's back. She means ill and he knows it as keenly as he knows every muscle in his arms and legs have tensed.

Her hands fly out from between them as she turns, and Mick sees a cup in her hands. A tin cup, with engraving on the sides—strange the small things you notice as the seconds split into fractions, each one ticking by as though it is an hour. And as she flings this cup towards him, a stream of liquid soars through the space between them. It is not water; it has a milky taint, and it is perfectly on course to connect with Mick's face.

Then those fractions of seconds are gone. There is no time to act, to move, to avoid the fluid as it splashes into his eyes and over his cheeks. And then all he knows is pain. Stinging, burning, fiery pain which takes him to his knees and draws guttural screams from his chest. It's like his eyes are being gouged out, like his skin is being peeled from his skull. Mick tries to wipe the liquid from his face, but now his hands burn too. The distinct smell of lye meets his

155

nose. Lye? She threw lye solution at him? How did she even get it? Of course she did. That is her specialty.

The burning is so intense; he feels himself fading. How did he end up here working in a prison with women who would rather see him dead? But even as that question rises, the answer comes. He remembers when the Lord showed him the way. The day when he sat in church and heard a sermon that changed his life. It wasn't so long after the incident in the pub, so perhaps God was already at work in his heart. But as he sat there that day, it seemed that the minister spoke every word directly to Mick.

He spoke about the sheep and the goats from Matthew twenty-five. He spoke of feeding the hungry and thirsty, giving hospitality to the stranger, clothing the naked, and visiting the prisoner. Although all of those sections spoke to Mick, the one that stood out the most was visiting the prisoner. If they did not look after these people, it was akin to not looking after the Lord. How could Mick not care for Him if He were before him? How could he ignore the injustice when he knew precisely how bad it was? Could he have watched Jesus go to the cross without raising a cry against such injustice?

To his shame, he knew the answer was possibly yes.

But even Jesus spoke of preaching deliverance for the captives, to set at liberty them that are bruised. Weren't they all called to follow in his footsteps?

That day Mick knelt at the altar and gave his life to the cause, to the Lord's cause in loving his neighbour, whomever that might be, even be he in prison. He committed his life to Him, to serve Him in this way. Mick just didn't know then how he might serve the needy prisoners in Hobart Town. And he didn't know it would lead to an attack from the very people he tries to support.

As Mick comes to from his swoon, he can no longer see what is happening around him, but he can hear. In between his own cries of agony, Mick hears noise. Much noise. At first there was just him, as though the rest were stunned into silence. But now women yell, guards bellow and the people move around, making scuffing noises. Mick gropes around in darkness, crawling, trying to find the door. Someone near him cries out, 'Water! Get me water!'

A crash from somewhere in the yard. Shouts of 'desist!'

'Get away from him, Mary.' That must be Ellen's voice, and close by.

More voices echoing Ellen's warning.

'He needs help.'

Ann?

'If you touch him, so help me …' He might be in agony, but he can recognise the sinister edge to Ellen's voice.

'He's the best of 'em here. Why would ya hurt him?'

'He married the Shank. This is for her. If I can't be happy, neither can she!' And with that, something collides with his stomach, knocking the air out of him. He's sure it is a full minute before he can breathe again, but before then he hears the angry grunt of women charging at each other, fighting.

Another thump and women roaring all around him. They've started a riot.

An acrid smell hits Mick's nose, but amidst his pain, he doesn't register. He is still curled up on the ground.

Until he hears the screams. 'Fire!'

'Help! Help me!' Mick is dragged by his feet. Intermittently. Slowly.

He tries to roll over, to crawl to his feet, but he can't see. Mick reaches out to find something to cling to, something to pull him up, but all his hands find is cloth, the hem of someone's dress. And for his efforts, he receives a boot to the face, and he is once again writhing on the ground.

More feet. More agony. They are running over him. In their haste and panic to escape, the prisoners trample Mick underfoot. This will be his end. *God save me.* The sea of pain and blackness takes over, the echoes of hate and panic-filled screams echoing in his ears.

CHAPTER
Nineteen

Olivia

It's getting late. Micky hasn't come back to the hotel yet. Olivia doesn't exactly know what time it is, but she knows two things. One, the sun has gone down and two, she is hungry. Normally, Micky comes in and has their supper brought up to them. Olivia had some leftover bread at dinnertime, but now her stomach rumbles a little.

Not that she's complaining. She's quite used to being hungry, what with the minuscule rations the Factory issued. But it's a sign that Micky should be here by now, and he's not.

Olivia doesn't want to worry. She doesn't want to believe that her fears have come true. She needs to distract herself from those thoughts.

She tries singing to the walls. They aren't bricks of stone like she's used to, and they don't each have a name. Even so, it works for a time. Singing to the walls brings back so many memories of her time inside the Factory though. Most of those memories are not happy ones. So, while she tries to distract herself from one lot of unhappy thoughts, she drowns herself in another.

She needs to focus on something merry. All of her memories of Micky over the past months, they are the good ones. They are the ones she needs to spend her time on. Olivia starts with that first day when she met him at the Factory, when he never flinched at her insults or sassiness. She smiles at that. She suspects she began to fall for him even then, though she didn't want to. Olivia tried to fight it. She did.

Oh, where is Micky? He should be here.

Perhaps he is working an extra shift. Maybe the Matron made him do more work to punish him for his kindness.

Olivia paces up and down the small room for a while. What can she do? Is there a way she can find out what is happening? She doesn't know anyone here, anyone she can trust to send a message or enquiry. Olivia wrings her hands and her heart beats in double time. She needs to calm herself down. Her worries are probably unfounded.

Just trust Micky, Olivia, she tells herself. Her mind doesn't listen very well. No matter how many times she tells herself Micky is fine and everything is ok, a picture of Ellen rises in her vision and she feels sick.

By the time she acknowledges Micky will not return tonight, it is too late to send to the kitchen for food. He did leave her a few coins in case she needed anything, but the cook finished hours ago. Besides, Olivia doubts she could eat anyhow. Her stomach churns, churns, churns.

She tries to lie down and sleep, but every single noise makes her sit up, thinking Micky is here after all. It's a hotel, for crying out loud. There are lots of noises—all night long. And not a single bump or scrape or footstep or soft voice calling is Micky.

Olivia tosses and turns. She continues to scratch at her arms until they are sticky with blood, but she can't stop.

Where is Micky? *Where is Micky?*

In the small hours of the night, she rises to pour herself a cup of water. She's so tired. Tired because she hasn't slept. Tired of feeling panicked. Tired of the restless waiting. She hopes a drink and a turn about the room will help her rest.

In the moonlight coming through the small window, she notices Micky's bible sitting on the sideboard. Micky is always going on about the Scriptures and how they help him. He has taught her to read some. Maybe she should try reading to help her sleep. It might distract her enough to doze off.

Olivia lights the lamp and sits close by its flame to see. She is thankful the nights are not too cold at this time of year, so she doesn't need to drag the blankets over. She puts the bible right in front of the dim light. Micky has left a marker in there, so she opens it to read.

> *Thou shalt not be afraid for the terror by night; nor for*
> *the arrow that flieth by day;*
> *Nor for the pestilence that walketh in darkness; nor for*
> *the destruction that wasteth at noonday.*
> *A thousand shall fall at thy side, and ten thousand at*
> *thy right hand; but it shall not come nigh thee.*

Olivia is not sure about several of the words, but what she can make out sounds comforting. Is this what God says to people, to her? Micky always tells her God is with her and cares for her, but these are such broad promises. And there is more.

> *Because thou hast made the Lord, which is my refuge,*
> *even the most High, thy habitation;*
> *There shall no evil befall thee, neither shall any plague*
> *come nigh thy dwelling.*
> *For he shall give his angels charge over thee, to keep thee*
> *in all thy ways.*

So, if Olivia can find refuge in God, he can give her rest and keep her safe? He will send angels to watch over her? And Micky.

Olivia blows out the lamp and crawls back under the covers of the bed.

Dear God, I know Micky trusts in ya an' accordin' to yer book, ya promise to look after him. Please keep him safe an' bring him back to me. An' please help me stop worryin' about him. I know I'm new to this, but I'm tryin' to believe in ya the way Micky does. Please help me.

Olivia continues to pray as she lays there in the darkness, with a few dull moonbeams giving a blue hue to the room. She prays about many things, anything she can think of, really. But at some point, she must have fallen asleep while doing so. The next thing she knows, faint sunlight takes place of the darkness. There is only one thing she can think of to do right now. *Thank you, God.*

That was one prayer answered. She got some rest. Now for the next prayer—for Micky to come back to her safe.

Olivia waits for as long as she can until she can hear people stirring in the inn. She figures the cook must be in the kitchen by now, beginning breakfast for people. She quickly gets dressed and splashes some water on her face, all the while keeping an ear out for footsteps outside their room. Micky will be back soon, surely.

If she makes a quick trip to the kitchen for food, hopefully she won't miss him on his return. It would be terrible if he came, and she was not there. He will be so tired. He will need her to soothe him, to stroke his brown hair while he goes to sleep.

Yes, maybe she shall get extra food for him, too. She hurries down the stairs, looking in every direction in case she has missed him in the building somewhere. But apart from a few workers who are preparing to start their day of labour or trade, there is no-one in the parlour or dining room. Olivia orders some eggs and bread, and then waits impatiently, standing on one foot, then the other.

Voices drift to her from the kitchen, not so easy to make out above the sound of banging pots and pans, and the hiss of meat on the stove.

'… such a shame. Dunnae why they cannae keep them girls in check. Somethin' needs ta be done.'

'They should be taken to Port Arthur an' put with the menfolk, that's what. Give 'em tougher punishment.'

'Maybe. Maybe. Still, there's no excuse for such behaviour. They should be grateful they got a roof over their heads. Not startin' fires an' riots.'

'Come on now, you ever been inside the Factory? It's nae pretty, I can tell ye that.'

What was this poison in Olivia's ears? Fire? A riot? At the Factory? When Micky was there? Olivia thinks she's going to swoon and sits heavily in a chair. One thing she knows—she must find out what's happened.

***

161

A young serving girl eventually brings Olivia's food out to her. Not that she is hungry anymore, sick again over what might be. She needs more information. She clasps the girl by the sleeve as she turns to head back to the kitchen. 'I couldn't help but overhear, miss. Somethin' happened at the Female Factory?'

'Aye.' She nods so hard Olivia thinks her head might wobble off. On any other day, this would have made her laugh. 'They say there was a riot, and the prisoners set fire to the yard.'

'Which yard? Do ya know?' Olivia's heart picks up speed.

'Dunno as I can say. They reckon it was the bad lot.'

That would be crime class, for sure. Micky! 'Was anyone hurt?'

'Aye. I heard there were too many to fit in the infirmary at the Factory, so some was taken to the hospital. The Factory's in chaos at the minute … '

Olivia hears no more of what she says. Her thoughts reel. What has happened to Micky? Have her worst fears come true? She refuses to believe it. He is busy helping get the Factory back in order and he hasn't been able to come back to her. That must be it. He's fine. He's fine. She tells herself over and over.

The girl's words drift back into the edges of her consciousness, like water leaks into a boat before it sinks.

'Miss? Miss? Are you all right?'

'Oh, yes. I'm fine.'

'You look a mite pale.'

"Yes, I think I might go and lie down for a bit.'

Olivia needs to think. No, she doesn't need to think. Her thoughts just do more damage. But she can't focus on a conversation either. Olivia thanks the girl and takes the eggs and bread that she probably won't eat now and climbs the stairs back to their room. Each step feels like it's three times its usual size.

She puts the food on the small table and drops onto the bed. What is she going to do? Part of her is sure Ellen has had her revenge, but it can't be true. It just can't. Fate wasn't so cruel as to let her have a few days of freedom and bliss with a husband, only to tear it all away again. God wouldn't do that to her.

Or would he? Olivia's mind goes back and back. He never saved her from Mary's machinations, or the Old Bailey, or from being sent to Australia. Why would he start now?

But last night …

That was a coincidence. Surely.

Her thoughts go back and forth for hours, or so it seems. Perhaps she dozed insensibly for some of the time. But now her head aches. If only she could get answers.

Should she try to walk to the hospital? Ask after Micky there? Or to the Factory? No, she can't go near the Factory, they'll likely drag her back inside.

Hospital it is.

Olivia tries to make herself look presentable, crumpled as she is from lying around in her dress, and tidies her hair as well she can. Then she makes her way downstairs. She takes a deep breath as she steps outside. She has never walked around Hobart Town before. At least, not without the escort of the police or, more recently, her husband. The truth is, she doesn't even know where the hospital is. She scratches at her arms again. She supposes she'll have to ask for directions.

Olivia comes across a man selling fruit on the street side and asks him for the way to the hospital. He looks her up and down for a moment. Can he tell she's a prisoner? Or does he think her something else? Is he friend or foe? She smooths her skirts, self-conscious. Where has her nerve gone? She used to spout impertinence with the ease that a teething baby dribbles.

'Ye wanta go south a block,' he points the way with his hand. Good thing too, Olivia doesn't know which way is south. 'Then turn left and follow Liverpool Street until ye see it.'

'It's on Liverpool Street?'

'Aye.'

'Thank you,' she nods and hurries off in the direction he'd pointed. She's glad he didn't give her a long string of instructions, for she would surely get lost. The way was simple enough, and it wasn't too far, either.

Soon enough, she arrives at the hospital. She is a little damp now as the sun is rather warm and she hasn't walked slowly. Beads of perspiration trickle down her back beneath her dress, and from the back of her neck. She stands at the entrance for a few minutes in an attempt to settle herself. The imposing gates don't make her feel any more at ease. But she needs to know. Her stomach swirls. Olivia passes through the gates and trudges up the pathway to the front door. She scratches her arm as she enters, dreading what she will find.

'Is Micky here?' she blurts out to the first person she sees—some kind of nurse in charge, by her guess.

The nurse gives her a blank stare.

'Oh, um, I'm lookin' for Michael Reeve. Do ya know if he's a patient here?'

Her face softens a little then. 'Let me check the register.'

She goes to a desk and runs her finger down a ledger. 'When did you say he arrived?'

'It would only be last night.'

She looks up at me then and shakes her head. 'Sorry, love, no one here by that name.'

'You're sure?'

'Yes, I'm sure.'

Olivia doesn't know whether to be relieved or more worried. No, she can't do that to herself. He must be fine. Still working at the Factory. Or he could be back at the Bull's Head already.

'Thank you.' Her words sound as breathless as she feels.

She ducks back out the door and walks as fast as she can back to the inn. For a moment she's not sure which street she needs to turn up to find the Bull's Head, but then she recognises a building she passed before. She arrives at the inn, fairly panting, and races upstairs to the room, sure to find her husband waiting for her.

But when she turns the knob, nothing happens. It's locked. Locked? She bangs on the door. 'Micky?'

Thump, thump, thump. 'Micky, it's me. Let me in.'

No answer. She lifts her hand to knock again and pauses. Maybe he's asleep after such a long night. He must be exhausted. She should let him rest then. It still doesn't explain why he would lock her out. Never mind. Olivia goes down and sits in the parlour for a while. There is nothing to do but wait and ponder what might be. When she sees a maid go past, she realises she could just ask.

'Excuse me, miss?'

'Yes?'

'Did Mr Reeve return to our room while I were out?'

She looks at me strangely. 'Room two?'

Olivia nods.

She looks uncomfortable. 'I, um, I was sent to clean that room not an hour ago. Mr Collins said the guests had left.'

'But we haven't left. I'm still here waitin' for Mr Reeve to come an' join me. I went out for a short while an' returned to find our room locked.'

The maid shifts from one foot to the other. 'There must be some misunderstanding. Shall I get Mr Collins for you and you can settle it with him?'

'Yes, please.'

It is outrageous to think that a person cannot go out for a walk without losing their room in an inn. It is Olivia who paces now. Agitated. Where is Mr Collins?

Ah. Finally, he comes out from wherever he has been and approaches her with a nod. 'Miss … ?'

'Cruikshank … er … Reeve. Mrs Reeve.' It will take her a while to remember she has a new name.

'What can I do for you?'

'There seems to be a misunderstandin'. I went out for a walk an' returned to find my room locked an' cleaned out.'

'Which room was that?'

Olivia takes a deep breath to hold back her irritation. Surely the maid told him all this. 'Room two. Mr Reeve an' I have been stayin' here for several days.'

'Oh, yes.' He raises his eyebrows. 'Unfortunately, Mr Reeve only paid for two nights, so unless he,' he clears his throat, 'or you, I suppose, pay further, the room is no longer available.'

Olivia grits her teeth and scratches at the scabs on her arm. 'Surely you can grant some leniency? Mr Reeve is due to appear at any moment. He's caught up in the trouble at the Factory ya see.'

Mr Collins shakes his head but looks resolute. 'I am truly sorry to hear that m'dear, but he will have to come and see me when he returns.'

Olivia clenches and unclenches her fists. What is she to do? With a deep, frustrated breath, she realises there is naught she can do. She will just have to wait. She gives Mr Collins a curt nod, not trusting herself to speak, lest she heap obscenities on his head. Then she walks back to the parlour, where she will wait until Micky returns.

But he doesn't.

Olivia waits for hours and hours. The sun is going down, she can tell by the long shadows and waning light. Several times today, the maids have asked her if she needs anything. She tells them no. The only thing she needs is Micky.

Several times she sees two or three of them gathered just outside the doorway, whispering and glancing her way. Perhaps they think she is crazy. Perhaps they think her husband has deserted her. But Micky wouldn't do that. She wonders what she will do come nightfall. Can she beg mercy from Mr Collins to let her stay another night? Surely, he would not send a woman out into the street?

On the morrow, she must face her fears and go to the Factory to find out what is amiss. That is, if Micky doesn't come back before then.

It is when the serving girls are lighting the lamps that noise comes from the front door. Immediately thinking it is Micky, or hoping desperately anyway, Olivia jumps to her feet and heads toward the entry. Her breath catches when she sees Mr Collins shaking hands with a police officer and gesturing toward her.

CHAPTER
Twenty

Olivia

Olivia shakes her head and backs back toward, toward where? She knows what this means. She has seen too much of it in her life.

'No, no, no,' she sounds panicked, which she is. 'Why would ya bring the police? I haven't done anythin' wrong.'

'This woman is trespassing. She slept in one of my rooms without paying for it. I suspect she is a … ' he clears his throat, 'a woman of the night.'

'What? This is false,' Olivia wails. 'I were stayin' here with me husband, Michael Reeve, what works at the Female Factory. He's been detained 'cause of the violence what happened out there last night. I'm just waitin' for him to return.'

The police officer looks Olivia up and down. 'You wear no ring,' he remarks casually.

'No. Not yet. We wed rather quick just a few days ago.' Her breath comes faster. How can she convince him?

'Do you have papers?'

'Papers?'

'A marriage license?'

'Micky, Mr Reeve has it.' This is not going well. Olivia scratches her arms.

'Will you pay your dues to Mr Collins for the night you spent here?'

'I don't have any money. Micky only left me with a few coins, which I used to buy supper an' breakfast.' This is it. They are going to call her a thief now. And a liar. And who knows what else?

The officer arrested her. He put her in a holding cell for the night along with a few prostitutes and a drunk woman. They think Olivia's one of them, and she's not talking about the drunk.

She begged and pleaded with the police officer as he shoved her out of the inn and toward the station. He was not inclined to listen. Olivia insisted she was married.

'Where's yer proof, then?' was his gruff reply.

'I dunno where the license is. Find Micky an' he'll tell ya. Or even his family, they was there.'

'So you say? Who might this family be?'

'The Reeves I tell ya. I think they're in New Norfolk.'

'A convenient distance away.'

'What do ya mean by that?'

'I mean it won't be easy to confirm what yer saying.'

He thinks she's making it up carefully so they cannot follow up in a hurry. The familiar sting of distrust burns in her. No one will believe her. They never have and just because she is married now, doesn't change a thing.

'It's the truth,' Olivia says sullenly, but without hope.

'Listen,' he sighs with impatience, 'we'll send someone out to the Factory tomorrow to see if we can find this Michael Reeve, and that will be that. If he confirms you are wed, you will be free to go. Provided he pays the debt at the Bulls Head, that is.'

'Of course he will. He's an honest man.'

'We'll see.'

Why, why, why does no-one ever believe the truth when they hear it?

'D'ya wanna know what I think?'

No, she doesn't.

'I think yer a convict yerself. Maybe even absconded and tryin' to make ends meet on the street. I reckon this Mr Reeve, if he exists, paid for yer services, and then left ya there when he'd had enough of ya.'

Olivia bites down hard on her lip, fighting against the rage and injustice that swirls like bile in her stomach. It will not help her if she screams at him like a raging lunatic. She shakes her head and mumbles, 'no, no, no.'

And that is why she now sits in a cell. Her arms have bled through her sleeves, she has scratched them that much. All she can do is hope and pray they find Micky in the morning.

In the meantime, she has to deal with her inmates. They, of course, recognise her. Well, at least one of them does, and that's enough.

'Well, lookee here. We've got the Shank in our midst!' The familiar one grins.

Olivia is not in the mood. She doesn't have the energy to put on that façade anymore. She just wants to sit here in silence with her thoughts. Try to work out a way out of this. But then again …

'Evenin' ladies,' she smirks, hoping she doesn't have to keep it up for too long. 'Rosie ain't it?'

'Aye, that's me. Run off again, did ya?'

'Ya know it.' Olivia manages a bit of bluster.

'Did ya stash some booty?' Rosie asks in a low voice.

'That's for me to know and you to find out.' Even if Olivia had something she wouldn't share. Not here. It was always the rule she had. She took her treasures back to the Factory and gave them out there. But she has no intention of going back to the Factory, so they'll never know.

'What did yer boss do this time?' Nosy woman.

Olivia shrugs. 'Same as usual.'

'Pigs!' She spits on the floor. 'My boss thought it fine to lock me in the cellar with the rats for the night. An' what did I do to deserve that? Dropped a piece of cheese on the floor, that's what. An' they blame me for runnin' off.'

Olivia grunts in sympathy and they are silent for a time, then Rosie speaks again, sounding wistful.

'I wonder what it'd be like to get a good one.'

Olivia squints at her in the dim hold. 'A good what?'

'Boss. Be assigned to a good boss.'

Olivia sighs. She cannot be bothered putting on a tough front anymore. 'I did once.'

'You did?'

'Aye. He were fair. Worked me hard, but fair. An' fed me enough. No harsh punishment or nothin'.' Olivia pauses, remembering. He was one of the early ones. Mr Quinn. He had a sheep farm in a pretty valley. Olivia worked from sunup to sundown, till she fell into bed exhausted. But he never mistreated her or tried to have his way with her. She was just a worker. Fed and housed and put to work. She had nothin' to complain about. Not even the other assigned convicts or servants.

'I ran away all the same.' Olivia shifts in her corner, trying to ease the ache in her back from leaning against the wall.

'Now, why would ya do that?'

'Have you ever been terrified by the thought of freedom?'

'What's that?' Rosie screws her face up at her.

Olivia should not have let that slip out of her mouth. She shakes her head. 'Never mind. Dumb question.'

She doesn't want to talk anymore. It all feels like a cycle. A mean, unforgiving, hope-sucking cycle. Why did she ever think that freedom might be possible? It was all happening over again.

Olivia had a plan, back when she was twelve. She intended to get out from under the manipulative hold of her mother. When Papa died, Mama focused her control on Olivia. Made her work in Papa's gardens. Made her feel guilty if she was too tired or sick, because Mama's poor back couldn't take it, or some such rubbish. How Olivia wished she had other brothers or sisters to take some of the load, but Mama never fell pregnant again after Olivia, and even she was a long time coming. So, she bore the brunt of Mama's selfishness.

But Olivia had a plan. She worked hard. Secretly, she did extra jobs for others in the village and saved coins so she might run away and find domestic work of some sort, far away from Mama. Maybe someone would even hear her sing and she could sing on the stage. She'd heard that Giuditta Pasta made lots of money singing. Surely Olivia could make a little. It was a good plan, and it gave her hope.

But then, of course, there came the dreaded market trips. She prayed that there wouldn't be any olives for sale. She begged God to keep her from this awful experience. After two stays in prison with hard labour, Olivia felt sick to her stomach from the moment they entered the streets of London. She was twelve years old but felt as though she might be forty.

Without Papa to do the distracting, Mama decided she would take that role and Olivia must steal the olives. This was the first time Olivia stole and committed a crime. Her palms were slick with fear, her throat dry in contrast, and her heart pounded so hard in her chest she could hardly breathe. Her stomach knotted tight, then swirled with nausea. But Mama had this way of putting pressure on, as though living with her and no olives would be worse than finding herself in gaol once again.

Olivia took the olives, but she was so full of fear that the act was a clumsy one, someone surely saw, and then she bolted, terror driving her feet. Of course, that made it even more obvious.

'Stop thief!' Olivia heard the shout behind her and knew she was done for. Why bother running? She stopped still and let them take her. Perhaps more prison time would at least give her a break from Mama's whining. How she wished she had the nerve to stand up to her. But it seemed she was as spineless as Papa.

Olivia knew not to expect her in court, to offer any defence on her part. She braced herself for the guilty charge and the sentence. She didn't bother trying to cry or even to say Mama coerced her into this theft. Olivia hung her head and waited. She would do her time—probably another three months in prison, winding the crank or treading the treadmill—and then she would go back and work harder than ever to put her plan into action. This would just be a setback, nothing more. Olivia breathed in deep and tried to settle herself, resign to the outcome.

But even in that, she was wrong.

'Seven years' transportation,' she heard the magistrate say, and her world fell apart. She was twelve! That was almost as long as she'd been alive. They sent her to the other side of the world for what seemed the rest of her life. The end of her plan. The end of her hope. God had it in for her. This was obviously the pattern of her life from now on. And every event from then on has proved her theory correct.

***

Olivia tries to paste on a smile as they lead her into the docks once again, but she fails. She seems to have lost the art of smiling.

'Who is the defendant?' the magistrate asks. You'd think he'd remember her by now. She's been here often enough. More than enough, to be honest. Olivia should have taken more notice.

'Olivia Cruikshank, convict,' the clerk drones.

Olivia wants to feign boredom, but she cannot. She knows what to expect. She is so agitated it is like there are ants running around inside her body, and she scratches her scabbed arms.

'Charges?'

'Fraud and trespass. Prostitution.'

The small courtroom is dark, what with all the wood surrounding her and the small windows high on one wall. She's not sure how the clerk can even read the charges. And it smells close—musty with the bodies of the unwashed—but she can still catch the scent of leather and paper. These smells bring the memory of every hearing she's been at the centre of flooding back, and she doesn't want to be here.

'Who is the prosecutor?'

'Mr Albert Collins, innkeeper at the Bull's Head Inn.'

'Mr Collins, please state your case.'

The innkeeper stands to his feet, his chair scraping the wooden floor, and clears his throat. 'Sir, I would urge you not to let this girl's looks deceive you. While she seems to be pretty and friendly, she is naught but a fraud.'

'I have seen plenty a wolf in sheep's clothing, Mr Collins. I doubt she will surprise me. Please state your grievances.'

A wolf? He thinks Olivia's evil already. She's done for. The air is too close in here, she can't breathe.

Olivia bites hard on her lip and scratches hard at her arm while Mr Collins tells the magistrate the same story he told the police last night. As much as she tries not to, a whimper escapes her. Will he allow her to speak for herself?

172

After Mr Collins is done, they invite the police officer to the stand to give witness.

He basically repeats everything Mr Collins said but has his own additions.

'I suspect Miss Cruikshank's story is contrived. I overheard her speaking with other prisoners last night. She admitted to absconding from her assigned labour and even hinted that she may have stolen from her overseer.'

'No!' Olivia's silent internal screams finally slip out of her mouth.

The magistrate frowns at her. 'Quiet, Miss Cruikshank.'

'But that were just bluffin' in front of the other girls.'

'Silence. You will have your say soon enough. From what I'm hearing now, you either lied to Mr Collins, or you lied to your cellmates. Either way, it seems your word is not reliable.'

Olivia grits her teeth as he turns back to the police officer. 'Who is she assigned to?'

The officer clears his throat. 'Er… we were unable to find the records.'

The magistrate glares at him. 'So, how do you suppose she absconded from assignment then?'

Olivia could laugh at the police officer's discomfort if it weren't her future hanging in the balance.

'What of her claims to be wed?'

'We have not located this Mr Reeve, yet. I have sent an officer to New Norfolk to see if he is with his family, but the officer has not returned.'

'And no-one else can verify Miss Cruikshank's claim?'

Silence. Except the shuffling of paper.

'No, sir.'

'What about Raff?' Olivia can't help herself. There's got to be a way to prove she's telling the truth.

'Miss Cruikshank!' The magistrate growls.

'But he were at our weddin'. He works here with, with you people.'

'Raff?' He raises an eyebrow.

'Um,' what is his proper name? Olivia scratches hard at her arm while she wracks her brain. 'Cardamone! That's it. Mr Rafaello Cardamone.'

The magistrate gives her a smirk and shakes his head. 'How convenient.

Mr Cardamone is currently transporting a prisoner to Launceston. He cannot verify your claims until he returns in a week.'

He stares at Olivia, rubbing his chin, like he doesn't know what to do with her.

She hears a door bang and some harsh whispers and turns her head to see what the commotion is about. Another officer enters the courtroom and makes his way up to the constable who locked her up.

'Excuse me. This is highly irregular. Who allowed this man to interrupt these proceedings?' The magistrate bangs his gavel.

The officer seems to ignore him but goes up to Olivia's prosecutor and whispers in his ear. Maybe this is the officer who went to New Norfolk returning with good news for her. She crosses her fingers and prays it is so. Micky will rescue her yet.

The constable clears his throat and shuffles his feet. 'This officer brings news of Mr Reeve, direct from the Female Factory. Miss Cruikshank is indeed a prisoner from the Factory, and by all accounts, Mr Reeve perished in the riots at Cascades Female Factory two nights ago.'

Everything freezes. Or explodes. Olivia can't tell. The noise in her head is so loud she can't make sense of anything. The noise might be her screaming for all she knows. Micky is dead? It can't be true. She cannot accept it. That would mean she has lost the only thing good in her life, and that means she has lost everything.

'No, no, no, no, no!' she cannot formulate any other words.

'Miss Cruikshank.'

Crushing pain envelops her chest. Micky? Her dear, sweet, Micky. The only love she's ever known, could ever know, gone? Gone. Forever. She can't breathe.

'Miss Cruikshank! Somebody get her under control.'

Olivia vaguely recognises there is commotion going on around her, maybe even hands on her, but her ears are buzzing. Is that the sound of blood rushing through her head? The throbbing. The darkness.

Her whole body rejects that word—perished. Even her knees can't take it. Her legs crumble beneath her and she sinks to the floor, the darkness closing in and the buzz now deafening. Until it all stops. Blissful escape.

When Olivia awakes, she finds herself in darkness. Her head pounds and it takes a few minutes to remember. But then …

Micky.

The grief overwhelms her, and this time she howls like a newborn babe. How could this happen to her? Why would God do this to her? She never asked for any of it. Nothing in her whole life.

Olivia cries for hours, hopelessness taking over. And eventually she sleeps again. It is a pattern she follows for a while.

Wake. Weep. Sleep.

Who knows how much time passes before she finally finds the strength to get up off the cot and look around? It seems she is in a cell, although there is no light to show what time it is. Her feet contact a tin of water and there is a small plate with bread on the floor. When they were placed there, she cannot recall. She drinks the water now, realising she is quite parched and hungry. She saves a small amount of water to splash on her face. Her crusty, tear-stained face.

So, they brought her back to the police station? She wonders if they will bring her back to court today to finish her. Well, finish the proceedings, anyway. And now she doesn't have a leg to stand on, as they say. Micky is lost to her. Raff is gone. Micky's family is too far away to help in any kind of hurry—as if the employees of so-called justice would even go to see them on behalf of a notorious convict, anyway. Micky and Raff are the only two people who would have helped her.

The tears well up again. But she is done. She has had enough of crying. It won't achieve her anything, will it? Olivia sucks in a deep breath. She will only allow the tears and grief in the depths of night. She must harden herself now. The future she dreamed of is gone, and there is nothing for it but to shove those dreams down hard.

For a moment, she thinks about praying, talking to God. But then she remembers he let Micky die. She's not talking to him. Maybe he is not even real after all. What kind of God allows so much suffering?

It is only a matter of time until footsteps sound outside her cell, and the clank of iron announces a visitor. A turnkey? Once that sound made her hope for a visit from Micky. Now, alarm bells ring in her ears.

'Well, good mornin', lassie,' the guard grins. A slimy grimace if ever she saw one. 'Welcome back to the Factory.'

The Factory? She's not at the police station? They sentenced her while she was unconscious?

Olivia purses her lips and glares at him, anger roiling.

She is about to unleash a tirade on him when she has second thoughts. None of that will achieve anything good. She sucks in a deep breath and matches his stupid grin. 'Yeah. Did ya miss the Shank?'

CHAPTER
Twenty-One

Olivia

So, it looks like she's back to picking and carding. Class Two. Thank goodness, they didn't put her in crime class, where she'd have to be on her guard all the time. Here, she can let her mind wander a bit. But then again, she doesn't want too much time for that either. Her thoughts eventually will turn to Micky, and she can't have the girls seeing her weak.

When she first came in, they all stopped and stared at her. No rousing greeting, or vulgar song, just silence. Some averted their eyes, some looked a little sympathetic, and a small number smirked. Obviously, they all knew. Everything.

Olivia forced a smile and held her trembling hands in fists. 'Mornin' girls. Couldn't stay away. Missed yas too much.'

With that, they returned to their work, some with a shake of their head, some with a murmur of welcome. Olivia took her place at the tables and began the finger-numbing task of working with the wool, ignoring those around her.

Problem is, she is desperate to know what happened in the riot. She isn't sure if any of these girls would know much, since they're in Class Two, and she's certain the riot happened in crime class, because that's where Micky had worked. Ann could tell her everything, but Olivia doubts she can get to see her, unless she makes trouble and gets herself sent back to crime class. Olivia sighs. She doesn't have it in her. She's too tired, so tired she could just lay down and die.

Then there is Mary. Trying not to make it obvious, Olivia looks around the room at all the girls. It appears her mother has not finished her stint in crime class, as she is not present. Olivia's pretty sure she would have noticed Mary when she walked in. Or Mary would have noticed Olivia.

Olivia sees Nancy on the other side of the dank room. She has previously worked alongside her, and they had the beginnings of a friendship. Olivia remembers that time she flirted with Micky. Pain stabs through her chest as she thinks of him leaning over them. That smile. Those gentle and kind eyes. The heat Olivia felt at his touch. She swallows hard. How long will she feel this torture? She shakes her head, trying to lose the memories. Anyway, maybe Nancy can tell her something about what happened here.

After the dinner break, Olivia wheedles her way into sitting next to Nancy. To her ruin, every time a warden walks past, that memory of Micky keeps coming back. She must ignore it. She must shove it down. Otherwise …

Otherwise, she won't be able to breathe.

After a brief hello, they work in silence for a long while. Olivia gets the feeling Nancy doesn't know what to say to her. At least that means Nancy cares a little. Olivia hopes so, at any rate. The questions burn on her tongue in equal measure to dread of the answers. They will cut wide open, those words, she knows it. She wonders if she can hold it together. And so she waits.

Olivia figures if she waits till the end of the day, she will only have to keep a grasp on the tatters of her heart for a short time, until they lock her in the dorm for the night. Yes, that is the best course of action.

Eventually, though, Nancy does pipe up. 'Sorry to hear about yer beau.'

Olivia clears her throat. Maybe she covers a whimper or a groan. 'Husband,' she whispers. 'He were me husband.' It's hard to even say the words. Olivia's hands tremble as she tries to work with the fleece, and her heart races.

'Ye were wed?'

'Aye.'

Nancy stops working for a moment, and from the corner of Olivia's eye she sees the older woman slowly shake her head.

'Did ya love him?'

What kind of woman does Nancy take her for? Anger burns. But then, she remembers that plenty of female convicts marry just to get out of prison, so it's a fair question. It strikes her that Micky's influence on her hasn't died with him, and anguish hits her again. Once, Olivia would have given Nancy a piece of her mind with that question. Now she feels a sense of grace toward her.

'Yeah, I did.'

'Oh luv,' the sympathy in her voice is real. 'I am so sorry. To have loved and lost so quickly is truly a tragedy.'

Olivia can do nothing but nod, and work fiercely at the wool fibres, tears pricking her eyes. Nancy reaches over and squeezes her hand briefly. That action says more to her than a thousand words. Olivia sniffs and must wipe her nose on her sleeve. She nods again and swallows her grief, which sticks like a large gobstopper in her throat.

More time passes as they work quietly again, a new understanding between them. Her silent company is all Olivia needs right now.

When the light fades in the small windows, Olivia draws up the courage to ask Nancy what she knows about the riot.

'We didn't see what happened in crime class of course, 'cause we was still in here,' Nancy began, 'but we did hear the din what grew louder an' louder.'

'What did you hear?'

'Yellin'. Screamin'. Crashin' noises. All that. An' then they was yellin' fire, an' we could smell the smoke. The turnkeys all started rushin' us outta here until we was all outside. Some o' them girls was rollin' on the ground, coughin' their lungs out—the ones from crime class, I mean. I think some got burnt even. I seen 'em cart a few away on stretchers.'

Nancy pauses with a gasp.

'What? Go on,' Olivia nudges her with an elbow, even though she doesn't really want to hear it.

'Sorry, just realised one of them stretchers probably had yer man on it. It was gettin' dark, so we couldn't see clear.'

Olivia nods and closes her eyes. 'It's all right. Keep goin'.'

'Well, I saw two of 'em guards tryin' to 'old one girl what was thrashin' about like a wild thing. Screamin' like a banshee she were. I think it were Ellen Smith, ya know. They're sayin' she's lost her sanity.'

Olivia grunts. She knows all too well. Olivia reckons she was probably behind the whole riot. 'What happened to her?'

'They took her away. Not quite sure. She ain't here at the Factory no more. Word is she were transferred to Lonnie.'

A memory triggered. 'I did hear of a prisoner bein' transported to Lonnie when I were in court,' Olivia confirmed. Was that who Raff transferred? Ellen Smith? Ellen Smith, who likely killed her husband. 'Good riddance to her,' Olivia spits. 'I hope she rots there.'

A wave of guilt shoots through her. *Micky, Micky, Micky. What have you done to me?* She can't even have feelings of revenge anymore? She is so angry she wants to scream. But Micky's words echo in her head. She can hear his voice in her ears. *Forgiveness is the only way.* 'Bah!' Olivia slams the fleece on the table.

'What's the matter?' Nancy asks.

'Nothin'.' Olivia switches the subject, not willing to probe anymore into these thoughts. 'I reckon it must be supper time.'

Sure enough, within minutes, the bell rings, and the turnkeys release them for the evening meal. Olivia keeps to herself while she eats and looks forward to the semi-solitude of her cot. There, she can turn her face to the wall and think through all she has learnt and felt and thought during this day. It isn't long before the sobs come again. She curls up as much as she can, and lets the grief roll silently, eventually falling into a dreamless sleep.

Olivia wakes up numb. It is as though her head is in a cloud of fog. Is this what happens when everything becomes too much? At breakfast this morning, the turnkey spoke to her and it took three times for her to register his words. He probably took it as insolence. She may end up being punished for it. But she can't help it, her brain won't work properly.

This time, Mary is back in the Class Two room, picking and carding like the rest of them. Their eyes meet. There is a yellow, faded bruise high on her

180

cheekbone. Olivia can tell Mary wants to talk to her. A pleading expression fills her gaze. What does she want?

What does Olivia want? Does she even want to talk to Mary? She should feel something right now, shouldn't she? This numbness has stolen her ability to feel—not an angry thought, or even a curious thought enters her head. Like her emotions have disappeared in the fog. Olivia is empty. She looks away from Mary and goes about her business. If Nancy and Olivia speak at all, it is mundane. Olivia has trouble formulating much more than a grunt here and there.

At dinnertime, she lines up for her plate of bland prison food, when Mary appears at her elbow.

'What do ya want?' It's not the friendliest greeting, but Mary doesn't seem phased.

'I want to tell ya how sorry I am.'

Olivia glances sideways at her. It surprises her to find her pulse doesn't rise in the slightest. Olivia sighs. 'Sorry for what? Ya buddied up with the very woman what wanted me dead. And then ya helped her kill me husband.' The words are harsh, but there is no heat in them. Olivia can't muster any.

'No, no. You've got it all wrong Livvie. I tried to save him.'

***

That got Olivia's attention, and she turned to face Mary fully. 'Ya tried to what?'

'Look, let's get some grub, and we'll sit an' talk.'

She's a clever one, is Olivia's mother. Knows how to pique her interest even in this dull state. They get their plates and find a bench together.

'Tell me,' Olivia mumbles.

'First, let me tell ya that I know I ain't been a right mother to ya. I know it's me own fault ya ended up here.' She fiddles with her food and Olivia notices the skin is peeling from red welts on her hands. She pretends she doesn't see.

'Yeah, when did ya realise that?'

'Selfishness. After the last few days, I've woken up to meself. How selfish

181

I've been. Yer poor dad must have suffered too. An' I know how much it hurts to lose a husband.'

Mary sniffs. Is she truly sorry and even sympathetic? Olivia sneaks a sideways look and notices Mary swipe at a wet cheek. Olivia raises her eyebrows. 'Huh.' A sound of wonder. It's all she's got.

'I didn't know how much Ellen hated ya. She's very good at pretendin' nice.'

Olivia snorts.

'The other day in the wash yard, I didn't know what she had planned. I reckon she told one or two of the other girls, but not me.'

Olivia draws in a deep breath. Mary was right there. 'What exactly happened out there?'

'Ellen got hold of some lye. She drew Micky's attention by huddling with the other girls, like she were plottin' somethin'. When he came over, she threw that lye in his face.'

Expletives fly out of Olivia's mouth then. Maybe she can feel something after all. She digs her fingernails into the bench. 'Then what?'

'Well, I knew how much he meant to ya, so I tried to get water to wash his face. But Ellen threatened to kill me then—she even pulled a dagger out an' waved it at me. For a minute I thought she were gonna stab Micky, but then she laid into him with her boots.' Her voice broke then. 'She stomped on his head, too. She were screamin' like a maniac all the while. It were awful. I ain't been able to sleep properly since. I just keep seein' him lyin' there.'

Tears spill over Olivia's cheeks too. It hurts to hear, but she needs to know. 'Didn't the turnkeys try to stop her?'

'The other girls—I reckon Ellen planned it all—started a riot 'round us, so the guards couldn't get close enough. They was throwin' stuff an' yellin'. Next thing I knew, smoke filled the yard. I dunno who started the fire, but the screams went from angry to panicked. They was all fightin' over each other to get outta there.' Mary paused and sobbed. 'Livvie, I tried to get Micky out. I tried to drag him, but he were too heavy. I didn't get him far before the turnkey pulled me away by force.' She sucked in a deep breath and wiped at her eyes. 'Next I seen him, I think he was on one of them stretchers, bein' taken away.'

'Where? Where did they take him?'

She shrugged. A forlorn movement. 'I dunno lass. I just heard later that he'd perished.'

Olivia sits in silence. The news has drained her too much, but she'd quiet tears.

'Will ya ever be able to forgive me for all I've put ya through?'

With a deep sigh, Olivia reaches over and grasps Mary's burnt hand. All the fight has gone out of her. Her lips tremble. 'I dunno, Mary. There's a lot. But, for Micky's sake, I promise to keep talkin' to ya.' Olivia slowly gets up from the bench. Her body feels so heavy. 'Thanks. For tryin' to help him.'

Olivia heads back to her workbench, ready to spend the afternoon thinking over all that Mary said, while keeping her hands busy with the fleece. But before she even gets there, the turnkey comes over and takes her by the arm.

'Come with me. Matron wants to see ya.'

Olivia sighs. Here it comes. The retribution for her insolence this morning. She shuffles after him without a word, and once again it surprises her how different she is now. What will Matron do? Send her to solitary for a few days? Put her in the wash yard? Who knows? Olivia even thinks she is beyond caring anymore.

Matron leans over papers on her desk as the turnkey shoves Olivia into her office. He shuts the door behind her, but Olivia knows he stands just outside, ready to take control if she tries anything. Olivia waits for Matron to speak. She has nothing to say of her own account.

Eventually, Matron seems to sign off on her document and looks up at Olivia from her writing. She stands up with the freshly scrawled page in her hand and grins at her. Mind you, a grin from Matron is never pleasant, a mere turning up of the corners of her wide mouth. 'I have an assignment for you.'

This is unexpected and takes a few moments to sink in. Assignment? No. Some part of Olivia still waits for the truth about her marriage to arrive and set her free. And besides that …

'I've only got a few months left to serve of me sentence.' Olivia has never, ever, used that argument before. It has never meant much to her before. Suddenly, it means everything.

Matron looks at Olivia sharply. 'Then you will serve them with Mr Stanthorpe.'

She will brook no argument, Olivia can see. So, this is her punishment for Olivia's lapse this morning. She grits her teeth. There is no point in fighting or trying to reason with the woman. Why would Matron listen to her anyway, when she has never made it easy to begin with? Olivia says nothing. She just stares ahead, fixing her eyes on the greasy smear on the wall behind Matron. *I hope Mr Stanthorpe is a decent man.*

With a swish of Matron's stiff skirts, she rounds the desk and leads Olivia out of the room, where, as suspected, the turnkey awaits. She hands Olivia over to him along with the document—Olivia assumes the assignment papers—and they walk toward the prison entry. No chance to say goodbye to her mother. The fragile and hopeful state of their relationship left unresolved. Mary will have to hear about her absence from others, and who knows what they will tell her?

Outside the prison doors, Olivia squints in the bright summer sunshine and the heat of the day hits her like the blast from a furnace. The stone walls of the Factory keep it a little cooler inside compared to this. The fresh air, though, no matter how hot it is, is very welcome, and she breathes deeply. A covered cart waits nearby with a gentleman standing beside it. She says gentleman because he's not dressed like a farmer. More like a, well, she doesn't know, really. He wears a long coat and a cravat. He also sports a top hat and carries a cane. Almost dandified, she reckons. Is this her new master? His appearance has Olivia's curiosity piqued despite herself. What kind of position has Matron assigned her to?

The turnkey hands the man—Olivia assumes Mr Stanthorpe—the papers and her new master hands her up onto the cart. Hands her up. If she weren't so numb, she might have laughed. He shares a few words with Matron and then he is up beside Olivia. With a flick of the reins, they are off, to who knows where.

It is a few minutes before he speaks. 'As you've probably guessed, I am Mr Stanthorpe. Mr Trevor Stanthorpe. And you are Miss Olivia Cruikshank, yes?'

She wants to tell him no. Mrs Olivia Reeve. But she doesn't have the strength. She merely nods instead.

Soon it is apparent they are heading out of town, which can only mean he lives on a rural selection, but that doesn't seem to fit with his attire. Mr Stanthorpe still drives in silence and she has no clue where they are headed, or what she is about to become.

'Ya don't look like no farmer,' Olivia finally says.

'You are very perceptive.' Sarcasm. That is unexpected. Olivia might have received a warning for impertinence, or an answer to her implied question. Instead, he seems to be sullen and cynical. Looks like she'll have to press him for information. Olivia sighs deeply. Maybe she is too tired for that. But she wants to know. She figures she can try once more and be direct this time.

'Sir?' Maybe she'll get a better response if she's perfectly courteous. 'May I ask where we're goin', an' what my position is to be?'

He is quiet. Olivia wonders if he even heard her, but he finally answers. 'North.'

All right. Short and to the point, but still telling her nothing.

'We will meet up with the rest of the troupe at the Black Snake.'

The rest of the what? 'Troupe?'

'Yes, Miss Cruikshank. Troupe. You now belong to a travelling troupe of entertainers. Stanthorpe's Extraordinary Entertainers, to be precise. I have heard good things about you, girl. That you can sing.' He looks at Olivia for the first time. 'Tonight, you shall prove your worth and sing for your supper.'

CHAPTER
Twenty-Two

Olivia

Sing? She sucks in her breath. She doesn't know what to think. Or feel. Didn't she always want to sing? But being forced to sing? And if she doesn't sing, she doesn't eat? Is that what he's saying? What if she refuses? She knows the penalty for insubordination. She will be back in the Factory before she can blink. In days past, she would not have hesitated. But now … ? Her stomach churns. She opens and closes her mouth but can't find any words.

'Is something the matter, girl? You seem pale. You can sing, can you not?' He is scowling.

She could deny it. Should deny it. It's not like she's trained or anything. What does she really know about singing?

'I don't know if I can.' It comes out almost like a whisper.

'What ever can you mean?'

Olivia swallows. And then she lets it all out in a gush. 'Me husband died a few days ago.' That's a good reason as any not to sing.

She lets that hang in the air between them, but she is met with silence again for a long while.

'My wife passed three weeks ago.'

So, he knows the grief.

'Unfortunately, life doesn't give us a reprieve from the need to eat or support others. And so, we must continue. We must work.'

Surprisingly, he speaks a language Olivia understands, even if she doesn't like it, and she has no argument.

Once again, they drive in silence, with only the surrounding wildlife disturbing the quiet. The sun begins its descent to the horizon to their left. She assumes the Black Snake he mentioned is an inn and they will stop there for the night.

'What do you have in your repertoire?'

Olivia jumps at his sudden speech.

'Repertoire?'

'The songs you sing. What are they?'

'I … ' What can she tell him? She's been in prison most of her life. She remembers a few children's ditties from when she was very young, but … 'Only songs from the prison, an' songs I've made up meself.'

'Hmph. Looks like the others will have to teach you some new songs. Sing me one of those you made up.'

'Now?'

'Aye now. I must hear before I set you before an audience.'

Olivia closes her eyes. There is nothing in her that wants to sing right now. All she would like to do is curl up in a cot somewhere and wait for her heart to stop beating. But singing is not the worst he could compel her to do. She is silently thankful she is not at hard labour, or even laundering for a farmer at this moment. She digs deep inside herself to find the spunk she once used to entertain the girls in the wash yard. And then she sings her song about the Female Factory.

When she is done, the corners of Mr Stanthorpe's mouth turn up. Is that a smile? Looks more like a grimace. 'You'll do.'

Olivia doesn't know if that means he thinks she's any good. Maybe it just means she won't starve. Not that she's overly hungry. Her stomach still swirls most of the time.

***

Mick

'Michael, lad. Are ya comin' back to us?'

A voice penetrates his consciousness. He groans. His head aches. His eyes seem heavy, stuck closed. No, swollen maybe. They feel like fire. But he can't open them. Where is he? He tries to voice the words, unsure if he succeeds.

'It's all right, Son. I'm here.'

His father's voice. His hand grasping Mick's. 'Do you know where Olivia is?'

Olivia? Who is Dad talking about? Mick's mouth is so dry he can hardly form any words.

'Wh … wh …' He seems to have little strength.

A pause. Dad is silent for long seconds.

'Rest, Son. There was an accident at the Factory. Yer safe now. I'm here with ya.'

***

Olivia

The sun is well down by the time they pull into the Black Snake Inn. Mr Stanthorpe quickly introduces her to the rest of the troupe—Mr Frith who plays the fiddle, Mr Brown who plays the whistle, Mr Carpenter with his accordion and Mr Johnson who says he's a magician. Mr Johnson is the only one who has a missus with him—she helps him with his act sometimes and then assists the others where she can. She says she can sing a bit, too.

They all seem friendly enough. Do they know Olivia is a convict? Or are they convicts, too? She mostly nods and tries to smile as they do the rounds of introduction, but when Mr Stanthorpe presents her as Miss Cruikshank, this time she interrupts. 'Mrs Reeve,' she says. 'I'm Olivia Reeve.'

Mr Stanthorpe gives her a grim nod. 'My sincere apologies, Mrs Reeve. That was a terrible omission on my part. Mrs Reeve is recently widowed, like myself.'

'So sorry to hear that, luvvie,' says Mrs Johnson with a dimpled smile. Olivia believes she is doomed to like this one.

Olivia learns the troupe has already procured rooms for them. Two rooms to cram the seven of them in. She is not a stranger to crowded sleeping arrangements, but it gives her some respect for Mr Stanthorpe, who doesn't seem to lord it over them. She's not met a boss like that before. They put her in with the Johnsons, and the rest are in the other room.

Mr Stanthorpe claps his hands. 'Let us freshen ourselves and see if we can get the innkeeper to pay us in kind.'

Everyone moves off to the rooms.

'What did he mean by that?' Olivia ventures to ask Mrs Johnson when they enter the room. Mr Johnson is kind enough to wait outside whilst they finish their ablutions.

'By what?' Mrs Johnson asks.

'Pay us in kind?'

'Well,' she grins, 'we entertain those what's in there drinkin' 'n' such, an' if it means more business for the publican, he might throw us a bone, if ya like.'

Olivia looks at her blankly.

Mrs Johnson rolls her eyes, but she is still smiling. 'He might give us our supper for free, or cheaper fees for the rooms.'

Understanding comes slowly. 'Oh. Mr Stanthorpe said I must sing for me supper, is that what he meant?'

'Aye, luvvie. But probably not as severe as you believed it. You'll still get yer supper, even if the innkeeper has a tight fist.' She pours water into a basin and starts washing her face.

Olivia breathes a little easier. So, she's not exactly being forced to sing. 'Is that how ya all survive?'

'Nah. It just helps when we're travellin'. In the towns, we usually put on a show in the town hall or one of the larger inns. Trevor, Mr Stanthorpe, sells tickets to those shows.' She waves Olivia over to wash her face whilst Mrs Johnson is drying hers off.

When Olivia is done, Mrs Johnson looks her up and down. 'I don't suppose ya got another dress what ya can wear?'

Olivia shakes her head. She's still wearing the dull serge clothing assigned at the Factory. She's not ready to tell her tale.

With a brief sigh, Mrs Johnson spins Olivia around, pulls off her mobcap and unpins her hair. 'Well, we'll have to make do with what we've got.' She releases Olivia's braid and collects a hair brush. 'You've got beautiful hair, luvvie.'

Thankfully, her hair is now past shoulder length again, and she doesn't have to answer questions about short hair. Not since her mother brushed her hair as a little girl, has she felt gentle hands on her head—apart from Micky running his fingers through her hair. The sudden memory brings a sharp gasp and Olivia's eyes prick with tears. Thankfully, Mrs Johnson is behind her.

'Sorry, didn't mean to pull so hard.'

'It's fine,' Olivia says. She cannot tell Mrs Johnson how nice this feeling is, even though it brings bittersweet emotions to the surface. For a moment she can close her eyes and imagine Micky is here with her. Only for a moment, though, she can't have Mrs Johnson see her cry.

Mrs Johnson makes two plaits down the sides of her face, then braids the rest at the back. In the Factory, her hair was always in a single braid, and mostly tucked up beneath the mobcap. And here, Mrs Johnson makes her hair look pretty. She winds the braid at the back into a bun, then brings the two side braids to loop beneath her ears and then wraps them around the bun.

Despite Olivia's best efforts, she still gulps down her emotion when Mrs Johnson turns her around.

'What's wrong, luvvie?' She seems genuinely concerned.

Olivia shrugs. 'I just miss Micky, er, Mr Reeve, me husband.'

Mrs Johnson's face melts into a sympathetic smile and she rubs Olivia's shoulders. 'There, there, dear. The Lord works all for good in the end, you'll see.'

At once Olivia switches from sorrow to anger and she blurts out things she should keep to herself. 'How can ya say that? Micky were the best thing that ever happened to me. We just got married. I'm supposed to be free now. But here I am, a prisoner again, an' he's dead!' The sobs shake Olivia's shoulders.

Mrs Johnson stands there for a moment, like she is shocked or something, then wraps her arms around Olivia. She stiffens. She wants to fight her off, but another part of her just wants to be held like this. 'How am I ever supposed to sing again?'

Mick

Voices drift to Mick from some otherworldly place.

'… he's sustained significant injury to his head. We'll have to wait and see.'

'What about his eyes?' That's Dad's voice.

'Again, only time will tell how bad the burn is.'

No, no, no. They can't be talking about him. He wasn't burnt. How would he have gotten burnt? He tries to open his eyes and groans at the pain in them and in his head. He lifts his hands to feel, but there are bandages wrapped around his head, and he tugs at them.

Footsteps rush toward him.

'It's all right, lad.' A firm hand restrains Mick's arms, restrictive but calming.

'Wh … what h … happened? Where … where am I?' His voice doesn't sound normal, like it belongs to someone else.

'There was a riot and a fire at the Factory.' His father's voice. 'But my main concern right now is finding Olivia.'

'What factory? Who's Olivia?' He doesn't know what Dad's talking about.

'Looks like he's got some amnesia.' Another voice. 'It's common to this kind of injury. Hopefully, as he heals, his memory will return.'

'What are you talking about?' Their words confuse Mick and the pounding in his head increases.

'Never mind now, Son. You just rest.'

He doesn't have the strength to argue further, so he just lies there.

***

Olivia

The Black Snake has a small enough crowd. Mostly travellers pausing on their journey for the night, but Olivia supposes there are a few local farmers here too. Men who've worked hard all day and have come in for some ale and mateship. It is almost her turn to sing, and she feels nervous. This is not something she's familiar with, as any previous singing has been on her terms.

Mr Stanthorpe took her outside with the three musicians earlier and made her sing her captive song to them. They quickly joined in on their instruments. It is hard to explain the way this made Olivia feel. Like her song mattered. Or like she is not just an amateur who made up a silly song.

Not five minutes earlier she had been venting her grief on Mrs Johnson and now she felt a warmth in her stomach, despite the gaping hole that Micky has left, that she cannot account for. Olivia is not used to such sweeping emotions. She doesn't know what to do with them.

So now she waits in the corner, watching the rest of the troupe do their thing. The mob seems like they're enjoying the show. Some tap their feet to the music, a couple even dance. Though, the innkeeper asks them to stop before the constabulary come in and put an end to the evening. Hopefully, Olivia doesn't wreck it for them when she gets up there. She swallows hard and scratches her arms. Mr Stanthorpe waves her over.

'Introducing our new vocalist, Mrs Reeve,' he declares in a big voice, with a sweeping gesture of his arm.

Olivia's heart pounds now that she looks into all their faces.

The band launches into the song behind her.

She takes a deep breath. The only way she can do this is pretend she is back there—at the Factory. 'Any you fellas been in prison?' she asks with a loud voice and a smirk.

She receives a loud holler of 'Aye' in response.

'Well, maybe ya'll remember then,' she grins.

And then she does it. She sings her song, just like she did to the girls in the Factory, pulling the same faces and swishing her skirts. After all, it was always an act. Next thing, the mob all stomp their feet on the floor, bang their cups on the tables, or clap. And by the time Olivia gets to the chorus the third time, they sing along. She guesses they like it.

When she finishes, they all cheer and whistle. Her heart swells. She is surprised to find she enjoys this. And then in an instant she feels guilty. How can she enjoy something when Micky is still fresh in his grave? It is so wrong. Thankfully, that is the end of her performance as she doesn't know any other songs, and she can escape to the room. She paces up and down for a while, confused by her feelings. Can't she just go back to being numb?

Later, when the Johnsons come in, she is already on her cot. Mr Johnson had hung a sheet from the ceiling earlier to give her a little privacy.

'Sorry to disturb you, Mrs Reeve,' Mr Johnson says quietly, as if he is unsure.

'It's alri'. I ain't asleep.'

'Well, you were the star tonight.' He speaks louder now. 'They wanted you to come back and sing again.' He sounds like there is a grin on his face.

'They did?'

'Aye. But there's plenty of time for that. We'll need to teach you some more songs while we travel.'

'Where are we goin'?'

'Launceston, I believe.'

'Oh,' Olivia replies absently. Her thoughts travel elsewhere. 'Did Mr Stanthorpe receive a good payment tonight, then?' She doesn't want to be the reason they go hungry or cold, ever. And she still doesn't really know what kind of boss Mr Stanthorpe is, although the others seem content. Is he likely to whip her if she doesn't perform to his expectations?

Mr Johnson chuckles. 'The innkeeper has given us a room for free and breakfast in the morning. That's not too bad if you ask me. He even suggested we stay another night, but I know Stanthorpe wants to keep moving. The best money is in the bigger towns and cities.'

'I suppose that makes sense.'

'Let her get some sleep now, my love,' Mrs Johnson tells him. 'Goodnight Mrs Reeve.'

'Goodnight,' Olivia replies.

***

Mick groans. So much pain. And then … 'I'm gonna be sick.'

Hands on him, pulling him to his side, rubbing his back.

'Where am I? What is wrong with me?'

'Yer in hospital, Son. There was an accident.' Dad's here with him.

'What accident? My head hurts.'

'Do you remember workin' at the Factory?'

'What factory? The mill?'

'No, Son. What about Olivia? I would have thought she'd be here by your side.'

His head hurts. 'Who's Olivia?'

Silence.

'Dad, you're not making any sense. What is going on?'

He tells Mick a story about the Female Factory and what happened there, but it sounds like he's talking about someone else. Then Dad tells him he's married and that he's wondering where Mick's wife is. It all sounds so foreign and confusing, and alarming as well. The problem is, he does have the injuries that result from the events Dad describes. Exhausted, he stops trying to remember.

CHAPTER
Twenty-Three

Olivia

The troupe split the next days between travelling and learning. The fellows teach her a bunch of new songs and they try them out on the unsuspecting clientele of whichever inn they stop at for the night. For the most part, they receive her well. It must be the combination of her singing abilities and her acting skills, because for sure all she feels is the gaping hole inside where Micky once lived. She's seen a couple of prim ladies shake their heads and cross their arms when Olivia performs. She reckons that would be because of the vulgar nature of some of the tunes they sing. A proper lady wouldn't cavort around, swishing her skirts, singing about lovers. Well, Olivia never had the chance to be a proper lady, so too bad.

Every night, though she's tired from sitting in a wagon or walking, practicing lyrics repeatedly, then performing, she still lies there and cries until she falls asleep. Silently, mind you. She puts her head under the blanket and lets the tears flow, but she doesn't want the Johnsons to hear her. Will this ache ever go away? She wonders if she will ever have the happiness she dreamt of with Micky.

Every morning, she wakes with a heaviness like she's never had before. It takes every ounce of strength to drag herself out of bed. For certain, if she weren't on assigned labour or even forced labour in the prison yards, she would not get up at all. Sleep is the only relief from this constant ache.

If only she could sleep and never wake up. If only she could tear this heart out that Micky awakened, or make it go back to being cold and hard as it once used to be.

Sure, this will probably be the best kind of assignment she could have hoped for, but without Micky, it seems pointless. She is still a prisoner. It all seems so unfair. All she can do is swing on a cycle of grief, anger, and listlessness.

'I dunno how to live without ya, Micky,' she whispers into her pillow. Her world seems emptier now than before she met him.

***

Mick

It is three days before he can sit up long enough to take in and retain all that his father tells him. He still doesn't recall the events that happened at the Factory within his memory, but he remembers the days leading up to it. And, more importantly, he remembers his wife.

'Have you found Olivia?' It's the first thing he asks Dad when he comes back to the hospital. Mick recalled enough to tell him where he last saw her.

'Sorry, Son.' Dad's voice is grim. 'It sounds like they took her in for trespass and failure to pay for her accommodation.'

'Dear God.'

'I went to the Factory, and she's not there either. Apparently, they've put her on assignment.'

'What do you mean, on assignment? She's my wife! She is supposed to be in my care now. Didn't she tell them?' Pain slices through his head.

Dad puts a staying hand on his forearm.

'Easy lad. I know as much as you.'

Mick pulls the blanket off to get out of bed. 'I have to find her.' The sudden movement makes him swoon though, and he lays back down with a frustrated groan. The futility of the situation hits him hard. He's blind. How is he going to do anything?

'Yer gonna have to leave the work to me. You need to get better yourself. Trust me to do this.'

Another tortured groan escapes his mouth. If only he could tear the bandage from his head and find that all is well. If only he could wash his face and find his eyes were just covered with dirt. This wishing will not get him anywhere. He knows God can heal him, but whether His choice is immediate, or through the ministrations of doctors, Mick must wait and see. Ha! See. He laughs scornfully at his unintended pun.

'What's that, Son?'

'Nothing, Dad.' He grimaces. 'Just feeling sorry for myself.'

'Try an' relax, lad. You'll mend better an' quicker if you rest. I know this is hard.'

Mick makes a noise that is a reluctant agreement and lies back against the pillow.

'Raff.' He sighs. 'You need to find Raff.'

'Of course,' Dad agrees. 'Your friend in the legal field.'

'Yes, he'll be able to find out where they assigned Olivia.'

He hears rustling sounds, and he suspects Dad is gathering his coat. 'I'll go right away.'

Mick tells him where he can find Raff and Dad leaves, and Mick is left feeling powerless, only able to wait for answers.

***

Olivia
December 1841— Launceston

It is Christmas. A Christmas Olivia was supposed to spend with her new husband and his family. It's these times she feels more the victim than ever. Robbed of things she never had. Some folks probably think she should get over it. But she doesn't want to. If she lets go of this sadness, she might forget Micky all together. She's trying to hang onto whatever fragments she can. It's bad enough that she struggles to remember how his voice sounds when he says her name. When he calls her his songbird. Called her his songbird.

They are in Launceston, performing at the various inns and such. Next week she hears they are performing a show in the Kangaroo Inn, where they currently lodge, every night. But, for today, Mr Stanthorpe has insisted they all attend St John's for church. Olivia's never been to church. Well, she's seen plenty of them from the outside, with their imperious spires, towers, and bells. If she'd had this opportunity even six months ago, she would have declined. God would surely strike her dead.

And a big part of her doesn't want to go today. God has forsaken her. He'd taken Micky away and left her empty and lost. Olivia doesn't understand how a God that supposedly loves and cares about her would do that to her. None of it made sense.

On the other hand, Micky showed her a grace she would never have expected. He believed in a loving God and lived in devotion to that. And if God had anything to do with Micky being the man that he was, she is game enough to see inside the church. Game enough to give it another chance. At the very least, it will help her keep Micky close.

They walk the ten minutes it takes to get from the inn to the church. Although it is quite early, the air is already warm and the sun burning hot. Still, she is happy to be outside for a time. No doubt they shall swelter inside the church. She imagines it will be close and airless.

It surprises Olivia to discover the opposite as they enter the large, towering building. The soaring domed roof means it is rather cool inside. She is both inspired and humbled all at once, even despite her doubts where God is concerned. Everywhere she looks, her eyes encounter arches which draw her vision upward. Windows of stained-glass depicting stories, which she supposes must be from the Bible, creating coloured streaks of light where the sun tries to shine through. Surely this place must be sacred.

In silence, she takes her seat with the others, one row amongst a hundred. So many people are here to worship, all in their nicest gowns and suits. Thank goodness she has Mrs Johnson to help her look presentable in a borrowed dress.

Olivia dares not speak, lest she say something that would offend. How she wishes Micky were here with her. She is sure she could whisper in his ear and he would not censure her for it. She has a thousand questions she would ask him. Like, what stories do the windows tell? She dares not ask Mrs Johnson and convince her she is an ignorant heathen. Although Olivia is exactly that.

Oh, but then …

The most heavenly sound fills the church. It is then Olivia notices the organ, pipes reaching to the roof, music rebounding from every angled surface, surrounding and enveloping her. Some notes sailing high, sweet as a blackbird, and other notes vibrating deep in the earth beneath her feet. Olivia has never heard music so close and so full.

A choir stands to sing. Melodies and harmonies mingle, forming a resonant chorus against the organ's music.

They sing songs of celebration, of the birth of the babe, Jesus, and the joy He brings. How even the angels rejoiced. Of course, Micky has told her about all of this, but she's never heard it in song. Every word and every note entrance her.

Although this is a church, and ordinary townsfolk make up the choir, this music somehow surpasses her memory of Madam Guiditta and her aria. Somehow Olivia feels as though the music draws her heart out from her chest, swelling with the volume of organ pipes and soaring harmonies.

Mrs Johnson must have heard her catch her breath, for she leans close and squeezes her hand. 'You all ri' luvvie?'

Olivia nods emphatically, probably looking like a child tasting candy for the first time. 'Merry Christmas, Mrs Johnson.'

***

Mick

Mick sleeps often. But when he is awake, he vacillates between praying for Olivia, his health, and everything else he can think of, and worrying about Olivia, his health and everything else he can think of. If the nurses could see inside Mick's mind, he is sure they would find it resembles a comedy routine. Or they would lock him in the asylum. Time drags by. An hour feels like a day. A whole day feels like a week. It is intolerable. And yet, he supposes he is learning, albeit grudgingly, to be patient like he never has before. He wishes he didn't need to learn this patience, though. This is all like one very sharp fingernail being drawn across a blackboard that is the breadth of this island on which he lives.

So, he is not sure when it is his father returns. Whether it has been a few hours or a couple of days is a matter of speculation. But Dad returns and his news is not what Mick wants to hear.

'It appears the court delegated Mr Cardamone to transport a prisoner to Launceston.' Dad's voice was flat.

'What do you mean?' Mick sits upright with a rush, his newly born patience wearing thin.

'Well, after the riot, they needed to remove the lass who caused all the trouble.'

Mick grunts and slumps back down. 'Probably Ellen Smith.' Though the events are still foggy, he has no doubts it was she who started the riot.

'How long is he gone?'

'I was told he'll be back in the next couple of days.'

Mick grits his teeth and clenches his fists. 'More waiting.' That powerless feeling is almost overwhelming.

'I tried to ask others for information about Olivia,' Dad clears his throat, 'but let's just say they weren't very forthcoming.' He sounds almost as frustrated as Mick. Almost.

After Dad leaves, promising to return as soon as Raff is back in Hobart, Mick cannot help but wonder where his wife is. Probably out on some farm, no doubt, working hard from dawn till dusk. Didn't she tell them she was married? Didn't she look for him? Could she be that fickle? The Matron suggested as much. Hurt sears through his chest.

No. She loves him. She wouldn't have just deserted him as soon as the first trial came their way. But then, how is she now out on assigned labour if she told them everything? It doesn't make sense. And it doesn't make the pain of betrayal feel any less severe.

Olivia

A week later, they are on a ship heading for the mainland, Sydney in fact. Olivia almost swooned when they told her. For a moment, she wanted to run and hide. How can she leave this place now, knowing her husband rests in a grave somewhere near Hobart Town? How can she desert him? And part of her just wants to go back to St Johns and hear the singing again. Indeed, she was about to ask Mr Stanthorpe for leave to do just that, when he tells her to pack her things for they are heading to the port.

On the other hand, Olivia is also leaving a place that has been a great torment. Van Diemen's Land holds mostly terrible memories, from which she would be glad to escape. She comes around to thinking it might be good to get off this island. New year, new situation, perhaps new life? Olivia grunts to herself. The less she hopes for a good future, the better.

Since visiting the church on Christmas Day, Olivia has found she's lost the taste for the bawdy singing in the inns. What was momentarily a bit of fun, despite her grief, now feels awkward and false. That choir singing in the church—that sounded real. But more than real, it was meaningful. What can she do about it, though? It's not like she has any say in it, is it? She'll just have to force the act, until either Mr Stanthorpe has had enough of her, or she finishes her sentence. And then what?

She stands near the bow, staring at the shifting blue that surrounds them, trying to ignore the way her stomach swirls in response to the movement.

'Nothin' like a bit of fresh sea air, is there?'

She turns her gaze sideways to see Mr Carpenter has joined her. Is there such a thing as too much sea air? Olivia's stomach seems to think so. Instead of saying this, though, she nods. 'Better than bein' cooped up below deck.'

'Aye. Being down in the hold reminds me of the trip from the motherland.'

She glances sideways at him again. Did he come as a convict, too? 'I didn't see much o' the sky on me voyage here neither. How many years did ya serve?'

'Seven. But I've been free for two years now.'

Free. There is that word again. In some ways, Olivia feels freer now than she ever has. But that's just an illusion, isn't it? She really has no say in her life's direction. She is bound to Mr Stanthorpe until her sentence is over. And then what? A few weeks ago, she had a future. Now, it is as though the ground has shifted beneath her, much like this ocean does. She grimaces as her stomach churns again.

'I still got a few months left to serve,' she mumbles, hoping he will move on before she needs to heave over the railing.

'What did ya get sent here for?'

Does she really have to tell everyone who asks? Shame still stalks Olivia every time she thinks about how weak she was, how she allowed her own mother to use her in such a way. She would love nothing more than to move on from that.

'You're lookin' a mite green, luvvie.' Mrs Johnson saves her from having to answer Mr Carpenter.

She turns away from the man to face Mrs Johnson on the other side of her. 'Yeah. I reckon I'm gettin' seasick.'

She offers a compassionate smile. 'Well, ya might think bein' out here is gonna help, but it won't. Better to come inside and lie down with yer eyes closed.'

Olivia allows her to take her elbow and lead her away.

'Excuse me, Mr Carpenter.' Olivia can at least be polite about it, she reckons.

He nods. 'Pardon me, Mrs Reeve. I didn't realise you were unwell.'

As they walk toward the steps that lead below deck, Mrs Johnson whispers in her ear. 'I think he's sweet on ya, luvvie.'

Olivia's stomach heaves again and she groans. She is most certainly not ready for that kind of complication again.

CHAPTER
Twenty-four

Mick

It is another three days before Raff comes. Though Mick has fought against it, his mood has become sullen. He is still confined to his bed most of the time. He still has frequent headaches. Once a day, a nurse leads Mick on a short walk through the ward and back to his bed. They removed the bandages from his eyes yesterday, and though he can open his eyes, he sees only darkness. The doctors cannot tell him if he will ever see again.

Added to the grief over his injuries are his constant worries about Olivia, both about her welfare and about whether she still thinks of him or cares for him. This not-knowing torments him day and night, causing terrifying dreams that are a mixture of broken memories of the riot and his fears for Olivia. Flames and pain. Pain and fire. He cannot escape the whirlwind.

So, it is with great relief he hears Raff's voice greet him, though he is probably less gracious than he ought to be. 'It's about time you showed up,' Mick growls.

Raff is silent, but Dad grunts a warning. 'Michael.' He only needs to say his name in that stern way, and he understands Dad wants him to behave.

Mick slumps back on his pillows. 'Sorry, mate.'

'If grumpiness is the worst you've got to offer, I dare say I shall survive.' Raff is more forgiving than he deserves. The bed shifts as Raff sits near his feet. His father must be sitting in the only chair nearby. 'I would have come sooner, old man, but I have been busy finding out all I can. I didn't want to come to you with empty hands if you catch my meaning.'

Mick cannot help but smile grimly. 'You know me too well.' He would have pumped Raff with a hundred questions and then been frustrated by his ignorance.

'I have much to tell you and you must try to save your questions until I'm done, all right?'

Mick sighs. 'Yes, sir.'

'Before I start, though, how are you faring?'

Mick grimaces at him. 'Isn't it obvious?'

Raff pauses a moment, perhaps choosing his words. 'I can see that you are injured, yes, and I have spoken to the doctor about your prognosis. My question is, how are you coping with all of that?'

'Not well.' Mick swallows, choking up suddenly. How can he put into words the fear he may never see again? The anger towards the women in crime class who caused this, and towards a system that would take his wife away from him. There are no words.

Raff's hand squeezes his shoulder. 'I understand.'

Mick sucks in a deep, shaky breath. 'Can we just move on to the story?'

'You don't remember much, do you?'

He shakes his head. 'A few flashes, but no.'

'It was Ellen Smith who started it all.'

'I knew it.'

'Yes. Seem she's had it in for you for a while, but after her son died, she turned psychotic.' Raff proceeds to tell Mick what happened at the Factory that night. 'Witnesses say Mary Cruikshank and Ann Finnegan tried to drag you out but came under attack from Miss Smith and her cronies themselves.'

'Mary Cruikshank?'

'Aye.'

'Hmph. And Olivia swore she had bad intentions. Are Mary and Ann all right?'

'A few bruises and minor burns, but yes, they are fine. They were released from the infirmary a few days later.'

Mick nods.

Raff clears his throat. 'This is where it becomes difficult.'

'Only now?' More sarcasm.

A half laugh escapes him. 'I guess not.

'Anyway, when they carried you out of the Factory, you were insensible. Blood was gushing from your head wounds. Most assumed you were dead. And that's the message that was passed around.'

He is silent then, as the full meaning of that hangs in the air, slowly making its way into Mick's comprehension. He sucks in a gasp. 'Olivia thinks I'm dead? No, no, no, no.' The urge to race out of this hospital and find her is back with full force. His agitation must be evident as Raff puts a steadying hand on Mick's shin.

Strange. His eyes can't see, but they can still create tears and one slides down his cheek. 'What did they do to her?'

Raff sighs. 'By all accounts, she waited at the inn for your return but was then arrested because she had not paid for the room. She tried to tell them she was married to you, but no-one believed her. She did not wear a ring and could not produce the license. At that point, no-one knew where you were.'

Mick squeezes his eyes shut, regret coursing through him. 'The license was with me. I didn't think to leave it with her.'

'This is not your fault, Mick.'

'So, they locked her up again.'

'She collapsed in court when she heard you were …'

'Oh, my darling girl.' Mick put his hands over his face. What his poor songbird has been through, as though she hasn't had enough hardship in her life already. This was supposed to be the turning point for her. This was supposed to be their happiness.

'They put her in Class Two, but a couple of days later, they assigned her.'

'To whom?'

Another long pause. 'Do you remember that gent we consoled in the pub that night?'

Mick scans his memory, which is still foggy in many areas, but he has a hazy recollection of this. 'The entertainer. The one who'd lost his wife.'

'Mr Trevor Stanthorpe, that's him. Well, he—'

'No. Do not tell me he has taken Olivia on tour with him.'

Raff lets out a frustrated sigh. 'I'm sorry Mick, but yes.'

'Where are they now? How do we get her back? We must go after her.' Mick is ready to jump out of bed this instant.

Raff's hand presses on his leg again. 'Hold on, Mick. Take a breath.'

'What do you mean, take a breath? She's my wife.'

'Settle down lad and listen.' This is the first time Dad has spoken all this time.

Mick clenches and unclenches his fists. Why should he calm down? He just wants to be with Olivia. This is all wrong. But they will not budge, will they? He lets out a begrudging breath. 'Fine.'

'First of all,' Raff says, all businesslike, 'Olivia is safe. We can rest in the knowledge she is with a decent master. And probably doing work she enjoys. It's not all bad, Mick.'

As much as he wants to rail against it, Raff is right. Mick nods his reluctant agreement. 'All right. So, what's the plan, then?'

***

Olivia
January 1842

Olivia has not cried herself to sleep since Christmas Day. Although she is still very sad about Micky, and she cries often, it is not the same feeling of despair she had before. Granted, she has been in the dumps on the ferry ride to the mainland, but constant seasickness caused that. Arriving in Darling Harbour after two weeks at sea, she is excited to see a bustling and thriving city. She is also relieved to be done with the swaying vessel.

'This is where the first settlers an' convicts came,' Mrs Johnson tells Olivia. 'Sydney is a decent city. Still a long ways from Old England, though.'

They disembark and walk west along the quay while Mr Stanthorpe and the other men take care of all their luggage. Olivia's legs feel unsteady and she wobbles.

Mrs Johnson takes her arm. 'You'll get yer land legs back soon, luvvie.'

'Aye, an' me stomach better settle down too.'

She pats Olivia on the arm with her other hand. 'She'll be ri'.'

They pass a throng of people, loading and unloading vessels, horses and carts by the dozen. There are men and women selling fresh fruit from wicker barrows, at which Mrs Johnson must stop and buy them both a banana. Olivia can't remember if she's ever eaten the crooked yellow fruit, but it is sweet and it seems to still her stomach for the moment. It's a darn sight better than the stuff they call food at the Factory, anyway.

The two women continue west along Argyle Street, passing the customs house and what looks like a fort on a hill to their left. Mrs Johnson says it's now a signal staff. Olivia takes it all in with few words. She's too busy trying to keep herself from falling over.

They've walked for about a quarter of an hour when they arrive at the Lord Nelson Hotel, a three storey, sandstone building which stands out from those surrounding it. Within minutes, the menfolk arrive with a horse and dray carting their belongings.

'This will be our home for the next month,' Mr Stanthorpe informs them. 'I daresay it will be where we perform most nights, too.' He is clearly yet to arrange the details of this, but seems hopeful.

''Ave ya done shows here afore, have ya?' Olivia asks Mrs Johnson in a side whisper.

'Yeah. He'll probably get us doin' shows at the Wool Packers out in Paramatta, too. They's both popular spots.'

When they are settled in their rooms, and again Mr Stanthorpe has placed Olivia with the Johnsons, Mrs Johnson rubs her hands together, apparently excited about something.

'Now that we're gonna be in the same place for a bit, it's time we got ya some new clothes sorted.' The older woman grins. So far, Olivia's worn the late Mrs Stanthorpe's dresses, taken in somewhat. And Mr Stanthorpe has never been too happy about it. Imagine seeing someone else in your dead partner's clothes. Olivia knew she couldn't have coped with another wearing Micky's shirts, or especially his fob. So, she was eager to have a dress of her own, but how could she?

'But I don't got … ' she argues. She is yet to receive more than a few pennies and, as assigned labour, that's more than she expected.

'Don't ya worry about any o' that. Mr Johnson's sister is clever with the needle an' such. She'll put somethin' together for ya.'

Out of the blue, tears well up in Olivia's eyes, much as she tries to stop them.

'What's wrong, luvvie?' Mrs Johnson frowns.

Olivia swallows and shrugs. She is still not used to her emotions running away with her. 'I don't see why yer bein' so nice to me.'

'Listen. I dunno, but what ya could have been me own sweet babe. I never was blessed with children.'

Olivia drew her brows together. 'Yer not that much older than me.'

Mrs Johnson shrugs. 'That don't matter none. Besides, it's good to have some female company, that it is. Not that Mrs Stanthorpe weren't amiable or nothin', but it weren't the same.'

Mrs Johnson was offering friendship. Olivia needed to swallow again. How many friends had she had in her life? The lady back at Newgate might have been, but they were on opposite sides of prison bars. Ann was certainly someone she'd relied on in the Factory, but Olivia never really trusted her enough. Same with Nancy. Then there was Micky, who still made her heart leap when she thought of him. He worked hard to gain her acceptance, and so far, he'd been the best friend she'd ever had. What if Olivia let Mrs Johnson get close? Would she die, too? At the very least, they would be separated when her sentence was over. She took a deep breath. It probably wasn't worth it. It was better to keep Mrs Johnson at a distance.

'Well, thanks. I'll be sure to pay ya back as soon as I get me own income.' And she would, too. Olivia would not be indebted.

'Don't be silly now,' Mrs Johnson waved her sentiments off like they were flies.

And so, the next morning, while Mr Stanthorpe is securing dates for their shows, Mr and Mrs Johnson take Olivia to his sister's home and have her measured for a new dress or two. One particularly for when she performs and another for general day wear.

Once again, Olivia finds their kindness overwhelming and feels like she wants to cry. Annoyed at herself, she becomes curt when they speak to her.

'Is everything all right?' Mrs Gallagher—that's Mr Johnson's sister—asks.

Even more annoyed, Olivia nods. Why is it she cannot put on her grand smile anymore? Why has it become so hard to bluff everyone?

'Do you not like the fabric?' Mrs Johnson asks.

'Any fabric is better'n serge.'

'Is it the colour?' Mrs Gallagher asks.

'The colour is perfect. Me favourite colour actually,' Olivia states matter-of-factly. And it is, too. She's always loved pink ever since she was a little girl. Not that she's ever worn a pink dress, let alone one made of shot silk. It is too much. Even the day dress is a lovely soft green cotton. That alone would have been more than enough.

And the thought hits her that Micky will never see her in these gowns. Never see how pretty she might look when not in prison clothes with her hair in a boring braid under a mobcap. The grief wells up in her again and she bites down on her lip.

'Something's wrong though, ain't it, luvvie? Yer lookin' a mite pale. Did ya eat breakfast this mornin'?'

Olivia shakes her head, desperately trying to keep the wave of emotion back. 'I'm still feelin' seasick.'

It's the truth. When she looked at the fried eggs and toasted bread put before her this morning, she almost threw up just from the smell.

Mrs Johnson looks at her strangely. 'That should have passed by now.' She presses the back of her hand to Olivia's brow. 'No fever.'

'I'll be fine. We just got off the boat yesterday. I'm just takin' longer to recover.' Olivia shrugs. But at least this argument has pushed thoughts of Micky out of her mind.

The two women look at each other, and an odd expression passes between them.

'What? If yer really concerned, give me a piece of bread an' I'll eat it. I ain't dyin' or anythin'.' Olivia tries to reassure them.

209

Mrs Johnson's lips twitch, like she's amused at Olivia's obstinance. She looks toward the door, craning her neck to look through to the other room, which is apparently empty. Then she asks Olivia a few very personal questions.

Confused at first, but becoming alarmed, Olivia answers her as best she can.

With a deep breath, Mrs Johnson eyes her intently. 'Olivia, luvvie, I think yer with child.'

CHAPTER
Twenty-Five

Olivia
Sydney – January 1842

A baby? She can't have a baby! How is it even possible? Olivia paces back and forth in her room, where Mr and Mrs Johnson have given her space to try to come to terms with this news. Of course, it's possible—Mrs Johnson explained the fundamentals. But she and Micky had been together only a few days. A few too brief, too lovely, too heart-breaking, days.

She presses her hands to her stomach. There is a life inside her. Micky's baby. Micky's son or daughter. Olivia can't decide yet if this is a blessing or a curse. How is she to provide for a baby? How is she to raise it on her own?

Olivia burst into tears when Mrs Johnson revealed the reason for her sickness and emotional fragility. They were quick to suggest Olivia could give the baby away, but there is no question of that in Olivia's mind. This is Micky's child. She will die before being separated from it. But the problem remains—what to do now?

She has asked Mr and Mrs Johnson not to tell this news to Mr Stanthorpe or any of the others yet, which they promised they will honour. Olivia needs to figure out what she is going to do first.

Her sentence will be over in a few months, perhaps before it is even obvious she is pregnant. Perhaps she can keep it a secret until then.

Her sentence will be over.

The heaviness of this truth hits her. No provision of food and clothing, as poor as it is, from the prison system or even from Mr Stanthorpe. Unless he wants her to stay on as an employed performer. In prison, they would look after her baby. They would separate her from the child, certainly, but it would still be fed and clothed. Outside of prison, what seems like an unlikely source of security will be gone.

Olivia reminds herself of the number of babies who died at the Factory. How would that ever be a better option? But did her baby stand a better chance outside the walls? She has no answer for that.

Panic threatens to rise in Olivia, and she scratches at her arms. She needs to find a solution. Should she talk to Mr Stanthorpe about the future? Will he want her to stay on? But does she even want to continue to sing in pubs filled with sometimes vulgar men and women? Does she even have a choice?

See, even in supposed freedom, she doesn't have a choice. Necessity forces her hand in order to survive. Freedom is a pipe dream.

Olivia remembers that Mr Carpenter has shown interest. He makes a point of speaking to her often. So far, she has hardly given him the time of day. Could she marry another for the sake of her baby and its welfare? Would he even offer for her? She certainly doesn't have any affection for him. Not in the slightest. But what if he's the only one who would stoop low enough to wed her? It's not as though she has time to wait for another, someone like Micky. She almost laughs to herself. There will never be another Micky. And just like that, grief overwhelms her again.

Why did he have to die? Why did he have to leave her alone with all these decisions? What would he tell her to do? She tries to remember his voice, his encouragement, his tenderness. But his voice has already faded. His face has become blurry in her memory. She's not ready to let go of him. She doubts she ever will. And this baby will make certain of that. Olivia hopes the little one looks just like him. This baby must be raised to be like Micky, as good and wholesome as Micky. And that won't happen singing in hotels.

Olivia knows what she needs to do.

That evening, as the troupe sits around a table while Mr Stanthorpe tells them of their schedule, a plan forms in Olivia's mind. And later, while she sings ribald lyrics, and moves her body in what would only be called a vulgar way, her plan becomes a determination.

This kind of singing makes her feel no better than a prostitute. She deserves every sling of the word 'whore' that is thrown at her. Even though it's all part of the act, this is not what she wants for her baby. Not ever.

After the show, she sidles up to Mr Carpenter, who has gone to fetch a pint of ale from the bar. 'The customers seem happy tonight,' she comments.

He turns to her, and there is no mistaking the light in his eyes. 'Aye. Can I get you a drink?'

'Just water for me.' She needs to keep her wits about her, not that something stronger wouldn't help her courage. She already needs to swallow down the guilt for what she is about to do. 'How long ya been playin' the accordion?'

'Since I was a little one. My dad taught me.' He hands her the cup of water.

'Did ya ever wanna do anythin' else?'

He laughs self-consciously. 'I started working in finance, but that's how I ended up here.' He pauses to chug some of his ale. 'Fraud. So, when I got out, I figured no-one would trust me in that field. And even if they did, I don't know if I trust myself.' He laughs again. 'What about you?'

'Yeah, I wanted to sing since I were a girl. Never imagined anythin' else, really. Course, I'm plenty good at all them domestic chores. Grew up with 'em. Done 'em on assignment too.'

Memories trail through her mind. Mama, the different landowners she worked for, prison. The one person she would have liked to set up home with and happily done domestic work for is gone. She holds her breath for a minute. This is not the time.

'So, I see just you an' me is goin' to Paramatta with Mr Stanthorpe next week.' The Redcoats Mess House is a feeding place for the military men. Seems they need some entertainment. Particularly, Olivia's been told, they want a saucy woman to sing for them. So Mr Stanthorpe will take her and the accordion player to make them happy.

Olivia scratches her arm. She is shaking. Can she trust this man? Will his interest make him blind enough to her purpose? *Come on, Olivia!* It's not like she's never pretended to flirt before, or lied, or cheated, or anything else that helped her survive. Why is she so hesitant now? Then again, why would she embroil this man in her problems?

Mr Carpenter's eyes light again. 'Yes, I'm looking forward to it. Might give us a chance to get to know each other better.' Question mingled with hope spreads over his face.

'That'd be nice.' Olivia swallows her guilt yet again, but then blurts out everything. 'Truth is. I don't think I can do this anymore. I need to get away. Would you … would ya take me … away from here?'

Now he looks alarmed and glances all around them like he's worried someone overheard. He grabs her by the elbow and leads her outside, where it's quiet.

'What on earth are you thinkin'?' he hisses.

Olivia summons tears. It's not that hard these days. 'I can't keep performin' like this.'

'So you want me to run away with you?'

She blinks at him. 'I thought ya liked me.'

He presses his lips together and runs a hand through his hair. 'You're not wrong. But running away? Olivia, you only have a few months left. I can wait. Can't you wait, too? Then we can be together, and I'll take you anywhere you want to go.'

'I don't think I'll survive a few more months.' Olivia draws away from him with a petulant look. 'Never mind. Sorry I asked. I'll do it on my own.' She goes to walk away.

'Wait.' His hand is on her arm. She turns back to him, wiping at her semi-fake tears.

'What if you get caught? You know they'll throw you back in gaol, don't you?'

'It's a risk I'm willin' to take. Ya could protect me, of course.' Olivia feels bad using these tactics, but she is desperate.

Mr Carpenter's face is stoic. 'Well, it's not one I'm willing to take. That's not what I'd want for you.'

'So yer answer's no, then?'

'My answer's no.' He looks sad, but determined.

Probably not as determined as Olivia, though. She moves in close so they're almost touching face to face. 'Do me a favour, then? When we're at the Mess House, make sure Mr Stanthorpe drinks too much.'

He looks a little helpless as he grasps both of her arms, and his voice is shaky. 'Please don't do this.' Then he brushes her tears from her cheeks with a thumb. 'But how can I refuse you. I will come and find you.' He presses his lips to hers for a long moment, whilst Olivia remains as still as a statue.

***

Mick
January 1842—Launceston

Mick doesn't think he's ever been so ill tempered in his life. These weeks of recovery have dragged on in ever-increasing frustration. Wondering every moment how Olivia is doing, considering she believes he's dead, wondering where she is, wondering if Stanthorpe treats her well. It has been a test to his patience beyond anything he's ever known. And then there was the vexation of his body not healing overnight. Days passed before his head stopped thumping. Weeks passed before he could breathe without stabbing pain. And a month passed before there was any hope he would ever see again. Without Dad and Raff, he thinks he would be nigh crazy by now.

But they took turns sitting by him in the hospital, talked him down whenever it became too much, prayed with him, consoled him, and even chastised him when he was out of line. When Mick was well enough to leave the hospital, they still refused to allow him to go after Olivia, claiming he needed further recuperation before he could travel. He supposes they were right. The journey to Launceston is long and bumpy. So, then it was Mum who tended to him at home, keeping a strict watch over all he did. His sweet mum bore with much sullenness and testiness in those weeks. He has much to atone for.

Of course, being blind makes everything that much worse. He's had to be led by the hand everywhere he goes. To think he might never see Olivia's beautiful face again was a crushing blow. To think he would stumble in darkness all his life made him want to throw things. And for a time, he teetered on the brink of despair. And then one day, the darkness became shadows. Mick saw light, granted it was grey light, but it meant hope and it meant a better future. Thank God for his grace.

Now, though, Mick can see blurry images around him, and every day there is a little more. And finally, his family has allowed him to travel. They have arrived in Launceston—Dad, Raff and Mick—and finally, *finally*, his bride and he will be reunited. They just need to find out where Stanthorpe is housing her. The anticipation is killing him.

Raff makes enquiries at every inn they come to and has done so ever since they left Hobart. So, they know the troupe went to the Black Snake Inn. They stayed in Jericho, Ross, and Cressy, and all reports told them they travelled to Launceston. There are many pubs in Launceston, so despite Mick's impatience, it may take a while to locate them.

'Anything?' Mick asks Raff when he returns to the buggy after one of these enquiries.

'Nah, mate,' is his dispassionate answer.

Dad flicks the reins and clicks his tongue to make the horses move. He is up front, driving, whilst Mick and Raff sit in the back. On to the next hotel then. They have been at this all morning and learnt nothing.

'They must be somewhere.' Mick's impatience leaks out again.

'Yes, and we'll keep looking until we find them,' Raff reminds him. 'It's just a matter of time, Mick. Hold on.'

Their own patience must wear thin. Mick is like a child who continually asks their parent 'are we there yet?' He apologises again. He has lost count of how many times he needs to say sorry.

Raff slaps him on the shoulder. 'It's all right. We understand.'

'Hmph.' That's about all Mick has to say.

'Do you know, I reckon I want to find her just as much as you do …'

'Not a chance.'

'… because then you will finally shut up.'

Mick can hear the laughter in Raff's voice, and he punches him in the arm, chuckling. 'Point taken.'

Dad pulls up outside another inn and Raff jumps out.

'How ya doin' back there, lad?' Dad asks.

'I think I'll be glad of a walk and a stretch soon.' Mick still gets sore, cramped up in the buggy for hours on end.

'Well, it's gettin' close to dinnertime. After this one, shall we get some food and then go down to the river for a walk?'

'Sounds good,' Mick says, although he's annoyed by the fact this will slow them down.

When Raff climbs back in the carriage, Mick can tell something is different, even though he can't make out any facial expression. Perhaps his movements are lighter.

'What is it?' Mick is eager to hear.

'They were here,' Raff says, and his voice sounds excited. 'At least, they performed here.'

Mick's heart almost bursts with the knowledge they are getting close. 'So, do they know where Stanthorpe has the troupe?'

'Aye. Innkeeper says they are at the Kangaroo Inn on Wellington Street.'

Mick nearly jumps out of his skin. They are so close. 'Can we skip dinner, Dad?' His voice sounds just as desperate as he feels.

'Heading to the Kangaroo Inn, now, Mick,' Dad answers as he nudges the horses away from the curb.

It feels like Dad's driving slower than ever these few blocks. Mick doesn't reckon they can get there quick enough. It takes everything he has to bite his tongue and not tell him to hurry up. He drums his fingers incessantly on the edge of the buggy. *Not long now, my darling Olivia.* Not long now.

The seconds drag by like they are hours, and the minutes like days. But it is only minutes till they get there.

'What if they're out performing?' Mick doesn't think he can cope waiting any longer or searching any further.

Raff puts a steadying hand on his shoulder.

'Breathe Mick.'

Mick is sure he's laughing at him. Raff's lucky he can't tell if there's a smirk on his face, or he might feel obliged to cuff him. He's probably going to cuff somebody if he can't find Olivia.

Dad has barely stopped the buggy before Mick tries to get out, which would probably have ended with him face-planting the cobblestones. But Dad's jumped down just as quick to assist him. Mick still can't judge the distance of the ground. But there is nothing in him that wants to be cautious right now.

Dad grabs his elbow and tells him when to step up or around, and they enter the inn without mishap. Raff was in before them and is already asking about Stanthorpe and the troupe.

'They was here, but they ain't no more. Mr Hinshaw,' the maid, Mick guesses, calls over her shoulder. 'These folks is askin' about them entertainers what was here.'

Mick's brain has stalled on the words 'ain't no more'. She's not here? *She's not here?* He can't believe it.

'What do you mean, they're not here?' He blurts. 'Where's Olivia Reeve?'

A man strides toward them from the other end of the bar, flinging a towel over his shoulder. 'The small, blond lass? She's a ri' sauce-box, that one. Nah, they've gone to Sydney.'

Sauce-box? Wait, Sydney? *Sauce-box?* 'What did you just call her?' Mick curls his hand into a fist and lunges.

CHAPTER
Twenty-Six

Olivia
January 1842—Paramatta

Olivia's plan is in play. She has sung those bawdy songs for hours tonight. Longer than usual. But she wants to keep Mr Stanthorpe drinking and Mr Carpenter has provided him with a continual supply. She reckons Mr Stanthorpe will pass out soon. So, she watches him while she sings, making sure her smile is bright, her laugh engaging, make them all think she loves doing this. She can feel her voice tiring though, so she hopes he drops in the next five minutes.

The good thing about putting her plan into action tonight is that the rest of the troupe is back at the Lord Nelson doing a show. So, it's just the three of them at the Redcoats Mess. Tonight, she will do it. She will escape and finally be free.

Her thoughts travel to the babe inside her. It must be tonight. She needs for him or her to have a life away from this degrading path. It needs to grow up in safety, surrounded by love, even if it's only Olivia to give it. Micky is gone, so she has no choice. Unless Mr Carpenter follows her after all.

Mr Stanthorpe keeps his stash of notes and coins in his spare shoes. She's seen him put it there one day when he didn't know she saw. Good thing, that. It helped her form her plans. As soon as he conks out, she'll get the cash and leave. She already has her few things packed in a bag. It's just a waiting game now. She only hopes Mr Carpenter doesn't try to stop her again.

Olivia growls out the words of the song with a vulgar wink at the nearest bleary eyed lad and puts her hands on her hips with a suggestive movement. The boys love it. They also love that the cut of her dress is so low it hardly holds her in. Many a time, they try to press a note in her cleavage. Extra money for her cause, for the future of her babe.

And then it happens. Mr Trevor's eyes roll and his head dips, and the next thing, he's out on the table, mouth hanging open, senseless. She pretends she didn't notice and winds up the song to much stomping, clapping, and ribald remarks. She offers a deep curtsy, to which they oblige her with more of the same cheer. Then she presses her forearm to her head.

'Oh lordy,' she says, blowing out her breath. 'I'm done in, lads. Time for me to retire. Come again tomorra, an' I'll sing you a merry tune.'

More cheers and whistles follow.

Getting to the stairs proves to be difficult. More than one fellow invites her to his room, or even out to the gardens, as if she doesn't know what that means. Olivia knows she can keep herself safe if she must. But thankfully Mr Carpenter is there to lend a hand.

One bloke grabs her by her braid, twisting it around his wrist. A curse on her ever-growing long hair. She smiles at him sweetly. 'Please unhand me, sir. Ya wouldn't want to hurt a tiny lass like me, would ya?' She pouts for effect. He seems to buy it and loosens his grip just enough for her to pull free and make her escape, just as Mr Carpenter gets to her side.

Out of the corner of her eyes, she notices Mr Stanthorpe stir. He can't wake up yet!

Another gent lunges for Olivia, staggering drunk by the looks of him. She sticks her foot out, catching his ankle, tripping him. He scrambles to his feet, his face burnt red, and goes for Mr Carpenter's throat. Olivia stumbles back a little, wearing an 'oh, my' expression, like she's shocked or scared. But this is just what she needs, even though she feels bad for Mr Carpenter. But he'll escape the drunkard soon enough.

The intoxicated fools all start aiming punches at each other. Soon enough, one fella falls on Mr Stanthorpe, knocking him right to the ground. Now's her chance to escape. She races up the stairs, with her skirts hitched almost to her knees. Checking both ways down the hallway, she opens the door to the men's bedroom and goes hunting for Mr Stanthorpe's shoes. It only takes a moment, and she has the purse in her hand. Her heart races. This is it. She slips into the room allocated to her and collects her small bag of belongings.

As she turns to flee, she glimpses her reflection in the mirror. That waif of a girl. Pretty, maybe, but fettered. Always chained. But hadn't God promised freedom? Hadn't the penal system promised freedom? It is only a few months away, they say.

If she runs now, chances are the authorities will catch her. And then what? Back to the Factory? Or another female prison? With additional charges and a new sentence. Does she really want to do that?

Olivia lays a hand flat on her belly. Does she really want to do this to her child? She's seen what happens to children of prisoners. They are separated, and the mothers sent off to assignment, while they keep the children at the prison. Though she hates to admit it; she doesn't want that. She can't imagine being torn away from this babe, even though she hasn't even met him. And her child would have little chance of survival in a prison nursery. She's seen one woman after another grieving over a dead infant.

Olivia sinks into the chair at the dresser. But this is all she knows. This running and returning to prison. She's never felt real freedom. Never believed she can have it. But supposed real freedom is only weeks away. A terrifying thought. What will she do with real freedom? When she has nothing to run from. When she must make choices about her future. This free future is more frightening than the thought of returning to prison. Why is that? It doesn't make sense.

But Micky said God promises freedom and future hope. Dare she trust in what he says? Dare she believe? Dare she hope? The thought makes her heart race even more than the anticipation of running away. The thought of hope lodges in her throat, hitches in her breath. Why is it so scary to hope?

Because allowing herself to hope opens herself to disappointment, pain, heartache—again. It's a risk, a risk of the soul.

All of a sudden, she can't breathe. She gasps, cries, bangs her fists on the dresser. She wants so much to let hope in, to dream again. To be truly free. She wants it more than she thought possible. And she knows she can't have it by running away. *I want freedom. Proper freedom.*

A gentle tap sounds on the door, which she'd left wide open. Quickly wiping her eyes, she turns to see it's Mr Carpenter. He scans the room, his eyes resting on her small bag of belongings. He opens his mouth to speak, but Olivia puts up a hand to silence him.

'Don't bother tryin' to convince me to stay. I've already changed me mind.'

He stands there, complete relief washing over his face. 'So, you're not running?'

'I'm not running.'

'Do you want to talk?'

Olivia raises her eyes to his. Now what will she do? She's led him to believe she might be interested. And maybe she will be several months down the track. But right now?

'I think I'd like to sleep. I'm tired.' She gathers her bag and fishes around in it for the purse of coins. 'Can you put this back in Mr Stanthorpe's spare shoes for me? Before he notices it's gone.' She places the purse in his hands, and he catches her fingers briefly.

'Thank you.' His smile is genuine and filled with hope.

Olivia takes a deep breath. 'No promises, Mr Carpenter.' There, she doesn't want him to hope too much. And she'll have to give him an explanation at some point. But right now, she is too weary.

When she finally slips under the covers, she cries for a long while, but a peace settles over her. This is the right decision. She will stay and see through her sentence. She will wait for her pardon to come. And when Mr Stanthorpe finally goes to his room, he will be none the wiser about what almost happened tonight.

***

On returning to Sydney, Olivia asks Mr Stanthorpe for leave to attend church on Sunday with the Johnsons, who seem to go regularly.

'As long as you're back in time for the evening show, you may do as you wish.' He shrugs.

She is not used to an overseer who is so flexible, not since one of the first landowners they assigned her to. That one gave all the convict labourers the sabbath to themselves. Not that they could go anywhere being out in the country, but they could sleep in and do as little as they wished. Thinking back now, Olivia should have stayed there, never should have started running and mucking up.

To be permitted to leave the hotel and walk around the city, that is something unexpected. Olivia feels a twinge of guilt, remembering how close she came to running away. She doesn't understand why Mr Stanthorpe would trust her to return.

'Thanks, sir.' Olivia bobs him a curtsy. Can't let him think she's ungrateful.

Going to church feels like it's the only way she can be close to Micky again. And right now, she wishes more than anything he was here to give her some guidance. She will see out her sentence, yes, but she is still unsure of the way forward after that.

The walk is only about ten minutes from the hotel, and she strolls along beside the Johnsons as they head straight down Kent St, past the military hospital and then head left till they reach St Phillips. They can't mistake the embattled church tower that looms over them, which is where they enter. There is a seating gallery at each end of the church, where scholars and soldiers sit. Wooden columns prop up the galleries. The pulpit is about halfway down the length of the building and the Johnsons head for the pews in front of that, although toward the back of the main seating area.

Olivia searches for the organ and finally spies it in one of the galleries. A woman sits at it ready to play and Olivia can't wait to hear church music again.

When finally they start, she is not disappointed. The building reverberates with the sound of the pipes and it immediately transports Olivia, just as it did in Van Diemen's Land on Christmas Day.

And more than that, the words the choir sings captivate her.

Just as I am, without one plea,
But that Thy blood was shed for me,
And that Thou bidst me come to Thee,
O Lamb of God, I come, I come.

Just as I am, and waiting not
To rid my soul of one dark blot,
To Thee whose blood can cleanse each spot,
O Lamb of God, I come, I come.

It is as though they sing about her. Tears spring to her eyes and her chest heaves. A hand slips into hers and she glances sideways to see Mrs Johnson's eyes are also moist as she squeezes Olivia's fingers. Does she understand? Does she have any idea of Olivia's turmoil of these last weeks?

Just as I am, though tossed about
With many a conflict, many a doubt,
Fightings and fears within, without,
O Lamb of God, I come, I come.

Just as I am, poor, wretched, blind;
Sight, riches, healing of the mind,
Yea, all I need in Thee to find,
O Lamb of God, I come, I come.

The beauty of this moment is almost painful. It is bigger than any of the moments she shared with Micky. But if not for Micky, she would not have recognised it. These lyrics the choir sing are Olivia's. As if she penned them herself. Something in her agrees with every line, every weighty word.

Just as I am, Thou wilt receive,
Wilt welcome, pardon, cleanse, relieve;
Because Thy promise I believe,

O Lamb of God, I come, I come.

Just as I am, Thy love unknown
Hath broken every barrier down;
Now, to be Thine, yea, Thine alone,
O Lamb of God, I come, I come.

Yes, Lamb of God, I come. I come. By now Olivia weeps to the extent that Mrs Johnson leads her outside to a bench near the church. Olivia figures she must be a disruption to those around her. Right now, there's not a part of her that cares what anyone thinks. Something is happening within her. Like she sheds years of hardship. The weight, the burdens, slipping away. She feels light. Like she could soar above the bell tower of St Phillips and dance in the breeze. Her sobs slowly change until she realises she now laughs.

Mrs Johnson, who sat with her arms around her the whole time, pulls back and stares at Olivia, her face full of question. Perhaps Mrs Johnson thinks she has lost the last remnant of her sanity. That thought makes her laugh even more. She shakes her head.

'What … ?' Mrs Johnson doesn't seem to know what to ask.

Olivia swallows back her giggles and pulls a handkerchief from her sleeve. She needs to dry her face and blow her nose. Then she looks Mrs Johnson in the eyes and smiles. 'I think I understand what Micky was tellin' me all along.'

Olivia has no idea what the rest of the service is like after they go inside again, what the reverend spoke about and such. Her mind spins with discovery, understanding and even the birth of new plans. *Thank you, Micky. Thank you, God,* she whispers under her breath.

After church, she convinces the Johnsons to take a walk to Miller's Point so she can stroll and continue to ponder on all that happened in her heart. Mrs Johnson asks her husband to stop by the hotel and collect a picnic basket for them. Olivia claps her hands in delight. The last, and only, picnic she ever had was her wedding day, which brings both happy memories and wistful yearnings together. How she would love to share another picnic with Micky.

The two women continue to Miller's Point where they stand and look across the bay in contented silence for a while.

'How are you feeling about your babe, luvvie?' Mrs Johnson eventually asks.

'I'm both excited an' a little scared if I'm honest. For now, all is well, but I've some decisions to make.'

'After you finish your sentence, you mean?'

'Yeah.'

'You're a wonderful talent. I'm sure Mr Stanthorpe will keep you on.'

'Maybe.' Olivia doesn't want to admit to her dislike of singing in the hotels, well their style of singing anyway. 'What would he be likely to pay?'

'Probably about twenty pounds per year plus most of your food and lodging.'

Olivia raises her eyebrows. That doesn't sound too bad, but again, she wasn't sure she wanted to continue with the troupe.

Voices behind them make them turn to see Mr Johnson, along with Mr Carpenter, Mr Frith, and Mr Brown, who all carry baskets of food.

'We thought we'd join you for the picnic,' the latter announces as they near.

'It's perfect weather for it,' adds Mr Frith.

Indeed, it is mild enough for a summer's day, so as not to make one feel like they are melting. Mr Johnson spreads out a blanket and begins to unload the baskets. They all sit on the grass and enjoy bread with slices of ham and cheese, fresh fruit and even jugs of lemon water.

As soon as she is finished eating, Olivia excuses herself to stroll along the seaside again. Almost immediately, she is joined by Mr Carpenter.

'You seem very tranquil today, Mrs Reeve.'

Olivia smiles. She feels tranquil. Probably the first time in she can't remember how long since she hasn't been agitated, anxious, or angry about something. 'It's a good day, Mr Carpenter.'

'Please call me Fred.'

She glances sideways at him. 'Very well, Fred.'

He walks with his hands behind his back, and he looks serious, like he doesn't know what to say.

Olivia keeps walking and waits, and he eventually speaks in a hesitant fashion.

'Last week, after … '

'After the Mess House?' Olivia has a good idea where this is headed. She doesn't really want to deal with it, but it must be done. She takes a deep breath.

'Yes,' he nods, brows furrowed. 'I'm … I'm not sure where things stand with … with you and me.'

It's a fair question. She did make him think there was hope and then gave him no guarantees. He deserves the truth. Olivia stops and sits in the grass overlooking the water, waving Fred to join her.

She turns her head to face him. 'I'm sorry, I weren't actin' the best for the last couple weeks. The truth is, I just found out I'm carryin' me late husband's child. I went a bit crazy-like.'

She lets the words sink in, watching the surprise on his face turn to—not disappointment or regret, or even distaste as she expected—but to understanding. He's not about to let her off the hook that easy.

'The truth is, I'm still grievin' Micky. I still think of him most o' the time. I'm not sure if I'll ever be ready to marry again.'

There, she gave him the truth. She won't blame him if he gives her a dressing down now. She deserves it. But he doesn't deserve her to keep leading him on.

Fred pulls up a blade of grass and fiddles with it in his fingers for a few moments whilst he digests her words. Eventually he looks at her again.

'Look, I'm not going to pretend your actions didn't trouble me, nor that your news hasn't jolted me, but I still think we could have a future together.' He reaches over and entwines her fingers in his. 'It's only been a couple months since your husband passed, give it some time. I am willing to wait, and I am willing to support you and your child. Perhaps, in time, you might even learn to care for me.'

Olivia doesn't know what to say. He is clearly aware that her affections still lie with Micky, and yet he's not ready to give up on her. She could do a lot worse than this kind of man, even if he never compares to Micky. All she can do is nod agreement to him.

'And in the meantime, will you allow me to pay special attention to you, Olivia?' He brushes his thumb over her fingers.

'All ri' then.'

CHAPTER
Twenty-Seven

Olivia
February 1842

'Your idea has some merit.' Mr Stanthorpe rubs his chin and Olivia can see the idea of success turning into wealth in his eyes. 'I would have to hire a piano player, of course, perhaps a violinist, and find better gowns, but they would pay themselves off quickly. Especially if we can get you before the wealthier members of society.'

Olivia grins. She has just suggested that Mr Stanthorpe allow her to sing more palatable parlour songs in folks' drawing rooms and maybe meeting halls. Rather than complain about the current music she is being made to offer, she came up with a better option. It will mean the difference between staying and enjoying the work after her sentence is complete, or leaving the troupe, thus providing an insecure future. The idea came to her after seeing an advertisement in Mr Johnson's newspaper for a similar event.

'I'm gonna need someone to teach me them songs, though,' she confesses. 'Remember, I didn't know any songs when ya first picked me up. But I learnt fast, didn't I? I can do so again.'

'Yes, and I daresay you will sing them very well. Better than most.' Mr Stanthorpe is excited, she can tell. Micky always said she sang like an angel, but Olivia always thought he was biased. Did she really have the kind of talent she's only dreamt about? All she knows is she loves to sing.

'I'll start making enquiries at once and we'll get some rehearsals going during the next few weeks. But until then, I'll need you to continue with our current shows. Understood?'

'Yes, sir,' Olivia nods, trying not to look as excited as he does.

'And until I find someone to replace you in this troupe as well.'

'Fair enough.' She isn't about to refuse him when it means his income as well as hers.

He walks away, rubbing his hands together, mumbling something about stars. Olivia shrugs. She never expected that meeting to go quite as well as it did. But she is grateful, nonetheless. She never thought she'd be able to look to the future with hope again since Micky passed, but although his loss still pains her, she can see definite possibilities ahead of her. Peace rests in her soul, like nothing she can understand. It can only be that which Micky told her of, that the Lord was indeed with her, despite setbacks and heartaches.

Olivia hums to herself, and words form in her mind. A new song. A very different song from those she made up in prison. And she smiles as phrases come together and she lifts her voice, her heart soaring with every note. This, *this* is what she loves to do.

That evening, she takes her place on the stage in the Lord Nelson and puts on her usual act, singing the songs that have become so distasteful to her. Her performance elicits whistles and hoots from the mostly male audience, responses that she is familiar with now. Not that she appreciates that kind of attention anymore. Once perhaps. But not now. Now, she would be happy enough with a simple clap and cheer.

She must ask Mr Stanthorpe and Fred to keep the fellows away from her after the show, as their advances are sometimes intimidating, distasteful, or downright alarming. But for now, she is safe on the stage, which is more like a temporary platform, with the three musicians behind her.

'This one's for all you what's been in a penal colony,' she calls out to the audience.

A loud cheer goes up and they stamp their feet. The stomping becomes the rhythm the band play to as they wind into one of the songs she created back at the Factory.

Welcome to this grand hotel, not so very far from hell.

They lock the doors an' ring the bell, but we can dance all night.

As she sings, Olivia sees images of the girls from the Factory flick before her memory's eye. Ann. Nancy. Ellen. Even her mother. People she is likely never to see again. And it strikes her that those memories are the past. She can separate herself from them. That is not who she is anymore, even though she sings about it.

Welcome to our palace hall, where we dine on bread an' gall.

The whip is large an' bed is small, but we still dance all night.

Mr Frith moves to the front of the stage and starts some elaborate fiddling, and Mr Brown puts down his whistle and joins Olivia to twirl around in a dance.

Welcome to this paradise. The cells they crawl with rats and lice.

Our sins they carry a hefty price, but we can dance all night.

The music slows. The last verse starts very solemn, and Olivia crouches low to look those men in the eye.

Welcome to our castle grand, one foot wrong, you'll surely hang,

You can't escape Van Diemen's Land …

Here Olivia pauses, straightening again for the finale.

And she pauses.

And she pauses, searching.

What was that she just saw?

Someone.

A familiar face.

Impossible.

It can't be. Is it a ghost?

She can feel the blood drain from her face. Why would he do that to her?

But then, there is another familiar face right at his side. And Mr Reeve is not dead as far as she knows.

The apparitions move closer, and her knees go weak. She reaches for something to steady herself, but there is nothing to hold and she staggers.

The light hits his face.

Micky?

But. But …

Micky!

Her breath stops, the song forgotten. Everything around her is forgotten. Except him. Olivia almost falls off the stage in her haste to get to him.

'Micky?'

'Yes, my darling songbird. It is I.' His voice, that dear sweet voice, is breaking. But then she is in his arms, holding her so tight she can hardly breathe. Not that she cares, she holds on just as tight, her mind spinning with confusion and utter elation.

'Yer not a ghost,' she murmurs into his chest.

She feels his chest shudder as he laughs. 'No, not a ghost.'

She pulls back from him to look up at his face. A face which bears scars that weren't there before. 'They told me ya were dead.'

Micky swallows, his face full of regret. 'I know. I'm so sorry you were made to believe that.'

Olivia can still hardly believe this is real. She wants to laugh and cry at the same time. She wants to reach up and trace her fingers over those scars, but she suddenly realises she is in a room full of people. With a deep breath, she steps back and summons her stage act.

'Well now, folks. This here is me husband come back from the dead.'

They all clap and cheer and whistle. Olivia gestures toward the band still on the platform.

'These fellas will finish the show for ya.' They can still make music without her singing. Besides, she knows Fred can hold a tune if he needs to. She mouths an 'I'm sorry' to him as she takes Micky by the arm and leads him out of the room.

In the hallway, the senior Mr Reeve puts a staying hand on her arm.

'Oh, in all the excitement, I didn't say hello.' Olivia curtsies to him.

'Good to see you, Mrs Reeve.' He grins. 'Now, I know you two need some privacy, but please keep hold of Michael's arm and guide him up the stairs.'

Olivia's eyes swing from him to Micky, who is shaking his head, and back again. 'Why does he need guidin'?'

'Because I've been blind for the best part of two months,' Micky grunts. 'I can see most things now, though.'

'The scars on yer face. What happened that night?'

'Ellen threw lye into my eyes.'

They are burn scars. Olivia presses a hand to her mouth, horrified.

'But we can talk about all that later. I'll be fine walking up some stairs. Thanks Dad.'

Mr Reeve puts his hands up like he's defending himself. 'All ri'. I'll take the hint. See you in a bit.' He goes back into the concert.

They are alone. Micky's right though, now is not the time to relive that night, no matter how much she wants to know.

'I can't believe it's you.' Olivia finally allows the tears to come and her whole body shakes with them. 'I thought I'd lost ya forever.'

'Not a chance.' Micky's voice is hoarse as he takes her in his arms again, this time his lips finding hers, their kiss conveying all that they could never put into words. It is a long while before he draws away from her and puts a steering arm behind her back. 'Come, before we are discovered.'

Olivia holds his arm close, leaning into him as they walk, giddy with delight to have him back. It is beyond her best dreams.

'You have turned me into a madman, my darling.'

Olivia chortles. 'How so?'

'I punched a man on account of you.'

Olivia glances sideways at him, incredulous.

'Well, I would have if I could see him properly. Unfortunately, I missed.'

She laughs out loud and then becomes serious.

'And you have turned me into an honest woman.'

Micky sighs. 'Wonder of wonders. But I doubt that is my handiwork.' He squeezes her arm.

'I'm free, Micky,' she says.

'I know, songbird. You've been free since the day we were married.'

They have reached the stairs and Olivia stops walking, turns, and places her hands on his cheeks, dragging his face towards her. 'No. Look at me.'

His gaze locks on hers with a grin. 'You're a little blurry, but still just as beautiful.'

'Then hear me. I am *free*.'

She waits for the realisation to come and sees a tear slip down his cheek. 'Oh, my love, that is the best news.' His arms slide around her waist again and he draws her in tight, lifting her, spinning around with her and setting her down again. Although this time she is on the second step and can look him straight in the eye.

'But I have some even better news,' she grins. 'Do you want to hear?'

'What can be better than that?'

Olivia leans in close and whispers in his ear, then stands back to watch the light spread across his face.

'You're what? Are you serious?' He is very loud.

Olivia doesn't think her smile can ever be bigger than it is right now. 'Yes, Micky. Yer gonna be a daddy.'

Epilogue

Olivia smiles as she steps to the altar of the church. She no longer needs to pretend; her smile is genuine and comes from a deep sense of peace.

She scans the congregation, many of whom she now calls friends. And family. Her sisters-in-law and their husbands, Mr and Mrs Reeve, the reverend who has been so supportive and taught her much, and their dear friend Raff.

Micky is there in the front row, bouncing their beautiful boy, William, on his knee. He takes Will's plump little arm and waves it, making her want to giggle.

The organist plays an introduction, and Olivia takes a deep breath, then opens her mouth and sings her song to the congregation, her heart soaring on every note as it does every single time. She can't believe where this year has taken her. Olivia is now a paid member of the church choir, not that she needs to work for an income with a loving husband who supports her so well.

She felt little regret in leaving Stanthorpe's Troupe of Extraordinary Entertainers. How could she when she had Micky back? She stayed long enough for Mr Stanthorpe to find another vocalist, and Micky stayed too. Mr Carpenter bowed out gracefully. Not that he had much choice in the matter. Mrs Johnson drew a promise from her to keep in contact via letters, and they had already exchanged several, with Micky helping Olivia to read and respond. Thankfully, Mrs Johnson relayed that Mr Carpenter was now courting a nice lass and seemed happy.

After the church service, the folk thank her for her song and tell her how much it means to them, which is a darn sight better than being whistled at. But even better is the Sunday tradition of going to the Reeves' for the roast dinner and family fun. At first, when they'd returned from Sydney, Olivia had felt a bit on the outer with such a close-knit family. She's never experienced anything like it in her life. Now, after a year, she can throw the banter about just as good as the rest of them. They've accepted her as one of their own. It still brings tears to her eyes even now and she quietly thanks God for her fortune.

'Wake up, sleepyhead.' Feathery kisses on her eyelids the following morning bring her out of her dreamless rest.

'Does Will need a feed?' It's the first thing she thinks about every morning. Motherhood has brought such exquisite joy, like nothing she could have believed, and along with it, endless fretting, which Micky always tries to soothe.

'Still sleeping soundly at this moment,' Micky answers, brushing loose strands of hair from her brow. 'But he will soon, I'm sure. Mrs Granger will be here shortly, and we must get ready to go to the Factory.'

Strange. That word doesn't make her stomach clench the way it used to. Micky no longer works in the prison. He creates beautiful furniture for the colonists. But on Mondays, they both go to the Cascades Female Factory to see to prisoners' welfare as much as they can.

At the same time as Mrs Granger knocks on the front door with a 'yoohoo', Will hollers for breakfast. Olivia has barely managed to put her dress on, but laughs as she welcomes Mrs Granger, while scooping her little man from his crib.

'Here, let me change him while you finish dressing.' Mrs Granger puts a basket on the table and reaches for Will. The generous older lady from church watches their boy while they visit the Factory.

Within an hour, Micky and Olivia are at the gates of the Factory with Mrs Granger's basket of scones. She often sends some baked treats with them to give to the prisoners. Micky squeezes her hand as they enter. It's his way of saying 'I know what this place meant for you, and I think you're brave to come back here.'

They undergo the familiar pat-down and Olivia recalls the times she had contraband hidden away in her stays. The girls often ask them to smuggle something in for them, but they always refuse, bringing only Mrs Granger's gifts or other things that might help their welfare, such as soap, or paper to write letters.

First up, they attend the prisoners' devotional service, where Olivia often sings a hymn or two. At first, some of the girls booed her and chanted for the 'Shank' to sing them one of her old tunes.

'That ain't who I am no more, girls,' she had to explain. She's told her story several times now, ending with, 'An' if there's hope for the Shank, then there's hope for all o' ya.'

And that's what she spends most of her time at the Factory doing now. Encouraging the girls to hope for a better future. To put their head down, behave themselves, and see out their sentence with diligence, and if they can, integrity. Just the same as Micky had always done for her, and still does for others.

After the service, they counsel women who are open to encouragement and then it is time for Olivia's special appointment. The Matron has agreed that every Monday, Olivia may meet with her mother for thirty minutes.

It is a small room with no windows and they bring Mary in to her. The first time, her mother broke down and cried as soon as she saw Olivia. 'I didn't think I'd ever see ya again.'

Olivia had been unsure how to respond. Back then, her wounds were still very raw where it concerned her mother. But over time, Olivia has realised her mother may have changed, after all.

'Morning Mama,' she says as they let the older woman into the room, the turnkey closing the door behind her.

'G'day Livvie. How's me grandson doin'?'

'He's perfect.'

'I'd love to see him.' She says this every week, of course.

'I know ya would.' No promises yet.

They talk easily enough, Mama always asking about her life 'out there', and Olivia always checking that her mother is not getting herself into trouble.

'No, I'm takin' a leaf outta your book,' Mama says. And from what Olivia can tell, she keeps to her word.

They have even had a laugh together from time to time, which feels nice. And makes Olivia wish they could have a normal relationship.

On their way home, Micky fidgets overtime with the reins. Olivia knows him well enough to know this means something bothers him. Just like he knows if she scratches her arms, it means no good. Although she hasn't scratched her arms in a very long time.

'What's wrong Micky?' There's no beating around the bush with her. No time to waste on pretence and insinuation.

He reaches over and takes her hand in his. 'I've been thinking.'

Olivia fails to see how this is worrisome. 'Yeah?'

'Well, our family is growing, right?'

'What do ya mean?'

'I, well, I presume you want more children, yes? As do I.'

'Of course.' She still doesn't understand what the problem is.

'Perhaps … perhaps you might need some help around the house … soon? What with me busy in the shop and you practising your singing?'

Olivia stares at him. She can practise any time. 'What are ya tryin' to say, Micky? On me life, yer speakin' in riddles.'

He squeezes her hand. 'I was wondering … what if … what if we got some assigned labour?'

Olivia sits back. 'Oh.' She lets the information sink in. 'I suppose it would be a way to help one of them women.' The idea grows on her.

'I was specifically thinking about … Mary?' He winces as though she might throw something at him.

Olivia's heart thumps. 'Stop the buggy, Micky.'

'I'm sorry. I didn't mean to—'

'Stop the buggy!'

Micky yields and reins in the horses, his face showing alarm and regret.

'Olivia, I—'

'Come here ya lanky mooncalf.' Olivia grabs him by the lapels of his jacket and pulls him close, slapping a rough kiss on his mouth. 'How did I get me such an excellent husband?' She laughs at his astonished face. 'Yes, assign me mother. A thousand times, yes. She'll need some very strict boundaries, but yes, I'd like nothin' better. I can't believe I didn't think of it meself.'

'You really like the idea?' Micky still seems surprised. 'You aren't angry or scared?'

'Scared, probably, but I don't want that stuff to rule me anymore. If she's in our home, there is more time to work on mendin' the past.'

His lips curve into a gentle smile, his eyes shining with pride. 'How did I get such an excellent wife?'

Olivia gives him a saucy grin as she pulls him to her again. 'You don't know the half of it.'

The End

Author's Note

Transportation of prisoners to Australia commenced in 1788 and continued, to Van Diemen's Land (Tasmania) at least, until 1853. Approximately 25,000 of the 164,000 convicts transported were women, convicted mostly of petty crimes, and 12,500 of those ended up in Van Diemen's Land.

Although my character, Olivia, and her fellow inmates are fictional characters, I drew from real women's stories who suffered at the hands of the penal system.

In 1841, an Inquiry into Female Convict Discipline was established which looked into areas such as rioting, trafficking, ill-discipline of convicts and also looked into the high mortality rate of infants in the nursery.

The results of this inquisition, along with the introduction of the Probation system, meant that after that time, women were kept in separate apartments, or light cells, two women per room. They lived in those small cells 24/7 with only a short break to walk each day, where they were made to stay at least four feet away from each other. They slept, ate, and worked in the separate apartments under strict watch and were not permitted to speak to each other, under threat of punishment if they did. If well behaved for six months, they were then given permission to be assigned to work outside the prison.

The Anti-Transportation League was indeed a movement that raised a voice to cease the transportation of convicts, although it did not begin until the late 1840s. However, there was growing opposition to transportation from 1837 and even more so after transportation ceased to New South Wales in 1840, so I thought it relevant to include those sentiments in this novel.

While the Iron Pot Lighthouse was run and maintained by convicts in 1841, I found no evidence that a female convict was ever sent there. But what is Rapunzel without a tower, right?

About the Author

AMANDA DEED is an award-winning author residing in Melbourne with her husband, her grown-up children, and several birds. Outside of her family, her life revolves around words, numbers (writing and accounting) and a healthy splash of music.

Her first novel, *The Game*, won the 2010 CALEB Prize for Fiction, and she has since had several novels final in the same prize. Amanda loves to write novels that explore her faith, Australian history, and romance.

For more information, go to www.amandadeed.com.

More stories by Amanda Deed

Unnoticed: Beauty for Ashes

9781925563061

Complete with an evil stepmother, a missing shoe and a grand ball, *Unnoticed* takes the time-old *Cinderella* fairy tale and gives it an Australian twist.

Unhinged: Joy for Darkness

9781925563245

Unhinged is an Australian retelling of *Beauty and the Beast*, complete with a mysterious curse and a precious rose.

www.wombatrhiza.com.au